FINAL 7

BOOKS BY KERRY DREWERY

FINAL7

KERRY
DREWERY

HOT
KEY
BOOKS

First published in Great Britain in 2018 by
HOT KEY BOOKS
80–81 Wimpole St, London W1G 9RE
www.hotkeybooks.com

Copyright © Kerry Drewery, 2018

A CIP catalogue record for this book is available from the British Library.

ISBN: 978-1-4714-0630-0
also available as an ebook

1

This book is typeset using Atomik ePublisher
Printed and bound by Clays Ltd, St Ives Plc

Hot Key Books is an imprint of Bonnier Zaffre Ltd,
a Bonnier Publishing company
www.bonnierpublishing.com

For my big brother, Colin

When money speaks, the truth keeps silent.

Old Russian proverb

PROLOGUE

Martha

Was that a heartbeat?

I don't know. Can't find it now. Can't feel it.

I move my hand, try again.

Nothing.

Try again.

Fuck, still nothing.

'He's . . .' I mumble, shaking my head. Can't say the word. Can't end it.

Tears drip from me.

Can't see for blur.

I wipe my eyes. My hands feel sticky.

I look at them.

Looks like blood.

Isaac's.

The car tears down the road. Streetlights flash through the window.

Light

dark

light

dark . . .

across Gus's face as he turns around in the front seat.

He's staring at Isaac; he stretches and puts a hand on his chest.

So calm.

Then he looks at me, takes my hand and puts it on Isaac.

'Feel,' he says. 'He's breathing.'

I nod but can't speak.

I'm shaking.

Don't know what to do.

I watch Isaac's face as light hits it.

Wish his eyes would open.

I close mine, imagine being with him, concentrate on my palm rising and falling as he breathes.

Stay with me, Isaac, I say in my head, willing every breath he takes.

Something, a truck or lorry, flies past us so fast and heavy it rocks the car and I open my eyes.

The car slows.

'What the –' the woman driving says.

I open my mouth to ask who she is, but as I turn to look out the window, I stop.

Not far ahead, at the boundary of the Rises, under a barrage of floodlights, are rows and rows of lorries and trucks.

I squint through the windows and the darkness, blinking to try to make sense of what I'm seeing.

Cranes in the sky. Orange flashing lights. Workmen all over.

And massive, ugly, concrete panels, stacked up to make a huge wall.

For what? To keep us out?

Stop our influence? Control us? What?

'Berlin,' I whisper. 'Israel, Belfast. Korea.'

'Now London,' Gus replies.

What the hell?

What the actual hell?

TV STUDIO

11 p.m. The programme – *Death is Justice: Late-Night Round-Up* – is beginning.

The screen shows the death row building – recorded footage from a CCTV camera. Throngs of people. Half-light. The blue eye logo above it all. The image shakes, distorts, blurs. A massive boom rocks the area and clouds of smoke rise into the sky.

GEROME SHARP (off-screen): This is Gerome Sharp, new roving reporter for *Death is Justice*, reporting live from the death row building. Viewers are warned that footage contains flashing images and scenes of an upsetting nature.

In the recording, clouds of dust plume towards the camera and the blue from the eye logo flashes and flickers.

GEROME (off-screen): As an earth-shaking explosion rocks death row we ask – did terrorists bring this carnage to the City?

The screen changes to a shaky image from a hand-held camera. People are screaming and running, some with blood pouring from them. Others stagger. The camera zooms in on the building. Bodies can be seen on the ground close by.

GEROME (off-screen): Countless injured as panic rips through the streets in what many are calling 'justice's blackest day'.

Blue lights flash over the scene. The wail of sirens and crying. The camera focuses on Martha on the ground with her hands in the air. Eyes wide and mouth open. Blood on her face. Police pointing guns at her as they approach.

GEROME: Fugitive, and prime suspect, Martha Honeydew is arrested at the scene. What may be a detonator is found nearby.

The footage fades and is replaced by live feed of Gerome Sharp at the scene: chiselled jaw, long dark coat and neatly tied check scarf. Running along the bottom of the screen are the words 'Terrorism in the heart of the City'.

GEROME: This important symbol of justice came crashing to the ground earlier today in a targeted and bloody attack. Only minutes after the final verdict had been given in the Isaac Paige case, an explosion rocked central London, threatening to bring the justice system to its knees. At present the cause of the explosion is unknown, although there have been unconfirmed reports that it was a bomb. We are also waiting for confirmation on the number of dead; however it's feared that the amount of people injured when the building crashed to the ground in clouds of smoke and dust, throwing the entire area into chaos, may well reach into the thousands due to the crowds the case attracted. Martha Honeydew, who has been the focus of a nationwide manhunt since her acquittal from death row a week ago, was arrested at the scene. While the exact nature of her involvement in the attack is as yet unclear, CCTV footage shows Honeydew approaching the building wearing a backpack, leading to suspicions this could have been a suicide bomb attack gone wrong. We'll go to the Prime Minister now for a live statement on the events.

The Prime Minister – Stephen Renard

'Where is Sofia?' the PM demands as he strides down a corridor, straightening his tie and flattening his jacket. He takes his phone from his pocket and taps the screen.

People scurry around him, staring at clipboards or mobile phones with frowns and shaking of heads.

'And why is nothing working?' he shouts as he throws his phone to the floor. 'You!' He points at a young man with close-cropped hair walking towards him. 'Who are you?'

'Err . . . I-I . . .' the young man stutters, 'I'm the new intern. Gino.'

'Gino, get me Sofia! Now!'

'We . . . We c-can't –' he says.

'What?'

'We can't . . . find her. Her phone's not connecting. She's not in her office.'

'Her phone's not connecting because the system's gone down, you arse. And she's not in her office because I said she could have an early night. Are you stupid?'

'Then . . . ?'

'There must be something wrong.'

'You don't think she's caught up in the . . . the . . . ?'

The PM stops and turns on him. 'Shut up,' he hisses, jabbing him in the chest, his face contorted, his jaw clenched. 'Shut the hell up.'

'Sir,' a gentle female voice comes from the side, 'we've sent a car to her apartment and we're contacting her friends and relatives.'

The PM looks to her, his face softening.

'In the meantime, sir, if you don't mind my saying so, the press are waiting for your statement.

He nods slowly, stretches his neck sideways and brushes back a loose strand of hair.

'That's very efficient of you,' he mumbles.

The Prime Minister walks away. Further down the corridor a young man opens a door for him, and as he steps through, his face turns calm yet serious.

On the other side rows and rows of chairs are filled with journalists and news reporters. The chatter stops, people pick up microphones, cameras, pens and notebooks, as the PM stands at the lectern at the front of the room, rests his papers in front of him and looks over the crowd.

'Ladies and gentlemen, it's with a heavy heart that I speak to you this evening.' He pauses and takes a deep breath.

'At precisely 8.57 p.m. today we, the law-abiding public, came under attack from forces who wish to unleash chaos into our society.' He speaks slowly and deliberately, pausing at the end of each phrase as cameras flash and reporters and audiences at home hang on his every word.

'I can confirm that a bomb was detonated directly outside death row, resulting in the collapse of one side of the building and serious and dangerous structural damage to the rest.

'This is a senseless act of violence.

'It is wanton disregard for the values we live by.

'It is an example of the hatred and barbarism that have been allowed to fester and grow within certain sections of our society.

'But we will *not* let them grow any more. Nor will we allow them to affect the freedoms we hold so dear.

'I publicly condemn the actions of the group that carried out this attack, who have no respect for the value of human life.'

He pauses, drops his head for a moment as if in sadness. Then lifts it again, takes a deep breath and looks at the audience.

'The emergency services, our best and our bravest, are at the scene and are doing everything within their power to assist the injured. At this point, however, I cannot speculate on numbers, but suffice to say that in the region of two hundred people were in the audience at Cell 7 tonight and, as yet, fewer than fifty have been accounted unharmed.

'Furthermore, it is believed that as many as three thousand members of the public had gathered outside the gates.

'We ask for your patience and understanding in this time of great pain.'

He pauses, looking over the audience, and slowly shakes his head.

'And great pain it is, but not pain we shall dwell on nor seek pity for. For we, society, the City, law-abiding citizens of the Avenues, will rise from the ashes, from the dust and the debris of this calculated, blood-thirsty attack, and we will unleash the full power of the law on those responsible.

'As you may be aware, the fugitive Martha Honeydew was discovered at the scene. She was found with a detonator in her hands.'

He pauses while a mutter ripples through the crowd. Then he raises his hands for silence.

'I'm sure you are all as shocked as I am that someone so young could commit such a terrible crime, especially against an institution that barely a week ago allowed her own release and was soon to acquit the young man she claimed to be involved with.

'Speculation has been rife, and I can now confirm that Honeydew did not act alone.'

As he pauses again, he glances around the room and spots Sofia standing by a door at the back. Their eyes meet for a second and she gives a brief nod of acknowledgement.

'There seems little doubt that a small yet dangerous group of individuals is plotting against us. Against the City, the Avenues, and the good people within it. The law-abiding, hard-working, family-loving citizens which we, *you*, all are. Plotting to destabilise our society, to attack the deepest roots of justice, and the very heart of what makes us human.

'This group of . . . and I hesitate to call them "people" because in my mind they are no better than animals . . . have been named as . . .'

He lifts his chin, squares his shoulders and takes a breath.

'. . . Eve and Max Stanton, Thomas Cicero, Joshua Decker, Gus Evans, Isaac Paige and Martha Honeydew. These seven, with their sympathies for the criminal, the lazy, the benefit-scroungers and the poor – the kind who we have tried many times to help so they might go on to help themselves, the kind who live in the Rises – will be brought to justice.

'Eve Stanton has been arrested. Honeydew has been sent

to prison. Evans is already there. We wait for confirmation on Paige, while emergency services secure the area. We are putting stringent security measures in place and we will hunt down Max Stanton, Thomas Cicero and Joshua Decker. Like animals we will hunt them down, and again our city will be a safe place to live.

'We must stand together and stand strong and we will prevail against this evil!'

He lifts his fist into the air and the crowd cheer with him.

'Thank you for your time and your support,' he says as they quieten. 'My thoughts are with those affected and their families on this terrible night.'

He collects the papers and, with a final glance towards Sofia, walks from the room.

Sofia edges around the chairs and follows the PM, nodding at journalists she knows. As she reaches out to push open the door she catches sight of blood on her hand and quickly wipes it down her trousers.

Isaac's blood.

The door swings closed behind her.

'Sofia,' the PM says and takes her by the shoulders. 'Thank goodness you're here. The systems are down, I can't –'

She looks up and meets his eye without flinching or betraying even a shadow of doubt.

'Nobody here knows how to reset them. I assume you do?' he asks in a whisper.

She nods. 'Yes, sir, of course.'

The Stanton house

The house is in darkness. Max and Cicero stand in the kitchen, the light from the television news flickering on their faces and around the room. The sound is low and subtitles stream along the bottom of the screen.

'TERRORIST GROUP AT LARGE ... RISES 7 WANTED FOR QUESTIONING ... THOMAS CICERO, FORMER HIGH COURT JUDGE, IN BOMBING SCANDAL ... MAX STANTON NAMED AS YOUNGEST EVER TERRORIST ...'

Pounding comes from the front door.

'Open this door or we will break it down!' a voice shouts. 'This is your final warning!'

Max picks up his laptop bag from the floor and looks to Cicero.

Silently he nods and, pulling their jackets around them, they head out of the French windows.

Behind them crashing sounds from the front door, but by the time the police are through, Max and Cicero have disappeared into the darkness of the garden and beyond.

Martha

The wall's going up fast.

The woman said it's too dangerous for her to go into the Rises so she dropped us off before it and we had to walk. Me and Gus carrying Isaac between us, causing God knows what damage to him. Supposing he had a broken rib and it punctured his lung? Or some head injury we were making worse by shaking him around?

I tried to persuade her but she was adamant. Kept saying Gus would explain later and that she had to go. I had the feeling I knew her face from somewhere but I couldn't work out where.

She kept saying she hadn't thought it'd happen that fast.

What?

The wall?

I glance back. Cranes rise into the sky, silhouetted by floodlights. Enormous sheets of concrete hoisted into the air. The creaking of it all and the groaning. The sounds of our freedom under stress. The shouts of men, the thunder of machines.

How long is it already?

How far does it stretch?

Will it go all the way around?

How will folks go to work, to the shops, to see friends?

How will we – I look down to Isaac – get a doctor?

We're trudging over the grass now, me and Gus, towards Daffodil House.

We've put Isaac in a supermarket trolley we found abandoned at the underpass and we're pushing him. Have to – there's no other way we can manage him.

It worries me.

It shakes and rattles like hell and it can't be doing him any good.

I want to pick him up and carry him.

Hold him.

Fix him.

He's gone blue around his mouth. I touch him and he's cold like stone, so pale and still. I pull my jacket off as Gus pushes and I throw it over Isaac.

The cold bites me, takes my breath and I tense and shiver.

'You'll catch your death!' Gus says.

'I can move to keep warm,' I reply. 'He can't.'

He shakes his head at me. 'Put in back on,' he says, and he starts pulling off his own coat.

'Don't try getting all chivalrous on me,' I say to him.

'Shut up and push,' he replies. 'This is nothing to do with chivalry. This is cos I've got a jumper on under and all you got is a T-shirt. Stop trying to be the hero and put your jacket on.'

As he places his over Isaac he throws mine back to me.

'I wasn't trying to be a hero,' I mutter. 'I'm just . . .' If I carry on I'm going to cry, so I shut up instead and lift my face into the cold wind.

He says something but I can't hear.

On the bar of the trolley his hand rests on mine.

I take a deep breath and nod.

Death Row

Eve stands barefoot in a tiny room made of old crumbling bricks and a cracked and dirty concrete floor. Moss grows in the corners and mould up the walls; a fusty smell hangs in the air. A draught through a high window sways the single light bulb hanging from the middle of the stained and peeling ceiling.

In her egg-splattered pyjamas Eve shivers and wraps her arms around herself.

The chains around her ankles and wrists clank against each other.

'Stanton!' a loud male voice booms, and a short chubby man waddles in through an archway at the side. 'Time to sort you. Come on.' He yanks at the chains and she lurches forward, following him out through the archway.

'Where are you taking me?'

'No talking unless instructed,' he says. 'You should know the drill.'

The next room is just as cold and stark as the first, but has a wooden table and chair in the middle. A long electric cable leads across the floor and to hair clippers resting on the table, along with folded prison overalls and a tub of white powder. The only other object is a metal bin.

'Where are we?' she asks. 'This isn't death row.'

He yanks on the chains and she stumbles forward.

'I said no talking,' he mutters. 'Now strip.'

'Pardon?'

'Clothes off. Hands on the table, legs spread.'

'What?'

'De-lousing. Hair off. Prison uniform on.'

She stares at him.

'Get on with it, or I'll have people come in here and do it for you. You haven't got nothing I haven't seen before, and I don't take no thrill in the body of some fifty-something wrinkly has-been.'

'I'm forty-two.'

'Like I care.'

She stares at him.

'I should've realised that someone of your ... *physique*,' she says twisting the first button on her pyjamas, 'would be less concerned with appearance ...'

'I told you –'

'... than someone,' she continues, interrupting as she undoes the next button, 'with a body they look after.'

'What?'

'Or is that unfair of me?' She unfastens the last one and slips the top from her shoulders.

He continues to stare as she lowers her trousers and steps out of them.

'Clearly your stomach hanging over your belt isn't as important as the brain in your head, is it? Just as my breasts are of no relevance to the person I am inside.'

He wipes a corner of his mouth on his sleeve.

'And the sagging of your male . . . *chest area* . . . is as relevant to your character as my lack of thigh gap.'

'Shut the hell up,' he mutters, wiping his top lip.

She walks over to the table, rests her hands on top and spreads her legs.

'You have no clue what I'm talking about, do you?'

Not taking his eyes off her, he lifts the tub of powder and twists the lid.

'Your brain has disengaged from your head, hasn't it?'

Without replying, he throws the de-lousing powder over her.

She closes her eyes. 'You are just the sort of Neanderthal they want. Cheap thrills, no questions. Not even any thought.'

'Put the overalls on,' he grunts, 'sit down, and for Christ's sake stop talking.'

The overalls are the same as she's seen so many before her wear, and as she pulls them up her legs and pushes her arms down the sleeves she fights the thought that she would've counselled someone wearing these exact ones, and that someone, at least one, would've died in these.

Once she's in the chair, the smell of damp floats up from them and she fights the nausea rising through her stomach and throat.

Behind her, the clippers buzz into action and the cold of the metal hits the back of her neck.

Her blonde hair falls to the ground.

Martha

The place is empty.

There's no one around.

Not a soul.

The sound of that wall going up, the sight of it, must've scared everyone off.

There weren't even any of the homeless folk at the underpass.

Daffodil House is above us now, but I don't even see any lights in windows.

We shove the trolley right up to the front doors.

Remember the first time you met? my head asks me. *Remember him walking you right to this door in the rain? You told him to fuck off. Remember that.*

I do, I reply, and I look down at him, sprawled across this decrepit trolley, his face bloodied, his skin tinged blue, his eyes closed.

Celebrity Chat's Teen Bachelor of the Year. The *National News* Junior Crime Ambassador. Son of celebrity millionaire. A star pupil at Anderson's Academy for the Gifted.

What have I done to him?

I want to drop to my knees and give up.

I want to die because fighting is too hard.

Not now, my head tells me. *You owe it to him to be strong. You are strong.*

Right bloody contrary thing you are, I tell my head.

Gus pulls the door open.

Strange to be back.

I push the trolley inside.

What's that smell? It smells . . . *nice.*

A gentle light flickers on and I freeze.

There's no rubbish on the floor; it's clean and shiny. The walls aren't smeared with grease and dirt from a million grimy hands; instead they're painted a gentle green. And the strip light doesn't flicker like some horror film.

Faces peer out at us.

Friendly, soft and welcoming.

Smiling.

A young girl moves towards me and puts a blanket around me. A shiver runs down me and I have to blink not to cry. I recognise her face but don't know her name.

Then an old man steps forward, his legs bowed like he's had rickets or something, and his face has lines and wrinkles so deep there must be a thousand stories hiding in there.

He takes my hand and he smiles at me.

'Welcome home,' he says.

I can't speak to reply, but I hope my smile says it all.

Max and Cicero

Through the suburbs of the Avenues they walk and walk, not daring to take public transport, keeping their heads low and their hoods up, scarves lifted to obscure their faces, keeping out of view of shops, streetlights and car headlights.

It's late at night, the last day of November, freezing cold, frost on the ground, the few people around hurrying and taking little notice of anything.

In a window to Max's side, lights on a Christmas tree sparkle and he turns away quickly; memories of his mum in his head, their tree at home, presents underneath, turkey and friends. He speeds up.

They walk and they walk, with fingers seizing from the cold and faces pinching in the wind, and eventually it looms ahead of them.

'What *is* that?' Max says, his voice hoarse and broken.

Staring into the sky, they both come to a stop.

'It looks like . . .' Cicero mutters, his eyes straining, '. . . like they're building a wall.'

'Why would they do that?'

Cicero shakes his head and starts walking again, faster this time.

Max scurries up alongside him. 'To keep them in there? To stop us going in? To control?'

'All of the above?' Cicero replies. 'Whatever the reason, we need to get in there before it's too late. Come on; we need to be quick.'

'But then . . . what if we can't get out?'

'What choice do we have? We stay here, we'll be arrested, we'll be dead in a week.'

DECEMBER 1ST

Death is Justice trailer

Kristina Albright, fitted trouser suit and perfect hair, stands to one side of the screen in the quiet TV studio.

KRISTINA: The headlines today, December 1st: residents of the Avenues fear for their safety as shops in the district continue to employ people from the Rises.

Images flash on the screen: well-dressed people clutching bags to their chests; people peering through gaps in curtains; mothers ushering children quickly down roads.

KRISTINA: We question if a recent spate of house burglaries in the area could be down to the same people.

The image changes to a shot of the destroyed death row building with police tape flapping in the wind.

KRISTINA: Police call for calm in the aftermath of the bombing, stating they will do everything within their power to bring the Rises 7 to justice.

The camera zooms in.

KRISTINA: And finally, with Isaac Paige's body yet to be recovered, and Patty Paige on life support following the explosion, questions are being asked as to whether Martha Honeydew will be placed *back* on death row. Join us tonight at six thirty, when we'll be looking at these events as well as revealing the site of the new death row.

Music plays and the screen fades to black.

Martha

They've tidied my flat, the folks here. Vacuumed, dusted, changed the sheets and that. Made it homely for me and Isaac.

Someone's even fixed the lift.

They lifted him out the trolley with such care, carried him into the lift and took him up. Then when it came back down again, they guided me so gently. Like I'm a person again. Like I matter.

I walked down the corridor and past Mrs B's. Still can't get my head round it being empty. She should hear me coming and appear at the door with honey cake and a big smile.

Am I angry?

Yeah, at myself. And sad. And disappointed with the whole world who follow like sheep. Who are selfish and blinkered.

Maybe not the whole world, but those with more to lose than to gain.

A woman I sort of remember from before steered me into my flat and I could've melted with the warmth and comfort of it.

I looked to her, her brown eyes and brown skin and her wide smile, and my eyes filled.

The sheer relief.

They'd made a bed up in the living room for Isaac, all manner of medical things lined up next to it, and by the time I got up there they'd settled him on it and folks were fussing around him.

'This way,' the woman said to me, nodding to the bedroom, but I shook my head.

'I need to stay with him,' I replied.

She didn't argue. Instead she turned to a couple of small children behind her and pointed to a wide chair filled with cushions and covered in a multi-coloured blanket and they pulled it up next to the bed.

I recognised it, the chair. I'd seen Mrs B sitting in it a million times; they must've brought it from her flat.

'Rest,' the woman said to me, and as I sat down it was like Mrs B was wrapping her arms around me. I closed my eyes and let her, and felt the blanket go over me and I imagined it was Mrs B just like she did before all this happened.

'A doctor's on the way,' the woman whispered.

My eyes shot open. 'Where from? The City?'

'Shhh,' she replied. 'Don't worry, he can be trusted.'

Trust? I thought. I don't know about that.

They brought me some hot soup and bread, then a mug of sweet tea and some biscuits, and after that I rested a hand on Isaac's and watched every single breath he took.

I don't know how long ago that was.

I don't know what the time is now.

I know I've slept, because now there's a drip in Isaac's hand, bandages around his arm and his face has been cleaned up.

Some guard you are, I think to myself. *They could've strode in here and suffocated him and you would've just carried on snoring.*

I stand up and walk to the window, ease back the curtains and look outside.

It's a funny light. The floodlights, on the right, are so dazzling you can hardly see anything else, but I put a hand up to shield their brightness and there, away to the left, is the pink of dawn breaking and the black silhouettes of the birds who've stayed to fight the winter.

It's a while till spring, I want to tell them, and I remember Mum scraping bacon fat or breadcrumbs onto a plate and sending me downstairs with it.

'For the birds,' she'd say. 'We help them survive the winter and spring will be sweeter with their song.'

'Did we help that one?' I'd say to her as we strolled through Bracken Woods with bluebells forcing through mud and a sparrow singing its heart out on a blossom tree.

She'd nod, and because I was looking for the sparrow I'd notice the bluebells and the blossom, hear the song of blackbirds and starlings and smell new green grass.

But because of that the Rises would look greyer when we went back home.

I think of the birds, remember the one in Eve's tree at death row.

I want to tell it I'm sorry I destroyed its home.

I move my hand and look back to the floodlights. The cranes have moved since last night; they're further round now, and the concrete wall spreads as far as I can see.

Ugly and grey.

A mess around it of piles of mud and rubble, grass torn up, trees pulled down.

We didn't have much to look at before; now we have even less.

Is this the future for us?

Separation and segregation?

Why?

We're not a different race, or colour, or religion.

They're separating us because of class. A virtual wall's been there for years; now it's physical.

Fuckers.

Next we'll have to carry ID all the time, or be forced to wear an armband.

What makes them think they're better than us?

They reckon they're more intelligent, but they bloody aren't.

And they sure as shit don't have superior humanity.

I shake my head.

It all comes down to money.

They think they're better than us because they have money.

Money equals power equals money equals power equals . . .

You get the gist.

Point being – it sucks.

'Good morning,' a quiet voice says.

I jump and spin around. A small, thin man is leaning over Isaac, white hair like a dandelion clock and skin dry and tight as if he's been slow-roasted.

He glances to me. 'I'm Dr Novak. How are you feeling?'

'Is he OK?' I ask.

'Mr Paige?' His fuzzy white eyebrows move up his forehead, two beady eyes peering out from deep sockets. He nods slowly. 'He's breathing.'

I know he's breathing, I think.

'But . . . is he . . . ?'

He knows what I want to ask. I see that look in his eyes, just like the paramedic's look when he lifted Mum into the ambulance on a stretcher. He could've told me there and then, that paramedic, but no, they had to make me hold on to that sliver of hope that she might actually live when he knew in his head it was hopeless.

Just like he is now, this Dr Novak.

'If he's going to die, if he's better off dead, then I want you to tell me. You don't need to protect me.'

He nods slowly. 'All right then,' he says, and beckons me towards him.

At the side of the bed I look down at Isaac. His face is cut and bruised, his bottom lip swollen, and at the side of his left eye is a massive lump.

His hands rest on top of the sheets and there's a drip in the back of his right one.

I think about breathing in, and I think about breathing out, cos if I don't I'm going to cry and I don't want to do that. I want, *need*, to be stronger than that.

'This . . .' Dr Novak says quietly, gesturing, 'the facial bruising, the cuts, is superficial. His leg is in a bad way, but we don't think it's fractured and it will heal fine. Problem is why he's not waking.'

His words hang in the air.

'Why?'

'Most likely head trauma.'

'But wouldn't there be some sign of that? A cut or lump or something.'

'Maybe, but maybe not. And without a CT scan we can't tell. All we can do is wait.' He looks at me. 'And hope.'

'And . . . and if it is some kind of brain trauma . . . then . . .'

His sigh is like air escaping a balloon. 'Who knows? Even if we did have the best hospital equipment and the best doctors, we could still only speculate. It could be swelling on the brain that goes down, it could be a bleed, a haematoma, it could be a fracture we can't see. Permanent, temporary . . .' He shrugs. 'Or it could be a coma he'll wake from in his own time. I can't say.'

I look away from him, down to Isaac then out of the window. *Breathe*, I tell myself, I can't focus, everything's spinning. All this crap, all this fucking crap we've been through, and we're here.

Here.

I wipe my eyes, clench my teeth and dig my fingernails into my palm.

'I'm giving him some anti-seizure medicine, just in case, and some diuretics which could help with any swelling, but apart from that –'

'When will we know?'

'It's impossible to say.'

I feel his hand on my shoulder but I pull away from it; I don't want his sympathy.

'Dr Novak, there's something I don't understand. Who was the woman who brought us here?'

His body nearly doubles in size as he sucks a deep breath in and his fuzzy eyebrows shoot right up his forehead. 'That,' he says, 'was Sofia Nachant, aide to the Prime Minister.'

'Why would she do that?'

He shrugs. 'Conscience? Sympathy? Who knows?' He glances sideways and I follow where he's looking. Max is standing in the doorway.

I smile, so relieved to see him, and I want to leap towards him and hug him but he doesn't even smile back.

'Where's your mum?' I ask, wanting, waiting for some kind of reaction. Something. Anything.

But he doesn't say a word.

He just turns and walks away.

Joshua

'I should come with you,' says Pete. Dawn light ekes through a gap in the bedroom curtains and falls across his face.

Joshua shuts the bathroom door and walks across the room to his overnight bag on the bed. 'No,' he replies.

'Don't you want me to?'

'Of course I do, but you have work. You're needed here.'

'There are other doctors at the hospital. Someone can cover me for a while.'

'It's not that simple, is it?' Joshua says, putting a handful of toiletries in the bag and moving to the wardrobe. 'If you come with me, you'll be branded as one of us – whatever "us" is: terrorist, enemy of the state.' He shrugs. 'You should stay here. It's safer.'

'You think it's safe?'

'I said *safer* –'

'You don't think that people are going to be pointing at me in the streets, accusing me of being a sympathiser? Throwing eggs at me?'

Joshua turns from the wardrobe with a handful of T-shirts. 'It's eggs, Pete, that's all. It's not knives, you're not going to be shot . . . and anyway, you should be used to getting pointed at in the streets.'

'I have no problem being taunted for being gay – I am – but

I'm not going to be hounded for being a terrorist sympathiser. Or a Rises sympathiser.'

'Because that's so shameful?' Joshua puts the T-shirts in the bag.

'Because it's not what I am.'

'You're saying you don't sympathise with these people?'

Pete stares at him. 'No,' he says at last. 'They made their beds. They want a better life, then they need to work their way up to it.'

'You are so deluded.' Joshua grabs his bag and walks out the room.

Pete stands up and follows him. 'I don't see why you're getting involved!' he shouts after Joshua. 'You've ruined your career. Next it'll be our lives!'

'And if you come with me, it'll be your career too!' Joshua shouts over his shoulder.

In the kitchen, by the back door, he puts the bag down and takes Pete's hand. 'When I met you,' he says, 'you were a breath of fresh air. You breezed in with your smile, warm attitude, openness to everything – different people, different views. You taught me to embrace that, that diversity makes life richer. You showed me how to be proud of who I am, even if I did keep that from the public for a long time, I'm proud of being me. I couldn't have done any of it without you. But . . .' He pauses and frowns. Shakes his head as he squeezes Pete's hand. 'Something happened. I don't know what, or when. Did my narrow-mindedness wear off on you? Did we swap places? I don't know.'

'You saying I'm narrow-minded?'

'In some things, yes.'

'Those people, they cause trouble – you only have to read the paper or watch the news. And now that girl –'

'When did you change?'

Pete stares at him. 'I woke up to what's really happening.'

'No, you let yourself be manipulated by the media.'

'That's –'

'I'm going, Pete. I want to come back and sort things with us, but right now I need to go, and I need you to think about things.'

'You're leaving me in danger.'

Joshua shakes his head. 'That's not right and you know it.' He leans forward to kiss him, but Pete pulls away and turns around.

Joshua picks up his bag. 'I love you,' he says to Pete as he steps through the door.

There's no reply.

Eve

For as many years as I can remember I've held on to the belief that after this life is another; when I die, I'll see Jim again; father and son, who couldn't be together in this life, will, at some point in the future, be together in the next, and for eternity.

For all those years that's comforted me, yet now I realise all it was was a plaster over a wound. Now that the plaster has been taken off, and I'm facing the end, I see the wound for what it is: infected and unhealed.

I see now that to believe in heaven is also to believe in hell, and whereas you, Jim, will have been welcomed into the arms of heaven for all the good you did, I will be heading to hell – I killed not just one man but two, because I killed you.

Will God forgive me for my sins, understand my reasons, look at the grey as well as the black and white, and will St Peter let me through the gates? My belief stands like a house of cards; has wobbled many times but not yet fallen. But now I'm removing one card from the bottom row.

All I believe in is love, and I cannot reconcile this with a god who would not allow us to be together, nor understand and sympathise with the reasons I killed that man.

Not a day passes without me wishing I hadn't killed him, that I'd found a different solution, and not a day passes without me wishing you were still with us; yet not a minute, not even a second, passes without my gratitude for the years I've been able to spend watching our son grow up.

I only wish there could've been more.

Martha

I've turned the heating up and I'm sitting with Isaac.

Have been all day now.

Fuck the bills, I thought. Probably won't be here when they come in anyhow.

And it needs to be warm for Isaac. There was damp on the walls last winter; can't have that again, can't risk him getting a chest infection or pneumonia or God knows what on top of whatever's wrong with him already.

I want to talk to him, but it feels weird. Can talk to him in my head, but not out loud.

I hold his hand.

Watch his chest move up and down.

And hope.

Mrs B would have me praying, but I'm past believing in that.

You pray for him, Mrs B, I think, and pray for me too, and for change.

Gus came in to see me. Hugged me for a long time, said he'd thought he'd never see me again. Made me cry.

Dr Novak has taken up residence in the next-door flat with the folks who live there. He comes in every hour, whistling a tune each time, checks Isaac's pulse, the drips, peels his eyelids open and stares into them. Then he nods and walks back out.

Last time he brought me a sandwich, but I couldn't stomach

it. It's still here now, but the edges have curled up and the ham's gone hard.

Folks'd be grateful for that, my head tells me. *You would've been yesterday too*. I pick it up and chew at a corner.

You need to be strong, that voice says to me, and I know it's right.

'Martha?'

I look up. Max is standing in the doorway, beckoning me.

I shake my head. I don't want to leave Isaac.

'Five minutes,' he says.

Dr Novak comes in. 'Go on,' he says, 'I'll keep an eye on Mr Isaac.'

I follow Max through to the kitchen, *my* kitchen, and as I get there Cicero stands up from the table.

An old-fashioned gentleman.

'Martha,' he says. 'It's good to see you.' He puts his arms out and I'm not sure if it's to hug me or to shake my hand, and I don't know what to do so I just sit down.

'How are you doing?' he asks, sitting back down opposite me.

I look at him. I don't know how to answer or what to say.

Good, thanks, I'm alive at least.

Glad, seeing as Isaac is too.

Angry, that Patty tricked me and I fell for it.

And tired.

Sad.

Lonely.

Scared.

'Pretty shit,' I go with in the end.

He nods. 'I can understand that,' he replies. His moustache twitches as he does some kind of stretched grin and behind his thick glasses there's worry in his eyes. 'I believe you've met Joshua before,' he says, indicating a man leaning against the sink – my sink.

'Joshua Decker,' I say as he looks at me. 'Never figured you'd be standing in my kitchen, drinking coffee from my mum's best mug.'

'Sorry,' he mutters, and goes to put the mug down.

'Doesn't matter,' I say.

'It's gin anyway,' he replies, and the effort of saying something light-hearted seems to almost break him in two.

'You here alone?' I ask.

He nods and gulps down the gin.

I won't ask any more; not my business.

He's hurting.

Everybody's hurting.

'We need to act,' Cicero says. 'We need a plan and we need to follow it quickly and efficiently. Ah –'

He stops suddenly, looking behind me.

I turn. There's a woman standing in the doorway shaking rain from her coat.

Suddenly my little flat is Piccadilly Circus.

'Who are you?' I ask.

She puts her hand out. It's thin to shake, like if I held it properly all the bones would crush to dust.

'Sofia Nachant,' she says. 'It was me in the car last night.'

'The PM's aide?'

She nods.

I don't know what to say to her. My head's so full of everything right now.

'Thank you,' is all I manage to mutter.

'I won't be able to come here again,' she says. She might be small, and her voice is too, but she stands there with her shoulders back and her head high, and even though she's shorter than me, I feel tiny and insignificant.

She's the *PM's aide*, for Christ's sake.

'It's too risky. I had to borrow a car today and pretend I was a delivery driver. If I'm seen here, all hell will break loose.' She reaches into her bag. 'I've got these for you all though. Fake passes to get you through the gates. Don't go through together though. They're all linked to the factory on the East Side Industrial Estate. Their database is never updated so they're unlikely to be checked.'

I'm not really listening to her now. I've just realised something.

'Where's Eve?' I interrupt.

Nobody says a word.

'Why isn't she here?' I ask.

And now they're looking at each other. Nervous, shifty glances.

'What are you not telling me?' I say.

'Eve . . . She –' Cicero begins, but Max strides in the doorway and butts in.

'They've arrested her,' he says.

'Yeah, I know that, for not telling them where I was. That was last week. But she got off.'

Max is shaking his head. 'No,' he says. 'They arrested her

again last night. For murder. But you already knew she killed that man, didn't you? You knew from when you read the letter at the dockside and kept it from me. *She* killed that man, not my dad, but she let him take the blame.'

'It wasn't like that,' I say.

'Were you there?' he replies, and I can hear the anger in his voice. 'No, you weren't, so shut up. You think you know everything, but you don't. You think you've got the right to tell people what to do, affect people's lives, read their letters, rip them up –'

'But –'

'No! You know how they found out? Hey? Do you? They read it over your shoulder using CCTV!'

'They probably knew already though; everyone did. That's not really my fault.'

'Everyone?' he shouts. 'Not me, not Cicero!' He turns to Joshua. 'Did you know? Did you?'

Joshua shakes his head.

'Everyone here, in –'

'So it *is* your fault!' he shouts, and slams his fist down on the table. 'But you don't think anything's ever your fault, do you? And you know what? *All* this is! All this shit started with you. *You* are the cause of it. And now look around. Look at the people dead and dying and suffering.' He jabs his finger in my face and I pull back. His face is red. Bits of spit fleck around his mouth.

'I . . . I . . .' I stammer.

'Jackson died, Mrs B died, Isaac's lying in there about to die and my mum's going to die in seven days, and it's all. Your. Fault!'

45

It's like a slap in the face.

'Max . . .' Cicero says.

'No, Cicero, don't pander to her because she's had a tough upbringing or whatever. Everyone's had some kind of shit to deal with!'

'Eve's on death row?' I whisper.

I glance up at Max. A lot of people lately have looked at me like they want to see me dead, but Max looking at me like that . . . that's . . . that's . . .

'I'm sorry,' I mumble.

'Sorry won't save my mum!' he shouts.

I have to get out.

I stand up and push out of the kitchen and out the flat. Down the corridor, and I can't see the lift buttons because my eyes are so bleary, but I pound one and the doors judder open, and as soon as it reaches the bottom I run out into the cold, frost in the air and on the ground, and I run and run, away from the lights and the concrete and from that fury in Max's eyes.

Because he's right.

It is all my fault.

6.30 p.m. *Death is Justice*

Lights dance over the clean, bright studio. Intro music plays and the audience applaud. The camera drifts towards a beaming Kristina as she bounds from backstage wearing slim midnight-blue trousers and an ivory silk shirt, with blue high-heeled peep-toe shoes. Her blonde hair is loose and bounces on her shoulders.

MALE VOICEOVER: Good evening, ladies and gentlemen, and welcome to tonight's episode of *Death is Justice*, with your host . . . Kristina Albright!

The audience cheer. Kristina pauses centre stage and waves and clasps her hands together as she waits for the noise to die down.

KRISTINA: Thank you. Thank you so much for such a warm welcome. It is so great to be here, back at the helm of this most iconic of TV shows!

The audience applaud again. She raises her hands for silence.

KRISTINA: You really are too kind. I thank you. I think it's true to say it's been a tumultuous time here on

Death is Justice over the past few weeks. We've had the execution of a drug dealer and a joyrider, the release of a wife-beater and an armed robber, but overshadowing all of that we've had the ongoing misadventures of Martha Honeydew.

To the right the screen illuminates with the eye logo, the words 'An Eye For An Eye For' gently turning around the iris. It moves to the bottom corner and the main screen is taken up with the image of Martha from her first day on death row: freshly shaven head, mugshot board in her hands.

KRISTINA: It was two weeks ago today that the miscreant Martha Honeydew first came to the public's attention in the shocking and bloodthirsty murder of the much-loved celebrity personality Jackson Paige. During her time on death row, we all saw the callousness of Martha's nature, the coldness of her personality and the deep-rooted hatred that had been allowed to fester throughout her formative years. Yet it wasn't until the final moments of her time in Cell 7 that we, the law-abiding public, learned the terrible truth – that her hostility towards the authorities, her jealousy of those with money and her spiteful lust for revenge had driven her to take advantage of the boy Jackson Paige treated as his own blood, his adopted son, Isaac, forcing him to pull the trigger on the man who had cared for him so much and given him every opportunity in life. Not only that, of course, viewers, but she would've known that coercing him into such an act would ultimately lead to his own death if justice was to be served. A direct result of her selfish behaviour, Isaac Paige was placed on death row. Yet not happy with the chaos she had already caused, with the help of Rises sympathiser Eve Stanton, Honeydew escaped, and a fortune in taxpayers' money – *your* money – had to be spent on her recapture before her final act was played out.

She turns to the screen and the image of Martha is replaced by video footage from outside the death row building. The explosion rips across the front of the feed, the camera shakes and smoke and flames fill the screen. It flickers and changes to the head-cam footage of a policeman on the scene as he runs towards a fallen Martha. The feed bumps along and then stares down at her bloodied face.

Kristina turns back to camera. Behind her the footage loops over and over. The audience are silent.

KRISTINA (quietly): Thousands were injured last night but we should be thankful nobody was killed. However, almost twenty-four hours on, there is still no sign of Isaac Paige, and his adoptive mother, Patty, is currently on life support. Should Isaac's body be found, or Mrs Jackson not survive, then Honeydew, already arrested at the scene, sentenced on *Buzz for Justice* and incarcerated, would be looking at returning to death row to again be judged. It has been quite the scandal and quite the adventure. But, I hear you ask, what of death row now? Well, here's where we have news for you.

She approaches the display. The recording of the explosion is replaced by the live feed of Gerome Sharp standing outside the Old Bailey. Wearing a woollen coat with the collar turned up, his shoulders hunched and his bare hands gripping an oversized microphone, he smiles to the camera.

KRISTINA: Hello there, Gerome, and how are you this evening?

GEROME: Cold, Kristina! It's more than a bit nippy out here tonight. But also very happy to be reporting live for you from what is the new, yet the old, death row.

KRISTINA: Explain . . .

GEROME: Well, as you can see, I'm standing outside the Old Bailey, which is where the accused are now being held. Of course, since the devastating attack, the purpose-built death row can't be used, so this has become the alternative.

He strolls towards the front doors. The camera follows him.

GEROME: As I'm sure many of you history buffs are aware, the Old Bailey stands on the site of the medieval Newgate Prison, an area which over the years has seen more than a thousand people executed! The court itself hosted the infamous trials of such as the Yorkshire Ripper and Oscar Wilde, the Kray twins and Dr Crippen and is the *perfect* location for our new death row.

KRISTINA: Ready made and purpose built, Gerome.

GEROME: Absolutely, Kristina, even though it was years ago. Why these weren't used previously, I have no idea, as thousands, *millions*, of pounds could've been saved. Certainly I'd question the need to rebuild death row now.

KRISTINA: But are they fit for purpose?

GEROME: I think we may be able to answer that, Kristina.

He smiles and winks to camera, rests his hand on the wooden door and pushes it open.

GEROME (whispering): Come with me . . .

The camera follows him through the door and into a huge

hallway. His shoes click on the marble floor and echo off the high painted ceiling and glass domes. He continues past murals of the Blitz, statues of long-dead monarchs and a huge staircase, turns down double-width corridors and passes under axioms painted around the walls. The camera pauses on one of them – *The Welfare Of The People Is Supreme.*

GEROME (loud, echoing): What a place of splendour!

The camera focuses back on him and follows him as he continues through a side doorway and the glamour is lost. He passes through another doorway, marked 'Do not wedge open' and down a narrow stairway. The light is dim, dirt is smeared on the walls and the warm breath of the cameraman condenses on the lens.

Gerome stops at the bottom. The upper half of the brick walls behind him are an old white, the lower, a dull green. Parts have crumbled away, leaving holes and gaps, while other areas are covered in black mould, and the concrete floor is dirty, chipped and appears damp. Thick pipes and ducting run the length of the long ceiling and electrical cables hang loosely along the walls. Above each of the seven open doorways a dull light flickers in a small, cracked plastic box.

Gerome wafts a hand in front of his face and turns to camera.

GEROME (smiling, gleeful): This, ladies and gentlemen, is the new death row! Once home to the worst criminals in history – a very fitting and apt place.

He continues walking, turns a corner, the walls now off-white painted brick, dirty and chipped, and he ducks to squeeze through a series of archways of ever-decreasing size.

GEROME: Historically known as Dead Man's Walk, this was the last journey of murderers such as Catherine Wilson in 1862, who the judge at the time said was 'the greatest criminal who ever lived'! Her execution attracted an audience of more than twenty thousand people! She, like her murderous fellows, took this final journey to the gallows. At the end of this corridor is the birdcage, an outdoor area where the public would get their final view, a chance to throw rotten fruit, hurl abuse and for them to feel vindicated.

KRISTINA (off-screen): And tell us, Gerome, is this something our public will have the chance to do?

Gerome stops in front of a large door, turns to camera and touches his ear.

GEROME: That certainly is the plan, Kristina, to take these cells and restore them to their former glory. To re-instigate the viewing areas and platforms. Yet in a slight twist from the previous death row, the accused will now be kept in Cell 7 until the final half-hour. Then they will be escorted along this walkway, under the birdcage, and out of this door into –

He rests a hand on the door.

KRISTINA: Like passing through the tunnel to a football match, or out into the gladiatorial ring!

He pushes the door open and steps outside.

GEROME: Exactly! I present . . . the execution room.

There's a flurry of activity; workmen in hard hats, some carrying clipboards, others with ladders or rolls of wire, banging and whistling. Wooden steps lead to a raised platform where men are perched on stepladders and surrounded by cabling. To the side is a gallery area, where railings are being attached, and on the high brick wall behind, workmen are installing cameras and a large screen.

GEROME: Imagine that buzz of excitement and the thrill of anticipation as the accused emerges into the light. The roar of the crowd, the blast of cold air! And not only will more people have access to see the accused meet their deserved end, but as the arena is roofless, we will have a drone above us feeding back live to subscribers of the service. For those lucky enough to have tickets, refreshments will be available from a number of retail outlets around the edges, which are currently being constructed. The perfect place to grab a quick burger or beer between stats. Not only that, but vendors will be passing through the crowd selling ice creams, and binoculars will be available for hire, for a reasonable fee, to allow a better view of the accused's face and the general goings-on.

KRISTINA: I need one of those tickets, Gerome!

GEROME (laughing): Well, Kristina, I hear rumours of a special media box being installed!

KRISTINA: Oh my!

GEROME: Yes, I thought that would be a grand surprise for you! You could have ringside seats to every execution. What more could you ask for?

KRISTINA: Gerome, it's a dream come true, and of course, will be of huge benefit to our viewers unable to purchase tickets or take advantage of our death drone service; we are truly an inclusive organisation, catering to all members of society. But tell me, when will this begin? Will there be a break in service?

GEROME: There will absolutely not be a break in service, Kristina. As you can see behind me, work is going on 24/7. Thankfully we have a day's grace as no one is currently in Cell 7, but tomorrow will be the final count for the prisoner Josef Constance, accused of beating an elderly lady to death. We wouldn't want to add to the pain of the victim's family by delaying the final count.

KRISTINA: Absolutely not, Gerome.

He moves back into Dead Man's Walk and begins retracing his steps. His voice is lower.

GEROME: It is a huge misfortune that we are currently unable to offer 24-hour viewing into each of the cells. However technicians have installed a camera above the entrance to the row, and there is constant viewing available through this. But don't be disappointed! We understand you, the public, need this information to make an informed decision, and so we have come up with an alternative.

He reaches the end of the corridor and stands close to the cells. The doors are closed, but the hatches are open. At some, fingers poke through and hold the bars; at others is nothing. He stops next to Cell 1.

GEROME: Yes, ladies and gentlemen, from tomorrow I shall be down here every day interviewing the accused, filming them in their cells, posing the questions you want to hear answered. And as the case is such a hot one, such a drama – a veritable real-life soap opera – our first interview shall be with none other than . . . Eve Stanton.

The camera moves off him and towards the open hatch. The bars blur and disappear from view as the camera zooms in to focus on Eve, sitting on the single mattress on the floor. With a shaved head, red eyes and shaking hands, she stares into the camera.

GEROME: How the mighty have fallen.

Daffodil House

In Martha's kitchen Max, Cicero and Joshua stare at the tiny TV screen screwed to the wall.

Behind his glasses, Cicero blinks and blinks, and the coffee cup in his hands shakes ever so slightly.

'Have you been replaced?' Max asks Joshua.

'I remember him,' Joshua replies. 'We had lunch once in the staff canteen. He was full of rhetoric about how corrupt the government was, how ridiculous the justice system is.' He shrugs.

'Could he be trying to infiltrate them?'

Joshua shakes his head. 'He was too ambitious. Offer that kind of man money and fame, and morals fall like autumn leaves. What does he have to worry about now?'

'Nothing,' Cicero answers, 'until the tide turns. Which it will. The public are fickle.' He turns to Max. 'You were rough on Martha,' he says.

Max shrugs. 'My mum's there because of her.' He nods towards the television: a close-up of Eve on one side of the screen while Gerome talks to camera on the other side.

'No, your mum's there because the system is corrupt and wrong.'

'Or because she killed a man and let my dad die for it,' Max replies.

'She killed him in self-defence,' Cicero says.

'And let my father die for it!' Max shouts.

'But –' Cicero begins.

'No, Cicero, there is no *but* – she let my father die and she lied to save herself. Fact. And Martha . . .' His mouth turns down and he shakes his head. 'She held that letter out for everyone to see.'

'They knew already.'

'*I* didn't!' he shouts, and he storms out of the room.

Cicero and Joshua flinch as the door slams.

Slowly their attention goes back to the television: photos and clips of Eve on loop while Gerome and Kristina talk to each other.

'How long have you been in love with her?' Joshua whispers to Cicero.

For a few moments Cicero stands in silence. Then he takes a slurp of coffee and sighs heavily.

'Since the day I met her,' he whispers. 'But I never told her.' With tears in his eyes he walks away.

Martha

Max is right.

Kind of.

Is it my fault Eve's on death row?

Kind of.

My fault that all this is happening?

Yeah, kind of that too.

I'm tempted to find a way over, past or through this wall and disappear into the distance and never come back. Chalk this all up to experience, start a new life in some remote Scottish village, or jump in the back of a truck going to Europe.

It'd follow me though, wouldn't it?

If not physically, then in my head.

Someone who didn't care would clear off, but I do care, you see. Maybe that's what's got me into all this trouble in the first place.

OK then, Martha, my head says. *So you do care and you're not going anywhere; then what are you going to do?*

I sit down on a log, close to the entrance of the shelter here at Bracken Woods, near where we made our fires, and shove my hand in my pockets. My right one hits something and I pull it out. Huh – an old piece of Mrs B's honey cake wrapped in foil. Lord knows how long that's been there. I eat it anyway.

Nothing's changed here in the woods.

But everything out there has.

'What do I do?' I whisper to the trees, the birds sleeping in their nests, the badgers and squirrels.

You're not fucking Snow White and this is not a fairy story, I tell myself in my head. *The animals don't listen and they can't help you. Buck up, and get on with it.*

'Get on with what?' I whisper. 'I don't know what to do.'

The moonlight on the leaves is like silver. Frost on the ground like diamonds. The undergrowth rustles quietly, then a rabbit pokes its head out and looks at me. Bold as brass it hops my way, its nostrils flicking at the air.

I freeze, watching it.

I've dropped some crumbs of food near my feet, reckon it can smell them.

It comes closer to me.

Why is it so brave?

Why does it trust me?

It doesn't, I think, *but it's hungry. Starving. It's weighed up the danger, knows it can run if you move, but it bets on you being that surprised that you won't.*

It grabs the food and runs off, and I do nothing but watch it go.

Clever rabbit, I think.

No, it's instinct.

I look up to the dark sky and the stars.

Our stars.

What do your instincts tell you to do? I ask myself.

* * *

I walk back the long way.

The very long way; out the back of Bracken Woods, down the alleyways leading to what was the shopping precinct – mostly boarded and shuttered up now – past the drunks and the homeless, so many homeless, and towards the wall.

It looms over everything.

Huge concrete panels slotted between upright posts, big floodlights at the top of maybe every third or fourth one. I go right up to the bottom of the wall, following it round; in some places there are piles of mud and rubble, broken pavements, knocked-down trees and street signs, even someone's garden fence.

It's a mess.

And it's ugly.

There's a break in it further along. Some kind of gateway like the entrance into some posh hotel complex or upmarket housing estate, only it's not, it's us. There's a red-and-white striped barrier across, a turnstile, and some kind of booth that a guard's sitting in. There's another guard at the barrier.

The floodlights blaze down and it's impossible to hide.

I back up, trying to disappear into the darkness where the lights don't reach.

Don't know if they can see me or not, but I keep quiet and I move slowly.

'This is boring,' the guard at the bar says. He takes a drag of a cigarette and flicks it at the booth.

'Pack it in,' the other one says as he comes out. He tucks a rolled-up newspaper under his arm and strides towards the other one.

'What are we supposed to do anyway?' the first asks.

'Get them in. Stop them coming out.'

'But what if they want to go out?'

'Our instructions are only to let them out if they've got work to go to. Weren't you listening?'

The first one mumbles something and shrugs. I step a bit closer. There's a broken bench so I duck behind that.

'Don't get why though,' the first one says.

'You should pay attention to what goes on around you. These are dangerous people, and we've been given an important, but dangerous, job.'

'What?'

'Read the papers,' he says, and taps him in the chest with his copy of the *National News*. 'Look at the front page. "Rises Layabouts Milk The Justice System". That's where your taxes are going. To give these lazy fuckers mobile phones and satellite TV! Look at all these boarded-up shops. They won't work in them, will they? But they'll come into the City and take jobs there.'

He nods his head. 'Yeah, I get you. Then we shouldn't let them out at all!'

'It would be safer if we didn't. There need to be tighter controls. We don't want another attack like the Rises 7 did, that's for sure.'

Stupid fucker, I think. He has no clue and he's spreading his ignorance.

Bloody newspapers.

Scandal sells.

And as long as it's selling, who gives a toss if it's true?

I take a step forward to go and argue with them.

'Who are the Rises 7?' the first guy says, and I stop.

'Where've you been? The moon or prison or somewhere? The Rises 7 – the terrorists who bombed death row and tried to kill all the people in it and the people outside. How do you not know about that?'

'I was out drinking last night. I haven't put the telly on all day.'

'And you just turned up for work without questioning why we're being sent to a massive wall and why it's there in the first place?'

The first guy just shrugs.

'It could've been carnage if they'd been clever enough to get it right.' His voice is lower now. I've frozen. Daren't move. 'Everyone in the City and the Avenues is talking about it. There's uproar. It's just been on the news – they found a car full of explosives near the Old Bailey, and another one at the Royal Courts of Justice. They say it was supposed to be a simultaneous attack – they found another trigger in the Stanton woman's handbag, another in that presenter's house – Joshua whatshisname.'

My stomach flips. I feel sick.

'Public are in uproar. But the PM was already on it, he'd already ordered this wall. Making plans to put anyone in here who's a threat to national security – any sympathisers.'

'What? Sympathisers are a threat to national security? Why?'

'Because they sympathise with this lot, you dumb fuck, and this lot are all a bunch of terrorists.'

I open my mouth to rant and argue. *Don't*, that voice in my head says. *Think carefully.*

'Jesus,' the man says, and he stands a bit taller, puts his hand on the gun at his belt. 'Man, you're scaring me.'

'You should be scared,' he replies.

Fuck, I think, and I shrink back into the shadows.

'The PM's a clever man though. And that Stanton woman's never going to be found innocent now. Public have turned against her. And people are scared, wondering who else is a sympathiser. Police are rounding them up, bringing them here.'

'It's a ghetto,' I breathe.

'We need to be on it. This job, here, this is a massive responsibility. The police need to make sure all the evil's in one place, and we need to make sure it stays in here.'

'A lie told often enough,' I whisper, 'becomes the truth.'

I walk on.

We're being demonised.

People who don't hate us already will soon enough.

They class us as one, lump us all together. Like a race, a nationality or a sub-section of society.

How can they hate us so much?

What have we done?

We, and that fucking irritates. It's not *we*. We are not one, we are not all, we are not responsible for each other's actions.

Good and bad are found in rich and poor, in black and white, in gay and straight. In everyone.

People are individuals.

Do the authorities fear us?

And there's that *us* now.

But it's easier to control like that, use the media to turn the public against *us*.

Manipulate into hating, and let the public do your dirty work.

It's shit, but I don't know how to fight it.

All I ever wanted was a fair justice system, without corruption, but this thing has grown arms and legs.

I walk on. My fingers are numb, the wind's like ice on my face. Sky looks heavy.

Things, words, ideas rattle round in my head.

I wonder if we'll have snow.

Newspaper headlines.

Not long till Christmas.

That everyone reads.

A white Christmas?

And everyone believes.

Wonder if it'll be a Christmas with you, Isaac.

And everyone talks about.

DECEMBER 2ND

Death is Justice: The Breakfast Show

In an outside broadcast Gerome Sharp smiles to camera as he holds an oversized, fuzzy microphone. He wears a green soldier's helmet fastened under his chin and a black bulletproof vest with 'PRESS' written in red across the front.

GEROME: Good morning, viewers, and welcome to our on-the-scene breakfast show. In light of the recent shocking and worrying events, we at *Death is Justice* have upped our coverage to keep you informed and to bring you all the relevant news and gossip from death row.

Behind him looms the grey expanse of the wall, the high-rise flats just visible in the distance.

GEROME: As you can see from my bulletproof vest and helmet, police are taking security *very* seriously, although even with these precautions they say they *cannot* guarantee my safety. It may be worrying, it may be dangerous, but it will not stop me from bringing you, the public, all you need to know.

The camera follows him as he moves along the wall.

GEROME: This wall may have been constructed in record time, but the importance of security has never slipped from the planners', and builders', minds. These concrete panels reach a height of twenty-five metres – far too high for anyone to scale. I am also assured that each panel is inserted into the ground to a minimum depth of five metres – far too deep for anyone to dig under without being noticed. But some have asked if this eyesore is absolutely necessary.

He stops walking near a break in the wall, the gap spanned by a security barrier and a turnstile. To one side is a small booth.

GEROME: Joining me first today is nearby resident Mrs Eva Wilson.

He moves sideways and an elderly woman wearing slacks and a padded jacket comes into view. She smiles awkwardly at the camera, then turns to Gerome.

GEROME: Mrs Wilson, I believe you and your family have lived in these parts for many years, and in fact you still live in the same house you were born in eighty-two years ago.

MRS WILSON: That's right. I live in that row of terraces over there.

GEROME: And do you consider that a safe distance from the Rises?

MRS WILSON: It might be now this wall's here. Now we won't get none of them kids walking through at all hours, singing and dancing down the road like they own the place. You'd think they didn't have homes to go to. Or parents waiting for them. And the girls? You should see the make-up on their faces, and the piercings. Even some of the boys wear make-up! Or have tattoos.

GEROME: How do you feel about the wall? Does it block out your light? Does it look ugly from your window?

MRS WILSON: I'm relieved. I've had eight new locks put on my front door in case them kids try to break in. I don't feel safe in my own bed with them around. It makes me shudder just thinking about what they might do.

GEROME: How many times has your house been broken into, Mrs Wilson?

MRS WILSON: I couldn't say it has, exactly; it's more the worry. You read all this stuff about what's happening and how these Rises folk are terrorising everyone and I lie in my bed in fear at night! But I tell you, that PM's done the right thing. He's got a heart of gold, spending all that money on this wall to make us safer. He'll get my vote again.

GEROME: Thank you, Mrs Wilson.

He strolls the other way, closer to the security gate, where a stocky man with a shaved head stands with his chest out and his hands behind his back.

GEROME: We also have the pleasure of being joined by the newly appointed Chief of Wall Security, Jed Gregory. Jed, to the uninformed this wall might seem like quite an overreaction, wouldn't you say? Especially considering that the perpetrator of the crime, Martha Honeydew, has already been arrested.

JED: Mr Sharp, let me explain something to you and your viewers. The purpose of law is not only to punish the guilty but to protect the innocent. Had this been applied adequately, and Honeydew been executed as she deserved, we would not be in this situation. We are now forced to shut the stable door after the horse has bolted.

GEROME: Then why shut the stable door at all?

JED: Because there are other horses, Mr Sharp. Three of the Rises 7 – Max Stanton, Thomas Cicero and Joshua Decker – are still at large, and they all pose a sustained and veritable threat to the safety of the innocent citizens the law has vowed to defend.

GEROME: You think they'd strike again?

JED: A leopard does not change his spots, sir.

GEROME: But surely it would be easier to arrest the suspects, rather than build this?

The camera pans out before focusing back on the two men.

JED: I don't think you appreciate the seriousness of the situation. I don't wish to alarm you, or your viewers, but thinking like that assumes no one else is a threat. And when we assume things we let our guard down, and that is when people get hurt.

GEROME: But after the police have arrested the suspects, will this be taken down?

JED: That's not my decision, but I would advise careful consideration. As I said, others may be a threat too. After all we don't know what influence the Rises 7 have had. We should remember the phrase 'One bad apple spoils the barrel.'

GEROME: Thank you, Jed, wise words indeed. Well, viewers, we've been offered an exclusive here on *Death is Justice: The Breakfast Show* – we are being allowed access into the Rises itself! Escorted by Jed and his hopefully very capable team. This is quite nerve-wracking. I'll just . . . adjust my helmet here and . . . tighten my vest.

The camera follows as Jed Gregory and three security officers lead Gerome through the turnstile and into the Rises. Two armed guards stand at the checkpoint.

GEROME: Viewers, the area in front of us is one you may be familiar with – the underpass where, notoriously, Jackson Paige was shot only sixteen days ago. The act that triggered this increase in violence in our city. To my left you can see the now-defunct railway station. Closing this, I'm told, will stop any stowaways getting into the City by hiding on the trains, or sneaking through. To my left you can see boarded-up shops, a symbol of the deprivation found here, and –

A loud bang sounds. The camera jerks and zooms upwards to sky, smoke pluming from the park ahead of them. It shakes then tips downwards, focusing on Gerome sprawled in the gutter. His cheek is bleeding and his chin is grazed.

GEROME: Oh my God, what was that? There was an explosion! Can you hear me back in the studio? There's someone running through the smoke towards us. I'm going. I'm going. This is Gerome Sharp, signing off and searching for safety!

The screen fizzes with static.

Martha

Did you hear that, Isaac?

They're letting fireworks off outside. Nutters. It's daytime.

Can you feel my hand holding yours?

I hope so.

I know Dr Novak is doing everything he can for you.

I know he'll do that whether I'm here or not, but I feel I should be, y'know? In case you . . . *when* you wake up. So I'm here.

I want to be the first person you see.

I want to be holding your hand.

And I want the first words you hear to be me telling you I love you.

But I've got to go for a while. I know I left you yesterday, but that was only half an hour; this time I'm going to be a while.

I want to tell you not to wake before I get back, but how selfish is that?

What if you were sitting up in bed when I walked back through the door? Smiling at me? Putting your hand out to hold mine?

Shouldn't let myself think that. Need to be realistic. Need to think what'll happen if you never wake up.

But Jesus, thinking that hurts.

I'm giving you the puzzle ring back. Eve put it on a chain

for me, and I'm putting it round your neck. Look after it for me, and show me how to solve it when you wake.

I'm going to go through the gates today, Isaac, and I'm going to do the best I bloody can to sort things out.

And I will be back.

I promise you that.

Eve

There are doors, but they keep them open now. I heard someone say it's to make it easier for the cameraman.

I'm chained to the furthest wall of the cell; I assume everyone else is too. The chains are heavy and thick, tied around my wrists and ankles; I can still move, but only to the doorway.

'Eve Stanton!'

I jump at the sound of my name and my stomach flips over. A guard stands in the doorway.

'Remember me?' he says. He strides into the cell and I step back until I'm up against the wall.

'I remember you,' he says, and he leans forward, his breath pungent in my face and the sweat from his armpits stinging my eyes. 'I remember you from all the times you told me and my men what to do. Thinking you were above us, Miss High and Mighty. Better than us.'

His fat, sweaty fingers run down my cheek.

'Look at you now. From grace to the gutter.' He reaches around me and I try to pull away but he grabs hold of me. 'You're mine, sweetheart. I could do what I like to you and nobody would ever know,' he hisses in my ear. 'You know what I want to do?' He pulls on the chains around my wrists and yanks me sideways. 'Hey, darling?' I close my eyes, but he grabs my face.

'Open your eyes and look at me!'

I peer at him, as a sneer creeps across his face. I feel sick. Is this what the guards did to the female prisoners when I wasn't around? Has it always been like this?

'You know what I'm going to do?' he hisses. 'Nothing!' He laughs in my face. 'Cos you're just some dirty scum. God knows what I could catch off you. God knows where you've been, or who you've been with. Dirtbags from the Rises probably. You could catch herpes from them, HIV, Ebola, rabies.'

'You really are ignorant,' I say without thinking.

His lips peel back against his yellow teeth and his eyes widen. 'Nah,' he says. 'I read the papers, see? They've been warning us for years about the Rises scum. Society should've stopped listening to the likes of you a long time ago.'

'It's lies,' I say.

'Shut up!' he shouts, and his hand slips down my face, onto my neck and I feel his fingers tighten.

'I could finish you, just like that,' he hisses. 'There's no camera in here.'

I reach to peel his fingers from my throat but he grabs the chains with his other hand and yanks them down. I can't move now. My face feels like it's swelling.

'But that would take all the fun out of watching you suffer.'

He lets go and I fall to the ground.

As one last insult he spits on my face.

'History will judge you,' I tell him.

Martha

I told Dr Novak I was going out.

I left him my phone number, told him to ring me if anything happened.

He nodded and didn't ask whether I meant if Isaac wakes or if he dies.

He said he'd update Cicero and Joshua when he saw them.

Said he'd tell Max too, but nobody knows where Max has gone. That worries me – it feels like I should look after him while Eve isn't here. I think Dr Novak saw that in my face, because he touched my arm with his parchment hands and told me that Cicero was doing what he could.

Cicero. Of course.

I'm walking towards the gates now, the shadow of Daffodil House on the path and over me. Hidden inside my jacket is the file of documents Isaac stole from his dad, that Max had shoved into his laptop bag and remembered to grab when they ran from Eve's house. Bloody hope the guards don't search me.

There's a queue of people waiting to get out, stretching back from the gates. I join the end. Nobody's saying anything. I keep my head down, but I watch the others, see a few make eye contact and a few carefully raised eyebrows of recognition of what an arse this is.

'Like Jews,' the old woman in front of me whispers.

I want to acknowledge her and agree, but I don't. Can't get drawn into conversation in case folk recognise me. Too risky.

Loose lips sink ships, and all that.

Except I haven't even got a ship any more!

There's some sort of commotion at the front, raised voices, and the folks in the queue peer around each other to see.

A middle-aged woman and what must be her teenage son are walking back this way. They've not let them through!

She's crying. He's got his arm around her.

I can't help myself. 'What happened?' I ask as they get to me, and I reach out and put a hand on the woman's arm. She looks at me, tears pouring down her face, sobbing and sobbing. She doesn't say anything, just shakes her head.

'They won't let us through,' the boy says, my kind of age, maybe a bit younger. 'They said we can't leave unless we're going to work, and that there's no other reason to go through.'

'But . . .' I say, wishing he'd hurry up and tell me before the guards notice us.

'My sister's in hospital. We wanted to visit.'

The woman in front of me spins around. 'Surely they'll let you through for that?'

'No,' the boy mutters. 'No exceptions, they said.'

I hang my head. I want to go and argue with the guards, but that would be suicide. This is shit. Complete and utter shit.

'We had a card to give her,' he whispers. 'My little brother made it.'

'Give it to me,' I say. 'I'll take it.'

The woman looks at me. Her tears stutter down her face. 'You'd do that?'

'I've got a pass to go to work. I can go via the hospital. Give it to me.'

She pulls an envelope from her handbag and I shove it into my jacket.

'Oi! You two, get out of here or I'll have you arrested!'

'Go,' I tell them.

'I said . . .' the guard carries on, his voice louder, and I can hear the stamp of his boots.

I look away from the woman and her son. I have to.

The guard stops shouting.

I look back and they've gone.

I'm through the gates.

Scanned the pass Sofia gave me, no questions asked. They didn't look at my face, just seemed happy that I was going somewhere to work. Or so they thought.

Would they have realised who I am?

Pretty certain they would. My face is still plastered on sides of buses as wanted even though I'm supposed to be in prison.

There was a name on the get-well card, thank God. I took it to the hospital, left it with reception.

A nurse promised it would get to her.

I'm in the City centre now, heading for a park.

There aren't many people about; too cold, probably. The trees are bare, the grass crunches under my feet, but it's clean and tidy and well looked after.

What else would you expect from a park in the heart of the City?

I edge through, keeping to the paths, trimmed bushes lining the way, and on a quiet stretch I sit on a bench.

I look up to the trees, tops of lamp posts, even the bins. No, I can't see any cameras. My back's against an old brick wall and there's nothing on that either.

Carefully I pull the file from inside my coat and peel back the cover. It's battered now, but thank God Max didn't leave it at his house or take it with him yesterday. And thank bloody God I managed to find it in all his stuff.

Suppose I could've looked through this at the flat, but I don't want to involve anyone else. I need to do this by myself.

I flick through it and stop on a page. Names and names of people everyone thinks are upstanding members of society, whatever that means.

Celebrities, do-gooders, national treasures.

But what are they really like?

Huh, well, I've got some of the answers right here.

But who gives a damn?

Jesus, Eve's got four days left. And I'm not bloody getting talked into some mad bomb idea this time! No, this time we do it properly.

I remember when Eve's husband was on death row. Everyone said he'd get off – they said everyone from the City or the Avenues always got off, so he was bound to as well. In his case I was glad about that – most folk I knew were, because we all knew the truth, and knew that he didn't deserve to die.

When he was found guilty, I remember the headlines were all about the case showing that folks from the City and the

Avenues are brought to justice as well. That it was proof there just *happened* to be more criminals in the Rises.

Eve stayed in my head that day. One of the only times I ever watched, or started to watch, the execution. She was so composed. Calm and . . . and . . . *respectful*. Even when the mother of the guy who tried to kill her gave her victim's speech. God, she kept a cool head when I would've lamped that woman one.

I was that cross I had to turn the TV off.

I suppose that's why I remember her first case as designated counsellor too.

Yeah. Nicolas Braden. Ran over some guy his wife just *happened* to be having an affair with.

He, Braden, worked in newspapers and it was all over the media. He got off and much thanks to her.

Huh.

He worked in newspapers . . .

Got off, *much thanks to her* . . .

Back of my neck prickles and my stomach flips with excitement.

Dare I?

Of course I bloody dare.

DI Hart

DI Hart steps out of the front doors of his Kensington home and strides to his black BMW, parked on the double yellow lines in front.

He doesn't see the figure slink across the road as he unlocks the door, and he doesn't notice him approach the passenger door with perfect timing to open it seconds before DI Hart drives away.

'Hey!' he says to the hooded figure in the passenger seat.

The figure, his face obscured, points something at him through the pocket of his jacket. 'Drive,' he says, 'or I'll shoot you.'

Without pausing to think, Hart turns the ignition and moves into the moving traffic. 'Who are you?' he asks. 'What do you want?'

'I have a proposition.'

Hart looks sideways at him.

'Don't look at me!' he shouts. 'Keep your hands on the steering wheel and your eyes on the road.'

'What do you want?'

'It's what you want.'

'I want you out of my car!'

'No. You want Martha Honeydew.'

Hart laughs hard and shakes his head. 'OK, OK, so you're

a bit slow on the uptake, or you don't watch the news. There was no need to jump my car and shove your finger into your jacket pocket and pretend it's a gun. I have Honeydew! She is safely locked up and won't be coming out for a very long time. *If* she comes out at all, as it looks very much like Patty Paige is going to stay a vegetable. Now,' he says, slowing down and indicating to the side of the road, 'get out of my car.'

'Not so fast,' the man says and, giving up on his pretend gun, he pulls a phone from his pocket, scrolls through the screen and holds it in Hart's line of sight.

Hart's gaze flicks from the road to the screen and back again. A few times. Making sure.

'See the time on it? And the date?'

Hart looks again.

'So she looks like Honeydew. So what?'

He touches the screen, zooms in and puts it back where Hart can see it.

'It looks like Honeydew because it is Honeydew.'

'It can't be.'

'Take a left here.'

'What?'

'Don't believe me? I'll prove it to you. Turn left here. We're going to the prison.'

'You've lost it.'

'Hold that judgement.'

'Why go there? I could phone.'

'And they could fob you off.'

'This is a waste of my time,' he sighs, but he turns left, drives through traffic lights and changes gear.

'If you believe that, then why are you still driving?'

They continue in silence, through traffic, across roundabouts and down side streets until they pull up in front of the prison.

Hart turns off the engine.

'Stay here,' he says as he gets out of the car.

The man in the passenger seat watches Hart walk over to the gates and his eyes don't move from the space until half an hour later, when he reappears.

Even from across the road, he can see Hart's face is stone and his chest is pumped out.

He watches him get back into the car.

The door slams.

For a moment they sit in silence.

'What do you want?' Hart asks eventually.

The man sighs. 'Safety. Guaranteed.'

Hart nods. 'I can give you that.'

'And . . .' he says, and he sucks in a deep breath and sighs heavily. Then he pulls down his hood and looks Hart square in the face. '. . . my mum out of prison.'

Hart stares at Max, unflinching and unsurprised.

Martha

I type the numbers into the phone.

Try to swallow but I've got a dry mouth.

A jogger smiles at me as she goes past, but I ignore her. I wish I could disappear into the undergrowth or be invisible for a while.

It rings.

My heart pounds.

'Good afternoon. *National News*, which department, please?'

I lean forward, almost doubled over, trying to hide from everything.

'Could you put me through to Nicolas Braden, please?'

'Who shall I say is calling?'

Holy cow, errr . . . my brain blanks. Quick, Martha, think.

'Errr, it's his child's school,' I blurt. 'If you could be quick, please.'

I get background music for a couple of seconds then a deep male voice cuts into it.

'Hello, this is Nicolas Braden. Is everything OK with the children?'

'The children are fine,' I say, firm and cold. 'Please don't hang up. This isn't the school, but I need to talk you.'

'Who is this?' he says.

'I have some information about you that I don't think

you'd want falling into the wrong hands.'

'I don't know what you're talking about.' His voice has gone from worried to curious to angry in three sentences.

'From your time on death row.'

Silence.

Then a sigh.

'That was a long time ago,' he whispers. And from angry to resigned.

'Meet me in five minutes. In the park opposite your work. The cafe there.'

I click the phone off.

Shit, I'm shaking.

You're at the pointy end now, Honeydew! my head tells me.

Huh, been at the pointy end for more than a fortnight.

The cafe's heaving.

I knew it would be.

Mums with buggies, crying babies, noisy toddlers, tourists poring over maps, businessmen chatting about work, teens using free internet.

One of those strange places that attracts everyone.

I grab a bottle of juice from the fridges and sit down at a table in the corner. I leave my hood up; some folks in here still have hats on, or scarves or winter coats; everyone fits in because everyone does what the hell they want.

But he doesn't.

I see him walk in, shifty eyes scanning faces and tables. Pausing at the women who look like they're dressed for an office. What's he thinking? That it's some kind of corporate espionage? Blackmail? Who knows? I know for a fact he won't be expecting me.

He orders a cappuccino, takes a seat at the bar that looks out over the pond and slips his jacket off. I let him stew for five minutes, then stand up, sidle over to him and sit down.

I leave it a moment, then in a low voice I say, 'You got on well with Eve Stanton then?'

He sips his drink. 'Who are you and what do you want?' He's still staring forward.

'Doesn't seem right, her being on death row, does it?'

'Why the hell should I care?'

'I think you do. She was good to you. She passed notes between you and your wife.'

'How . . . ?' His eyes flick sideways for a second, then straight back to the window and the pond.

'And your son. Although your daughter was a bit too young. In fact, she probably doesn't remember any of it. Maybe she doesn't even know.'

'So?'

'Do you ever lie in bed at night thinking that if it wasn't for Eve Stanton you'd be dead?'

'It was a *public* vote.' His voice is firm.

Outside a swan lifts his magnificent wings, flapping them as his black legs splash uselessly at the water until he lifts into the sky.

This guy next to me wants to be like that, but I'm a pike in the water, and he knows I'm there. Knows I'll have those feet if he even tries to flap away from me.

'So her telling your wife that the guy going under your car

90

was an accident – just bad timing, unlucky – had nothing to do with you getting off?'

'I didn't –'

'Then your wife going on *Death is Justice* and telling them some sob story, that missed out key points – like she'd been having an affair with the guy and you'd just found out – to get the public on your side. And taking your baby daughter with her, that did nothing, did it?'

I feel him looking at me. I don't move.

'What is your point?'

'I don't care if you killed that guy on purpose or not, but I do care about Eve Stanton. I care what people think about her, and I care that she's going to be killed for acting in self-defence.'

I turn to him, staring at the side of his head until eventually he looks at me. I see him gulp, then his eyes widen.

'Honeydew?' he whispers.

I don't answer.

'You've got some bloody balls contacting me. Wait . . . hang on, you're supposed to be in prison. How the hell . . . ?'

His voice is getting louder. I lean towards him. 'Shut your face or I'll shut it for you.'

'You can't threaten me.'

'I fucking can, and I fucking am.'

'I could have you arrested,' he hisses, leaning towards me. 'I could stand up and shout that you're here. Claim a reward. They can't know you're not in prison, surely? Or is this some cover-up?'

'Just for a minute, shut your mouth and listen to me. After that, if you still want to stand up and shout out and have me arrested and all that crap, then be my guest. OK?'

To my surprise, he does as he's told.

'Like it or not, me and you have a lot in common; we've both been on death row, both faced death, both survived it. And we've both been supported by Eve Stanton. I'm pretty sure you were guilty, and I know there's CCTV footage that looks like you steered towards that guy –'

'I didn't.'

'But for whatever reasons, they never used it. If I wanted to, I could land you back on death row and most likely have you executed.'

I pause for effect and take a slug from the bottle. 'I don't want to do that. Eve helped you a lot – she must've had her reasons – and she helped me too. We both owe her.'

I look him straight in the eye.

'Do you think she should die?'

'Of course not,' he says, 'but it's not my problem.'

'It wasn't her problem that you were going to die either. But still she went above and beyond what she was supposed to do.'

He lifts the teaspoon and moves it through the froth on his cappuccino.

'For what it's worth,' he whispers, 'it *was* an accident. A complete coincidence. People don't believe in coincidences though, do they? Eve understood that.' He puts the spoon down. 'But there's nothing I can do to help.'

'Yes, there is. You can help me help her. Use your influence at the newspaper. Run a story in there.'

He laughs and shakes his head. 'They won't touch it.'

'I'm not asking you to get their permission. I'm telling you to put it in. You must be able to hack the printing system or computer or something. Take one story off the front page and put something else there instead.'

'That's professional suicide. I'd lose my job.'

'Who's going to know it was you?'

'There'd be a witch hunt.'

'What, even if it sells well? Even if it gets everyone talking about your paper?'

He shakes his head. 'No,' he says. 'I won't do it. I'm not risking everything to put some sob story in the paper about Eve Stanton.'

He stands up.

'That's not what I'm asking,' I whisper and I grab his arm. 'I've got some stuff on the Prime Minister, other folk too, people like Hart, even your editor, DeLonzo. *That's* what I want you to publish. Corruption stuff. Crimes these people committed that were never brought to justice. The PM, he –'

He leans towards me. 'That's even worse,' he whispers. 'If I put that in, and they found out it was me, do you know what would happen?'

'You'd probably be arrested.'

'That's an understatement. You're not the only one who knows all about corruption and lies at high level, but nobody – *nobody* – is going to do anything about it. If I did that, then I'd disappear. So would my family. No. There's no way I'm doing that.'

'I'll see all the information on you is leaked.'

He pulls his arm away from me. 'I hope you don't. But at least that way my family would be safe, and they'd know what had happened to me.'

He goes to grab his jacket from the back of the chair but I stand up and block him.

'Please,' I say.

He looks at me and I'm sure I see genuine sadness in his eyes. 'I'm sorry,' he says, and I really think he is, 'but I can't. I can't risk my family.'

'You're risking them by *not* doing anything.'

'Maybe indirectly,' he says, and he rubs his eyes and face. 'I'd like to help, Eve's a good woman, but . . .' His voice trails away and he sighs.

'You're her only hope.'

He shakes his head. 'No, I'm not. You could try DeLonzo.'

'DeLonzo's implicated. He knows it exists.'

'Of course he does, and of course he's implicated – otherwise he'd have splashed this story all over the *National News* already.'

'But DeLonzo, he . . .' I pause because what I'm thinking sounds so pathetic.

'Scares you?' Braden asks.

I nod my head, glad he said it, not me.

'He scares everyone. But he's a businessman. Approach him that way. What if . . . ?' His voice trails off again, and he rubs his chin as he thinks. 'Do you have all the copies?'

I shake my head. 'Not all. No.' Subconsciously I move a hand over the file hidden under my jacket.

'Could you get them?'

I look at him sideways. 'What are you suggesting?'

'I bet DeLonzo would jump at the chance of publishing this. Like I said, he's a businessman. If he could publish it, it would be such a coup for the paper. Sales would go through the roof –'

'But you just said yourself that it would implicate him.'

'Not if the evidence of his involvement was destroyed. Not if you got all the copies, all the evidence, and contacted him and proved it. Let him destroy it all.'

'But then he'd never be brought to justice.'

He shrugs. 'What are you trying to do?' he asks. 'Bring everyone to justice or bring down the system? Or save the life of one person?'

'All of the above,' I say.

'Maybe you'll have to compromise. Turn a blind eye to one man to change the future for everyone.'

Jesus, why is everything so hard? What gives *me* the right to decide this?

'All the evidence?' I whisper. 'But . . . but that would be in . . . Where would that be?'

'I know where it is,' he says. 'But if I tell you, then I want your word you won't use any of it against me. You'll leave me alone.'

'As long as I'm safe, then you are,' I say, and I hate myself for making deals like I'm one of them.

'Fair enough,' he whispers, and in all the hubbub of the cafe he leans forward, the two of us in our own bubble. 'It's all kept together in the PM's files at Downing Street.'

A shiver runs down me. 'Then it's impossible.'

'Is it?' he asks, and he turns away.

The Prime Minister

Sofia closes the door of the blue room behind her and the voices in the corridor on the other side disappear.

The leather swivel chair creaks as she sits in front of the banks of screens, and as she leans forward it groans as if hissing through its teeth at what she's about to do. After a quick glance behind her, she types in the name 'DETECTIVE INSPECTOR HART', and after a moment a red dot appears on the map on the large central screen. Slowly the picture zooms in, refocuses, and zooms again until it reaches street level and is following Hart as he walks away from the rear entrance of Downing Street, towards his waiting car.

She frowns, watching as the red dot moves through the streets of London.

'Don't bother me,' a voice booms from the corridor outside the blue room, and Sofia jumps. 'Talk to Sofia.'

She reaches out to the control panel, but pauses.

'I don't know where she is. I'm not her keeper. And I don't care for your tone.'

The handle inches downwards.

The door opens.

The PM, sharp suit, perfect hair and freshly shaven, steps inside. 'Oh, Sofia. People have been searching for you all morning.'

She taps the exit button and pulls her hand back from the

panel. The red dot vanishes. 'I had a few important things to check,' she says.

As the PM approaches her, a young man carrying a pile of papers follows close behind.

'Sir, I'm sorry, but I need to interrupt,' the young man says, thrusting one piece of paper out as he balances the rest.

The PM stares at him. 'You need to learn some manners,' he replies.

'I'm sorry, sir, but I've been asked to pass you a message.'

The PM tilts his head and looks down his nose at the young man. 'From whom?'

'I'm not allowed to say.'

The PM's eyebrows raise and he snorts. 'And who are you?'

He blushes. 'I . . . I . . . thought I'd told you before, sir, I'm the new intern,' he says. 'Gino Wills.'

'Well, Gino Wills, new intern, Sofia deals with *messages*. You should know that.'

'Yes, sir, I do, sir, but the gentleman who –'

'Here,' Sofia says, standing up, 'give it to me.'

'But the man said only to –'

The PM waves a dismissive hand and leaves the room.

'– to take it to the top,' Gino finishes.

He turns to follow the PM. Sofia takes one step and swipes the note from his fingers.

'I am the top,' she says. 'I'm his buffer. I decide what Stephen needs to know, and what he doesn't.'

Shadows of doubt flit over his face.

'Did you read it?' she asks, as she unfolds it and scans the words.

He doesn't reply.

'So you think it's acceptable for you, an intern, to read confidential messages, but not me?'

'He didn't tell me not to read it.'

'I imagine he didn't tell you *not* to do lots of other things too.'

He ignores that comment. 'I think the PM should know about it,' he insists. 'You are going to tell him, aren't you? If it's true, that she's not there – Honeydew – then how did she get out? There might be a sympathiser in the police force, or in here. And where is she now and what's she doing? She could be plotting anything. Blowing up the Houses of Parliament, or this place. We should start a campaign. Get someone on the *National News*, issue a reward for sightings.'

She lifts a hand to silence him. 'Of course Stephen knows,' she whispers. 'He was informed the moment Honeydew went missing from the police station. But think about it, Gino, how would it make us look? The public would think we, and the police, are incompetent. That's not going to do anything for their trust in us, is it? What you should understand is that this needs doing quietly and with care, or we could lose a lot of support.'

'The PM's not acting like he knows. And the man who gave me this, I probably shouldn't tell you who it was, but he of all people –'

'I know it was Hart.'

He frowns and shakes his head. 'How?'

'And as you said yourself, anyone in here, or in the police, could be a sympathiser. We need to keep this close. We shouldn't be discussing this, but I'm trusting you, probably more than

Stephen would be comfortable with, so don't let me down. Don't let on to him that you know; he needs to be confident we run a tight ship.' She lifts the folded note and tears it into pieces. 'And that we don't leave this kind of information unguarded.'

'What do I tell Hart if he comes back to me?'

'That it's being dealt with,' Sofia says, and she turns back to the screen and sits down.

Gino nods slowly, but as he retreats from the room he looks back to Sofia. 'You have a lot of power,' he says to her.

Her fingers pause over the keyboard. 'I've earned a lot of trust.'

As the door closes she takes her hands from the keyboard and leans back in the seat with her arms crossed over her chest and a frown on her face.

Then she takes a phone from her pocket and types in a message.

6.30 p.m. *Death is Justice*

Lights dance over the studio. A heartbeat theme tune plays. Kristina, wearing a fitted black dress with silver trim, steps from backstage and strides across the floor, eyes bright and smile wide; a spotlight follows her. The audience applaud.

She raises her hands; the applause and music die down.

KRISTINA: Ladies and gentlemen, welcome to this evening's episode of *Death is Justice*!

Another brief round of applause.

KRISTINA: How wonderful to see so many excited, expectant faces in the audience. And I imagine there are even more excited faces tuning in at home! I for one am just *thrilled* with all the latest updates and developments – Martha Honeydew thought she could destroy us, but no, we rise from the ashes like a phoenix.

The audience cheer and whoop.

KRISTINA: Our system will not be brought to its knees!

We will continue to operate the fairest, most democratic system in the world. We will continue to allow the public their God-given right to affect the safety of our nation. We will continue to empower our citizens! And we will to continue to rid our country of those who choose to flout our laws and steal the most precious thing that exists in this world – life.

The camera swings around to the cheering and applauding audience. Many stand, nodding their agreement with Kristina.

KRISTINA: And we will continue to give you, the viewer, the audience, all the inside information on those crimes, so you, the voting public, can reach the most thorough and considered decision.

Her heels click on the shiny floor as she steps back to her desk and takes her position at the high stool at the side.

KRISTINA: Ever innovative and always looking forward, on tonight's programme we have something new for you. Yes, and I can feel that sparkle of excitement running through the studio! What can it be? Well, ladies and gentlemen, we are bringing you a series of one-off, once-in-a-lifetime opportunities. The chance for you to own not only a piece of history, but an iconic reminder of justice served.

On the oversized screen to the right of the stage, the eye logo zips into the bottom left corner and six boxes fill the rest of the screen, each with a lot number in the corner and an object at its centre.

KRISTINA: Yes, ladies and gentlemen, welcome to *Death is Justice* auction day! We are giving you the opportunity to purchase key elements from the crimes featured on death row. In each of these boxes is something pertaining to a crime, and you can own it. Have it on display in your home. Have your guests gaze in awe at the knife held by Alfie Duprey, the jacket worn by Alexia Brown, the gloves, still stained with blood, owned by Zillah Hallamy. These are priceless artefacts yet available for you to own.

An intake of breath sounds from the audience and a low mumble of chatter.

KRISTINA: Our very first auction will be for none other than the actual gun used by Isaac Paige to shoot his father, Jackson.

She pauses, and an 'oooh' drifts from the audience.

KRISTINA: But that, ladies and gentlemen, is for later in the show. Do not adjust your sets and do not skip channels, because, believe me, this kind of opportunity comes around very rarely in life. But before that, viewers, and giving you a chance to check your bank balances in the break, we'll be talking to our reporter on the ground, finding out what our most interesting villain is up to, and what she's thinking as she approaches her imminent death.

The screen changes, now filled with the face of Gerome, the cells underneath the Old Bailey behind him, a microphone in his hands.

KRISTINA: Hello there, Gerome. Tell us, how is it down there today, and what is the notorious Eve Stanton up to?

GEROME: Well, hello there, Kristina, studio audience, viewers at home. I must say, I'm utterly thrilled, Kristina, at the prospect of being able to own the gun used to kill Jackson Paige! I'm already trying to tot up in my head exactly how much I can afford. I presume credit cards will be allowed?

KRISTINA: Oh yes, all major credit cards.

GEROME: Excellent! That is a piece of history I'll definitely be bidding for! But away from that for just a moment. As you can see, we are deep in the bowels of the Old Bailey, a place that has housed some of history's most notorious and audacious killers and criminals. Along the corridors to my left, Dead Man's Walk, where the last steps were taken by so many hardened criminals. While underneath us, and you may be able to hear if you listen carefully, flows the River Fleet; this very hatch in the floor next to me leads down to it, and often, according to the guards, when the wind is in a certain direction and the tide at a certain height, there is a veritable waft of old London town where such criminals resided and carried out their atrocities. But of course, none of those criminals were any worse than our very own Eve Stanton.

He winks and beckons to camera.

GEROME: Come with me and see.

The camera follows him down a labyrinth of enclosed corridors, white paint flaking off brick walls, condensation dripping from thick metal pipes running along the ceiling, rat droppings in secluded corners and dirt smeared up the walls. He stops at a doorway. Moths bump repeatedly into the light above and, as it flickers, eerie shadows are cast onto Gerome's face.

GEROME: This is Cell 2. In a marked difference from the previous death row, the door has been wedged open, allowing a cooling breeze to drift through, and for conversation between prisoners. In this cell is Eve Stanton. Let's step inside.

His eyebrows lift in mock jeopardy as he walks through the doorway. The cell is barely a metre wide. High on the back window an old metal-framed window is wedged open. There is no bed, just a mattress, and no toilet, just a bucket.

Sitting on the floor, dressed in dirty off-white overalls, is Eve. Her head is shaved and covered in small, blood-stained nicks and grazes, and the chains around her ankles and wrists are attached to the wall behind her.

Gerome bends down. Eve shuffles upright and looks at him sideways. As she lifts her hands to rub her face, the camera catches sight of her bloodied wrists, rubbed raw by the chains.

GEROME: As you can see, Mrs Stanton has been struggling against her chains and has injured herself. Fortunately, for the safety of the guards, she was adequately restrained. Let's talk to her, shall we?

He turns to Eve.

GEROME (gently): Eve, tell us, how are you doing today?

Her eyes are wild as she looks at him.

GEROME: The guards tell me you had lasagne for dinner this evening, followed by apple pie and custard. They seem to be treating you well.

She doesn't reply; only frowns and glances around the cell.

GEROME: I understand from them that following health and safety guidelines and protecting your human rights, while also taking into consideration that as a prisoner and an accused offender you are here to be judged, is a difficult balance to get right. Do you think it's a balance they have achieved?

Still she says nothing.

GEROME: Many think conditions should be harsher, and indeed, viewing the menu you have here, the library trolley which is brought down every day, and hearing rumours that visitation rights are likely to be introduced in the next few months, it does seem more like a holiday camp than a prison!

He laughs awkwardly. Eve stares.

EVE (croakily): What library trolley?

GEROME: You're also looking like you've lost some weight there. Mind you, can't say that's a bad thing – you were a fraction on the . . . *pudgy* . . . side before coming in here! Perhaps this regime is good for your health!

EVE: Am I hallucinating? Or are you really a moron?

Gerome laughs again.

GEROME: Seems Mrs Stanton has finally found her voice! And her sense of humour. Now, Eve, the viewers at home are very keen to hear from you, and to understand you. I'm sure you, of all people, appreciate the necessity of such in deciding whether or not to vote you guilty. Although to me your guilt seems a given, we do need to go through right and proper process. Eve, is there anything you'd like to share with viewers at home?

She nods, sits up, wipes her hands over her face and rubs her eyes.

GEROME: Please, then, to camera.

As she struggles to smile, her lips crack and bleed.

EVE: I'm sorry –

GEROME (interrupting): I'm sure the family of your victim will be pleased to hear you say that.

EVE: I'm not talking to them.

GEROME: Are you saying you're not sorry you killed him?

She stares at Gerome.

EVE: I didn't want to kill him. I'm sorry he's dead, but I'm not sorry I hit him.

GEROME: You're *glad* you hit him?

EVE: You're putting words in my mouth. That's not what I meant. It wasn't my fault. He attacked me. I hit him with the metal bar to defend myself. And my husband. It was the only thing I could do. I wanted to say sorry to Max!

GEROME: The husband who died for you? Who you allowed to lie on your behalf so that you could live? Doesn't that make you responsible for *two* deaths?

EVE: No! No, it doesn't –

GEROME: Many think it does. In fact, some are going so far as to call you a serial killer. What, I wonder, is the definition of a serial killer? Is two sufficient? There has been some debate as to whether you *enjoyed* watching those you counselled go to their deaths.

EVE: What?

Eve lurches forward to grab the microphone but Gerome side-steps out of her reach.

EVE (shouting): That's ridiculous. I fought for that job so I could help people!

GEROME: Or you fought for it so you could get close to them and bask in their suffering before they died.

EVE: That is utter bollocks!

Again Eve lurches forward to try to grab the microphone, but Gerome moves swiftly out of the room, the camera trained on him.

GEROME: Ladies and gentlemen, did we get a true picture of Eve Stanton there? Was the truth too much for her to bear?

EVE (shouting in the distance): I just want to speak to my son! I need to explain to him. Please!

GEROME: The price of crime and the sting of guilt. No sob story from Eve Stanton, begging forgiveness from her victim's family, and I'm sure you heard those all-important words – "I hit him with a metal bar." Yes, Eve Stanton has just admitted her guilt live on air. Is there any more we need to know? Join us again after a short message from our sponsor, Cyber Secure, when we will be filling you in on all those auction details. In the meantime, don't forget to vote, and I'm certain you know which way.

As he smiles to camera, the padlock logo of Cyber Secure replaces him on the screen, streams of data flowing over a blue sky and into a white cloud.

Martha

They'll vote her guilty after that.

Heartless man.

Cruel and selfish.

Narrow-minded, vindictive bastard.

When will folks look beyond the black and white, the guilty or innocent? When will they see the grey, or ask for a proper explanation?

It's not that folks are stupid; they've just been subject to the media's slow-drip hate campaign for the last God knows how many years.

Better off killing folk than trying to understand them, they think.

I slurp the last of my drink and put it down on the table. It's busy in here. Some kind of cross between a cafe and a bar. The only reason I remember it, and remember the story, is because of its name – Beth's Place. Like my mum. Except I'm not looking for the woman it was named after. It's a long shot, but right now even a long shot seems better than trying to get into Downing Street.

I'm sitting right next to the TV, keeping my head down and my hood up, and folks are leaving me alone.

They were all sucked into *Death is Justice* as much as I was.

'What I'd do for the gun that killed Jackson Paige,' some man in a football shirt says, pint of lager in front of him. I wonder if he knows what a stereotype he is.

Someone with him laughs. 'Nah,' comes the reply. 'I want the dress that woman was wearing, what was her name? Brigid? That dress she had on when she was done in.'

'You're a sick bastard,' the first man says.

I step quietly around their tables.

Takes one to know one, I think.

I didn't much like Nicolas Braden's idea – can't see how I can get all the evidence from Downing Street without being caught. This is the only other option I can think of and it's bloody lucky the woman I need to speak to still works here.

There she is.

'Empty the bins, Michelle,' the manager says to her, and my ears prick up.

I head outside.

There's a frost on the ground, and it's the kind of cold that makes your face feel like it's being shrink-wrapped. She won't be out here for any longer than she needs to be, that's for sure.

I nip down the alleyway at the side, follow it round and I hear the back door of the cafe open.

I run around the corner, and there she is, lifting the lid of the bin, throwing the bag in.

'Michelle?' I ask. 'Michelle Scali?'

She spins round, freezes.

'What do you want? I haven't got any money. I'll scream. My boss'll hear.'

I put my hands up in peace. I must look like a thug, but

there's no way I'm pulling my hood down to show her who I am. 'Nothing like that, I promise. I just need to ask you something. You're Lisa's mum, yeah?'

There's barely any light, just what's coming from the door she's left ajar, but I see her expression change.

'Leave me alone,' she says, and she slams the bin lid down.

'I'm not here to cause trouble,' I say. 'I just need to speak to you. I know your daughter didn't commit suicide; I want to tell folks what really happened.'

'I told you to leave me alone.' She storms off towards the back door.

'Please. Folks should know the truth. I know who killed her. I can prove it.'

She spins around to me, right up in my face.

'*I* know who killed her!' she spits at me. 'I've known for eight years who killed her, but I can't do anything about it!'

'I can. I can get it in the newspapers.'

'No, you can't. And you know why? Because I tried. I rang them. Rang and rang but nobody would even talk to me. So I went there. Marched in, straight to the office of that cocksucker DeLonzo, told him I knew who it was. Would he print anything? Would he bollocks. So I asked him why, and you know what he said? Said that they'd never print it, never, not even if I had photographs of the bloke actually doing it, because they *couldn't afford to*. They'd *lose his advertising contract*. The money's more important than justice for my daughter. So I went to the police, and you know what they did? They laughed at me.

'You know what they said? "As if the owner of a business empire, with all his wealth, is going to bother kidnapping your

113

daughter when he could choose any woman in the world." Like they were saying that my daughter was ugly, or nasty, or worthless or something. Or that her life didn't mean as much as someone else's.'

'But if everybody stood up to them –'

'You're living in a dream world,' she says. 'No, in fact, you're off your rocker. People with that sort of money and influence are above the law. They can do anything they want to people like me and you.' She walks back and pulls the door open, and light floods her face, lined with years of sadness.

'Leave it in the past,' she says, and she disappears inside.

The door slams and I'm left in darkness.

No victim's story.

Nobody from the *National News* to help.

I can only see one way forward.

But I don't like it.

I walk through the streets, my head a million miles away from everything.

I've been in the City all day.

I want to go home now.

Be with Isaac.

Supposing he's woken and is asking for me?

Supposing he's . . .

Dr Novak said he'd ring, I remind myself.

I take the phone from my pocket.

No missed calls, but there's a message.

I click it open – 'Hart knows you're out. Be careful.'

I stop.

Shit.

My chest goes hot and my head pounds like someone's squeezing my brain and I close my eyes from it all and stumble to the side. Knock into someone and stagger back the other way.

I glance up, but everything's spinning.

Someone shouts something at me – I don't hear it, can't understand it – and they shove me sideways.

Shit.

I bend down, hold my head.

Breathe, Martha, calm, come on.

'Are you OK?' an old woman asks, her wrinkled face leering at me.

I nod and pull away from her.

'It'll be drugs,' someone else says. 'Keep away.'

I feel myself sliding to the floor.

'Do you want me to call an ambulance?' she asks.

'We should call the police!' the other voice says.

I shake my head. 'No . . . no . . .' I mutter. 'I'll be fine, honest.'

I stare down at the phone again and they leave me be.

Jesus, fuck, how does Hart know? How long till everyone knows? The PM even. What if they find out it was Sofia who let me out?

And what if this phone's got GPS on it too?

What if Sofia's tricking us all?

Who the hell can I trust?

Come on, Martha, I tell myself. Pull yourself together.

I take a couple of breaths. Stand up. Calm myself.

I don't want to chuck the phone, but what if they're tracking me?

I tap in a number and press call. It's picked up straight away.

'Max?' I say. 'I need your help. Can you –'

'Where are you?' he snaps at me.

'I'm in the City. Where are you?'

'You should be with Isaac, or don't you care about him now? You're just going to let someone else die.'

'Jesus, Max, did you get out of bed on the wrong side or something? What the hell are you talking about? Of course I care!'

'Not about my mum you don't.'

'I don't want to argue, Max. Can we talk about that some other time? Right now I need you to do something for me. Will you meet me back at the flat?'

Silence.

'Max. Max? Are you there?'

'Yeah.' His voice is quiet.

'Will you meet me back at the flat? Please.'

Silence again.

'Jesus, Max, answer me!'

'I'm busy,' he says.

'*Busy?* What are you *busy* with?'

The phone goes dead.

'What the hell?' I say. Too loud, and folks turn to me.

I stride off down the road. I'm so bloody angry I want to toss this bloody phone. Busy? I'll give him fucking busy. What the hell is he up to? Jesus.

I march away, kicking at kerb edges and stones. Sighing and grumping. Wasted day. What the hell now?

Jesus Christ, am I bloody angry.

I get my phone again, scroll through the contacts and type in a message.

'Meet me now, or I'll hand myself in and tell them you never took me to prison.'

Doesn't take long for the reply.

'Where I dropped you off the other day. Twenty minutes.'

Isaac

Blackness.
Warm.
Soft.
Dark.
Whispers from people.
Wind rattles windows; takes voices, takes people.
Alone.
Scared.
Clamp around head, squeezing.
Pressure, pain.
Coffee?
Sound, piercing.
Shrill.
Whistle?
Bright light, white.
Pain.
Scans.
Green flashes on black.
Calm.
Voice.
'Isaac? Isaac? Can you hear me?'
Hurts.
Too much.

Dark.
Soft.
Warm.
Blackness.

Martha

I jump on a train.

It's full of tired faces staring out into darkness, watching the lives of the 'haves' disappear behind them, leaving a landscape as barren as most folks' wallets.

Everyone ploughs out at the last stop. Not the underpass any more because that's inside the wall. No, we have to all walk through individually and be scanned.

I don't go the same way as them though. I cut around and head to the road that leads back to the City. It's odd – there are loads of parked cars. Don't know why there would be. Good ones too. Not the old heaps of junk you usually get round here.

The headlights of one flash; I stroll towards it, carefully looking around.

The door opens.

'Get in.' Sofia.

The door thuds as I pull it behind me and the light inside the car fades.

'Don't ask me to meet you again, and don't ever threaten me.'

'Sorry.'

'And for the record, I don't give a damn if you do try to tell them it was me who let you out. Nobody's going to believe you.'

'Why did you come then?'

'What do you want?'

'How does Hart know? And why are you so sure he does?'

'He came to Downing Street today and handed a note to the intern, telling him to give it to Steve. I managed to intercept it.'

'Are you sure it was him?'

'Certain. How he knows is anyone's guess.'

'What about prison staff?'

She shakes her head. 'There's sufficient *confusion* about which area you're supposed to be in that unless he went there personally he'd never find out. And he won't do that.'

I sigh and shake my head. 'I met a reporter from the *National News*. Maybe it was him.'

'What? Why are you meeting reporters?'

'It was only one,' I reply. I stare out the window and to the wall, the massive queue of folk standing in the cold waiting to be allowed to go home. It's so slow. Something must be going on. 'No,' I say. 'I don't think he would anyway.'

'Hart came in the back way.' She lets the words hang. 'And he didn't sign the note.'

I look at her, but all I can see is her outline and a vague light in her eyes.

'What did you want anyway?'

A car goes past, its headlights flashing through, and I catch a better glimpse of her. She's younger than I thought. The car parks further down the road.

'He went in the back way?' I ask. 'I didn't know there's a back way.'

'Where do you think the bins are? Or deliveries come in? Cleaners. There are over a hundred rooms, you know. And what about caterers for functions?'

'There are functions?'

She sighs. 'All the time,' she says. 'One tomorrow, a couple more later this week.'

Her fingernails drum on the steering wheel, I can just make out the dark nail varnish is chipped. 'It's a nightmare. Caterers, waitresses . . .'

Another car goes past. More headlights.

'This isn't where your mum was killed, is it?'

I shake my head. 'No, that was at the underpass. That's inside the wall now.'

I peer through the windscreen. The queue's getting longer.

'There are a lot of people who agree with your thoughts about Jackson,' Sofia says.

I turn to her; I wasn't expecting that.

'Your mum wasn't the only woman he took advantage of.'

'I know,' I whisper.

She stares at me. 'Follow that train of thought some time.'

Another car goes past.

'What *is* going on?'

'Is that all you summoned me for? To ask me how Hart knows?'

I'm still staring through the windscreen, trying to make sense of the crowds of people, things sticking up in the air, some kind of lights . . .

. . . and I'm thinking . . .

. . . wondering who I can trust and if . . .

'Theoretically speaking . . .' I say, and I pause again because I'm still not sure.

Do I?

Should I?

'Theoretically speaking, what?' she asks.

Takes a strong person to ask for help, Mrs B's voice echoes in my head. *Thinking you can do it all yourself is weakness sometimes.*

I remember arguing back, saying I *could* do it myself and I didn't *need* anyone's help.

But this?

She got you out, I say to myself. It's not much of a leap to trust her with this.

'Can you get me a job with the folks who do the catering for the functions?' I splutter out quickly.

Even in the darkness, I can see her frowning at me.

'Are you asking me to get you a job or to get you into Number 10?' she whispers.

'The second one,' I mutter.

The words hang between us. Suspended in clouds of warm breath in the cold of the car. There's time to watch them drift away before she replies.

'I should ask you why.'

I don't say anything.

I can hear my own breathing and the thud of my heartbeat.

What do I say?

Do I tell her?

Can I trust her?

I open my mouth to speak, but she does first. 'But I won't. Leave it with me. I'll text you in the morning.'

I open the car door. I can't speak.

'Martha,' she says, and reaches out towards me, 'be careful.'

I nod and close the door. I'm not really paying attention any more; I've got what I needed from that meeting.

I hear her engine start but I don't look around; something's going on at the entrance to the Rises.

I pick up my pace.

My heart's thudding. I start to jog.

'Shit,' I say out loud. 'Shit, the . . .'

People are everywhere, some with banners, some are lighting torches. Actual burning torches like they're the Ku Klux Klan or something.

Jesus Christ.

Some have got front pages ripped from newspapers, saying 'Arrest the Rises 7' or 'Rises 7 Bomb Our City' and pasted to boards they're thrusting in the air.

Whoever mans the floodlights on the wall has tilted them outwards and down now, illuminating this . . . this . . . *horde* of . . . God, you can't call them people . . .

Haters. Discriminators. Pack followers. Sheep.

Their faces leer at me as I push through them.

Their voices ring in the air with revulsion.

'Death to terrorists!' one shouts.

'Kill the Rises 7!' bellows another.

This is why there are fancy cars parked all over. They've driven down rather than slum it on trains with us, banners and placards and bloody paraffin for their burning torches, all in the boot along with their flasks of *connoisseur* coffee and probably tartan fucking picnic blankets and camping stoves they bought specially for the occasion!

'Burn the evil!' someone yells, and I feel the heat from a torch on my face.

Whoa.

124

I spin round, see TV cameras, journalists snapping photographs, microphones shoved in faces, Rises folk cowering as they are forced to queue just to go home.

Can't see them wanting to come out again in a hurry.

Jesus, hatred reported to spawn more hatred. When will it ever end?

I'm shoved one way, into a crowd of men, then shoved another. I slip and fall over. Someone barges into me, stumbles and kicks me. I can't get up. Boots tread on my fingers, something hits me and I fall back down.

Get up, Martha! my head shouts. *Or you're dead. Get up.*

There's another kick in my legs.

I scream, grab someone's jacket, hang on and haul myself up.

Faces loom around me. I hold my hood tight around my face. Lord knows what they'd do if they realised it was me.

'Rises scum! Rises scum!' they chant.

I run away from them, closer to the wall. If only I can get inside, maybe I'll be safe.

More people swarm forward. A bottle explodes on the ground near me. I stumble on. There's the checkpoint. I breathe.

And what the hell is that?

Next to the checkpoint seven people are lined up, all wearing white prison garb, all with their hands and legs shackled. I can't see their faces, but I stare at them . . . they're wearing masks.

Masks of . . .

My feet stop moving. I stare at them. Disbelief. Utter disbelief.

One of them wears a mask of me; another, one of Isaac; the rest, Cicero, Max, Eve, Joshua, Gus.

Seven of them.

And they've all got nooses around their necks.

They're staring at me. All of them, from behind their masks. I'm sure of it.

Next to them is a sign – 'Death is Justice – Hang the Rises 7'.

I stumble away in shock.

My hands are shaking so much I can hardly hold my pass for it to be scanned, and I'm so frightened, frightened to my bones, that I tear through the underpass, run across the stubby grass, past the park and don't stop until I reach Daffodil House.

I want to hide in there and never come out again.

DECEMBER 3RD

Death is Justice: The Breakfast Show

Gerome Sharp perches on the edge of a desk, wearing a blue suit with tie and waistcoat. A cut on the side of his face has stitches and his chin is thick with make-up in an attempt to hide a large graze. He fills the left side of the screen, while the right shows recorded footage of his trip to the wall the previous day with running commentary along the bottom.

GEROME: Good morning, viewers, and welcome to today's show. It's good to be talking to you from the warmth and safety of the studio after the recent shenanigans both at the wall and in the bowels of the Old Bailey! Let's see what today's headlines are . . .

Music thuds between the headlines he reads as images flash on the right side of the screen.

GEROME: Riots on the streets of the City as residents clash with Rises workers. Pickets in front of the East Side Industrial Estate gates as the unemployed from the City and the Avenues protest that Rises workers have taken their jobs. Calls from leading professionals and high-profile celebrities for further segregation of Rises inhabitants and City dwellers, following a spate of attacks. And at the wall itself, protestors call for permanent closure of the gates.

The screen changes, filling only with Gerome.

GEROME: Last night *thousands* of people took to the streets to protest about Rises migrant workers, insisting that those living in the City and the Avenues should be given priority for jobs in the area over those coming in purely for work. Although Rises residents have been allowed past the wall for job purposes, calls are now being made for them to work within their *own* society. A spokesperson for City Business, City People explained that this would encourage the regeneration of the Rises area as shops and business would be reopened, and that it would also lead to a substantial drop in unemployment figures within the City as jobs are freed up for their own citizens. And Vincent Clairborne, the leader of Peace be Apart, predicts that further segregation of this kind would lessen the sense of antagonism the City dwellers are feeling right now, while also giving a safe space for the Rises to develop their own communities. With anger towards Rises residents at an all-time high, many believe this may well be the best long-term solution and could put an end to scenes of carnage and chaos such as those seen last night both within the City and at the wall itself, where as many as thirty City protestors were injured in attacks.

Gerome pauses and touches his ear.

GEROME: It seems we have a live statement regarding this, coming from the Prime Minister right now. I'll pass you over.

The Prime Minister – Stephen Renard

The PM, with Sofia on his left, strides from the shiny black door of Number 10 and out onto Downing Street.

He stops at the lectern set halfway across the road and looks to the journalists and reporters gathered in front of him.

A couple of cameras flash.

He places a file on the lectern and his hands grip either side of it.

To his left, and slightly back, Sofia glances carefully around. Whitehall to one side, Horse Guards Parade on the other, and the buildings behind them are all quiet.

'As I am certain you are aware,' the PM begins, his voice firm and calm, 'last night saw a number of disturbing incidents shake our City. The safety of you, the public, concerns me greatly and, I believe, must always be our first and main priority.' He pauses for effect, taking a breath, standing tall and looking around.

'Taking into account the recent attack by the Rises 7, the injuries sustained by our people, and the prime factor – that this attack was carried out both by Rises residents and by sympathisers – I have made the decision that for the peace and security of our city, from this point on, anyone deemed to be a sympathiser, and therefore a threat to our nation, will be removed from the City and placed in the Rises.'

Journalists shuffle, cameras click, phones are taken from pockets and buttons are pressed.

'As Prime Minister,' he continues, no hint of quiver in his voice or shake to his hands, 'I have a responsibility to the people I serve and that responsibility is one I take very seriously indeed. Therefore there is no shadow of doubt in my mind that this is the best way forward in order to protect the lives of each and every one of you.'

'Prime Minister!' a voice shouts. 'Mr Renard.'

'The Prime Minister isn't taking questions right now,' Sofia says.

'Just one,' the voice insists. 'For the people at home.'

The Prime Minister nods.

'You say that sympathisers will be taken to the Rises. Are there any circumstances in which they would be arrested?'

'Our aim isn't to unnecessarily arrest people. Our aim is to keep the public safe and protected. If arresting a particular sympathiser and sending them to prison was thought to be in the best interests of the public, then that may be needed. It would depend on why they are classed as a sympathiser and would be for the police to decide on a case-by-case basis. But I will stress again that safety and security are always our priorities.'

He starts to turn.

'One more thing!' the journalist shouts. 'If Rises people are causing so much trouble, why let them out at all? Surely the safest measure for us, the voting public, would be to keep those gates shut. Wouldn't that eradicate any threat? People out here are scared.'

'It's a valid argument,' the PM says. 'And something we will consider if necessary.'

'And is it true that while the people in the City are being terrorised, you are still going ahead with plans to entertain the legendary footballer, Rik Midona, and his family this afternoon?'

The PM's head tilts slowly to the voice. 'If we stop leading our lives, if we cancel things important to us, if we change our plans because of fear, then the terrorists and the sympathisers have won. We must *not* let this happen. We must show strength of character, we must show perseverance and we must show that we are united in our fight against fear.'

He pushes his shoulders back and stands tall.

'Together we are strong,' he says. 'We must remain that way.'

Martha

What utter bollocks.

Round them up.

Ship them in.

Stop us going out.

No work, then soon no money, no food.

What about doctors, hospitals, colleges and universities for Christ's sake?

Regeneration my fucking arse.

'They'll never get away with it,' Cicero says, taking a bite of toast as he sits in the kitchen.

'They already are,' I reply. 'And enjoy your bread while it lasts. This keeps up we'll be bloody milling grain and kneading dough.'

I walk out, a cup of coffee in my hand going cold. I've drunk mugs of the stuff but it never makes anything better.

'Nothing from Max?' I say over my shoulder.

'Nothing,' Cicero replies.

I wander through to the living room and sit down next to Isaac.

'Did we cause this?' I ask. 'Or was it inevitable?'

He doesn't reply.

I wish he would.

I wonder if he hears me.

You see reports of people waking up from a coma saying they were aware of everything going on, but not able to do anything.

Bright lights and tunnels and voices telling them it's not their time and all that kind of thing.

Maybe it's the drugs.

I shuffle the chair closer to him and take his hand.

It's clammy.

The drip in the back has pulled and there's dried blood down it.

I get the wipes Dr Novak has left and I draw one gently down his bare arm, across his wrist and onto his hand.

Carefully I dab it around the needle going into his skin, the one filling him with stuff keeping his body alive while his head fixes – I hope – and then I ease it down each of his fingers in turn.

I take another wipe out, turn Isaac's hand over and run it down his palm, easing open his fingers and stretching out the lines some folk think tell you about your life.

Which is your lifeline, Isaac?

I hope it's not that short, stubby one.

But I refuse to think life's laid out for you like a map and what happens to us is predetermined.

I could kill myself tomorrow and make a liar of a long lifeline, if I really wanted. Y'know, just to prove a point.

I hold his hand again.

Close my eyes and go over stuff I wish I'd done differently.

Worry what'll happen tomorrow, next week, next year.

Today.

What'll happen is what you make happen, Martha, my head tells me.

I want him to wake up, and for us to forget all the shit that's gone on and clear off to the countryside and live there without all this . . . this . . . *crap.*

Me and him.

Him and me.

Let someone else take up this fight, someone stronger, cleverer, wealthier. After all, all I am is an orphan girl from the Rises. That's it. I said that way back, and that's still how it is. All I've done is fail. And now look at us. I'm guilty of murder by proxy.

Fuck it.

Fuck the lot of it.

I cannot –

Wait . . . What . . . ?

Oh my God . . .

'Dr Novak!' I scream at the top of my voice. 'Dr Novak! Quick! Quick! He squeezed my hand!'

I stand up, peer into Isaac's face looking for movement, recognition, the flutter of an eyelid, something. I keep hold of his hand, waiting for it to squeeze mine again.

My insides flip and turn, and my head spins.

'Come on, Isaac,' I say. 'I'm waiting for you, I'm here.'

'Dr Novak!'

Pulling a T-shirt over his head, Dr Novak tumbles into the room. He plucks a pair of glasses from his pocket, perches them on his nose and stands over Isaac.

Cicero's at the doorway now.

Joshua too.

It's silent.

No footsteps from the flat above, no voices from the one next door – nothing. As if the whole building is holding its breath.

'He squeezed my hand,' I whisper to Dr Novak.

He nods but doesn't look at me.

I watch as he peels open Isaac's eyelids, one at a time, and shines a light in them. Then he takes his pulse, checks his heartbeat, and then studies whatever information is bleeping away on the monitor.

I can hardly breathe.

Finally he looks at me, and I know the gist of what he's going to say before his mouth opens.

'I'm afraid it must have been a spasm. An involuntary movement. It happens sometimes – the body is full of nerves and reflexes. That is all. I'm sorry.'

It hits me like a brick.

'Didn't it mean anything?'

He takes his glasses off. 'Maybe. Maybe not. It's impossible to tell. There is still hope, Martha,' he whispers. 'For now. But the longer he's in this state . . .' He lets his sentence drift off, but I know what the rest of the words are. *If we had proper medical facilities . . . could scan . . .*

Cicero's in front of me all of a sudden and I realise there are tears pouring down my face. I can't see. Can't breathe. God, I'm sobbing.

He puts his arms around me but I pull away.

Shake my head.

And I wipe the back of my hand across my eyes and step

back to Isaac, looking down at his face, which seems so small and his mind so far away.

Jesus, I hope he's in there still, somewhere, somehow listening, aware, feeling.

I lean forward and my tears land on his face.

I sniff and blub. Touch the tear from his cheek with my thumb.

God, this is hard.

So

fucking

hard.

Isaac . . .

And I wish, God, do I *wish* I could talk to him and know that he

can

hear

me.

Someone puts a tissue in my hand and I hear the soft whistle of Dr Novak get quieter as he leaves the room.

Then Cicero's footsteps.

Bless those men. Good men.

I squeeze Isaac's hand and lean in close to his cheek, my mouth next to his ear.

I can smell the wipes I used to clean his skin, feel the stubble of his chin on my lips.

'I'll do it,' I whisper in his ear. 'And it'll either go right, or hideously bloody wrong.'

The sob in my chest is fighting to get out but now I won't let it. 'If it goes wrong, then I'll never see you again.' I run my hand over his shaved head, my fingers crackling on it like a match on a file. 'I'm doing it for all them out there, but most of all I'm doing it for us. Because when you wake up –' my chest judders and I pause, breathe, calm myself – 'there . . . there's going to be a future for us that isn't holed up in here.' I run my finger down his cheek and over his lips. 'Because . . . because I love you.'

And I kiss him.

Eve

They executed someone yesterday.

The barbarism of it.

The doors are still open and I'm still chained to the back wall, but yesterday I dragged the chains behind me and at full stretch I could reach the doorway and peer out.

I saw a prisoner being taken down Dead Man's Walk, a TV crew following close behind him, and after the final stats were read, I heard the cheer of the crowd ring out.

The electrical system here must be ancient because, soon after that, the lights flashed and flickered as his scream ripped through the air, and when he stopped, the lights steadied again.

A terrible smell of burning slowly filled the cells, which I hope was the old wiring, but fear hangs around us all now.

I sat down in the doorway for a long time afterwards, and although my faith is in flux, I prayed for the man.

Who will pray for me?

Time stretches on around me but I don't know if I want it to speed up or slow down even further.

'Sunny day at last, but I'm in this stinking place.'

I think I recognise that voice; I open my eyes.

It's cold in here; there is no duvet or even a sheet. I rub my arms and I can feel the goosebumps under my fingertips.

'And I was here till gone midnight last night.' His voice

echoes – I think he must be down the corridor. 'How is anyone supposed to look their best?' His footsteps are getting louder. 'And the public think we lead glamorous lives!'

My eyes are still blurry from sleep. I rub them, and my face. The chains clank against each other and are cold against my skin. I look towards the open door. Someone is standing there. A man. I blink again and strain my eyes to focus.

'Well, you look more shit than I feel,' he says.

Gerome is standing in the doorway wearing what looks like pyjamas with a winter coat on top. In one hand he's holding a bacon-and-egg bun, and the yolk and tomato sauce are dripping down his hand and onto the floor.

It smells divine. I swallow hard; I'm sure I'm salivating.

'Oh, fuck, sorry,' he says. 'That's really insensitive of me, isn't it?' He laughs and I watch him take another bite. 'What did you have last night? A roast dinner with trifle for dessert?' He shakes his head. 'I totally didn't get what it's really like down here. It's a shithole! It's not what it looks like on television, is it? Was the other place the same? It can't have been, surely.'

I ignore him; he's not really interested.

He licks yolk from his fingers.

'My mates in the pub all think I've landed a good number, but if they could see this dump for real – Jesus. How the hell they manage to make it look anything like decent for the show is beyond me! But it does. I mean, it doesn't look like you're in a holiday camp, but it looks OK.'

I follow his eyes as he stares around with his nose turned up.

'I'm sure I saw a rat last night.'

He looks back at me and sneers.

'You look shocking. I mean *really* fucking shocking.'

'Thanks,' I mutter.

He takes a couple of paces closer, holding the last piece of bun in his hand as he stares down at me.

'We're going to have to get make-up to see to you before we start shooting. That could take a while.'

He puts the last bit of food in his mouth and chews.

'Alice!' he shouts. 'Get your butt in here and sort this woman out. And get a move on! I don't want to be stuck down here all goddamned day.'

Alice, a girl with thick long hair and clear skin, walks into the cell with a square case. It has wheels but she's holding it off the floor by its long handle. She looks practised at it and doesn't flinch at the sight of the cell, nor of me.

She's dressed all in black and oozes style.

'Sort her out,' Gerome says, and Alice looks at me and nods. No hint of disgust. I wonder if she's been in here before or is used to dealing with strange situations. She reminds me of a nurse who's learned not to flinch at wounds.

She puts her case on the mattress and flicks it open.

'We'll soon have you sorted,' she says.

'Why?' I ask, looking to Gerome, not Alice.

'What?' he says.

'I presume you're doing this so the public don't know the conditions in here. To make them think I'm well and being looked after. An attempt to stop them realising exactly what it's like down here, facing death, so you can still demonise us and claim we are being treated better than we deserve.'

'Hey, darling, don't shoot the messenger, all right?

'What if I refuse?'

The both stare at me blankly.

'What if I refuse to let you make me up?'

Gerome pulls a face. 'Why would you do that? Are you being awkward for the sake of it?'

'I want people to see it how it is down here.'

'We could put a time delay on it.' I look up to another voice in the doorway, a young man with a camera. My cell is suddenly the hip place to be. 'That would allow us to put some filter on her.'

Gerome looks to me and back to the man with the camera. 'You'd need a bloody long delay. And we'd have to explain it. No. Alice, just shorten her chains so she can't move, then you can grab her and do it whether she agrees or not.'

Alice glances to me and I see a flicker of panic behind her eyes. She doesn't want to have to force me, even if they do shorten the chains so I can't move or threaten her.

Poor girl.

'OK,' I say to Gerome. 'I'll do it.'

Martha

A text message comes through from Sofia.

Tells me where to be and what time.

But how can I leave Isaac again?

I watch him.

Waiting for another squeeze from his hand, a flicker of his eye, a twitch to his mouth.

Cicero brings me another coffee; that one goes cold too.

He brings me sandwiches that turn stale.

Cola that goes flat.

Then my legs go dead.

And my bum goes numb.

Cicero's hand rests on my shoulder.

'Come and look at this a moment,' he says.

I shake my head.

'I think you'll want to see.'

Reluctantly I move; everything aches and creaks and I feel like some old woman.

He leads me to the window. 'Can you see them?' he says, and points to the exit in the gate.

I peer through, my eyes bleary. I blink. 'They were there last night,' I mutter. 'Loads of them from the City and the Avenues protesting about us.' I shrug.

'Look closer,' he says.

I wipe the window, lean right in. 'What? Queues of folk waiting to get in. Probably coming home from work.'

'Yes, you're right. Except they never did any work; they were turned back. All the people who work at the factories on the East Side Industrial Estate. How many families is that?'

'A lot,' I reply. 'So? What do you want me to do?'

'I don't know, Martha. Shall we stand on the rooftops chanting? Shall we storm the wall and knock it down? Dig a vegetable patch so everyone can still eat in six months' time? I don't know. What do you think? Because I'm out of ideas right now. And I don't know about you, but I feel kind of responsible for this.'

'We didn't build the wall. We didn't make the new laws.'

'No, we didn't. But we didn't stop it either.'

'Everyone's responsible,' I mumble, more to myself than to Cicero. 'Not just us.'

'True,' Cicero replies. 'But that doesn't let us off the hook.'

I look back at Isaac. So vulnerable. I don't want to leave him. I look back down at the message from Sofia.

'There's something I was thinking of doing. I'll need to go somewhere though. I don't really . . .' My words drift away.

'Do you want me to come with you?' he asks.

I look to him, back to Isaac. Think.

'Judge, you know what I'd really like? If you'd stay here. I know you want to do something, but if I could choose, I'd really like you to stay here, just in case . . . he . . . wakes.'

Or dies, I think, but I can't say those words.

'Of course,' he replies.

* * *

146

Cicero gave me the kick up the arse I needed. And someone I trust to look after Isaac.

I trust Dr Novak but if, *when*, Isaac wakes he won't know who Dr Novak is, or where he is, and the doctor won't be able to tell him where I am.

I don't want to go, but . . . if I'm going to do this, I need to get over there and quickly.

I've still got my hood up and my coat bundled over it; my hands are shoved in pockets, sun might be out but it's bloody cold, and I traipse away to the gate and the checkpoint.

It scares the living daylights out of me.

Loads of folk are coming back in – there's that whirr-thud of the turnstile as they push through it. Nobody's waiting to go out though.

I walk up to it, trying to look like it's the most normal thing in the world.

I imagine I'm going down into the underground, putting my ticket in, waiting for it to spit it out, push through the turnstile.

That's all.

The pass Sofia gave me is in my hand.

But what if this turnstile doesn't spit it out?

And there's no whirr-thud?

Shit.

Folks stream past me like flies, all heading back to the flats.

God, they look desolate. Eyes down, shoulders hunched, feet scuffing along the concrete.

'Wouldn't bother,' someone says to me. 'They're sending everyone back.'

'Who is?' I ask.

'Factories.'

'What about other places? Has anyone been allowed to work?'

'Not the folk at the car plant. They've been sent home too. Said they're *prioritising locals*. They won't work in those conditions. Won't want to work nights. Bloody snobs, all of them.'

I carry on.

I'm a few steps from the checkpoint.

Folks from here are now stereotyping all the folks from there. What good's that going to do?

We're all layabouts, and they're all snobs.

Yeah, right.

A guard's watching me. My hands are shaking, I put the pass in the machine, it's snatched off me.

I wait.

'Don't know why you lot are bothering,' the guard says. 'But you can have a nice little walk in the sunshine.'

Come on, come on, come on.

'No jobs for thieves and scroungers.'

Fucksake.

It pops out.

I breathe again, grab it.

Whirr-thud.

Through the checkpoint, pushing through bodies chanting for my demise. Thank God they don't realise who I am.

I've no patience now.

'Fuck off and let me through,' I say.

148

'Foul-mouthed whore,' someone shouts.

'Teenagers nowadays have no respect.'

'In my day . . .'

Oh, fuck off.

Isaac

Beep.
    Beep.
    Dark.
    Beep.
    Beep.
    Swirls.
    Beep.
    Colour.
    Beep.
    Memory.
    Voice.
    We hold hands.
    Will walk together.
    Get to Bracken Woods and
    you will smile until we have to go
    back.
    Beep.
    Beep.
    Voice.
    Martha, I say. She
    is looking at me.
    Waiting for the words
    she hopes I feel. And I hope she

loves me too.

You are my world, I say.

Beep.

Dark again.

Beep.

Martha

I didn't really think this through.

Well, that's not entirely true. I just overlooked the part where I've still got a shaved head and a look like a thug. Blending in like this isn't exactly easy.

I nicked a wig from one of those hairdresser's head model things, didn't really have much choice. It's a brown one. Lord does it make me look different.

I try some cheap clothes on but sneak double into the changing room; nobody notices when I come out that I'm giving back exact versions of what I've got on. And they don't spot that the clothes I went in wearing are shoved in a plastic bag. I nip into some discount make-up place as well and throw some lipstick and eyeshadow on.

So I'm a thief now too.

Tell you what, Isaac, you'd never recognise me!

It's weird though; suddenly I'm just an ordinary person and I'm walking through the streets with my head up and some folks even smile at me. And men look at me.

I want to shout at them, Hey, I'm that Martha Honeydew – y'know, the one you had pegged as a terrorist. The one folks said was a whore, a slag, a foul-mouthed bitch? Well, look at me now.

We can all dress up the outside, but the inside – that's who you are.

That's what no one ever bothers to see.

And by some bloody miracle, some God that I don't believe in actually smiling down on me for once instead of lobbing thunder and lightning in my direction, I made the meeting point Sofia told me about, and they didn't recognise me, and they didn't ask loads of questions and now I'm in some kind of catering minibus heading for Number 10.

Thanks to Sofia.

Thanks to her trusting that I'm doing the right thing.

Daffodil House

Cicero gently lets go of Isaac's hand.

'Was that your eyes flickering, son?' he whispers. 'Do you hear me, wherever you are?

'We will get you back,' he continues. 'Fight your way through the darkness in your mind and come back to us. We're waiting for you.

'Martha loves you. She's a good person.'

Martha

'Take this to the Pillard Room,' they say, 'the Terracotta Room. Not the Small Dining Room,' they instruct me, 'the larger State Dining Room.'

Lemon walls, Persian carpets, portraits, velvet chairs . . .

How the other half live.

Can't believe I'm here.

I do as they tell me for a while, then I manage to creep away. I take off the white pinny so I look more like a guest.

It's massive, this place. Doors and rooms and corridors and lifts and staircases. Where to start? I don't know how I'm going to find anything.

I duck in and out of rooms, trying to look inconspicuous. Not succeeding.

I go up and down stairs, purposefully but not running.

Jeez, my palms are sweaty. Heart's thumping. Try to look normal, Martha, act normal.

I find myself going into rooms I'm sure I've been in before and I'm so confused.

I'm panicking.

Come on, Martha, think, my head says. *Calm.*

It's a maze, that's all, a puzzle. Think of it like the warren of alleyways and narrow streets in the Rises, cut-throughs and hiding places.

I go back down a flight of stairs, paintings lining it, there's a chequerboard floor at the bottom, a big grandfather clock ticks and ticks. I swallow.

Suddenly there's laughing.

I freeze.

Footsteps.

Sweat prickles my top lip.

Someone in a suit appears at the bottom, tall and straight, an air to him. I can't see his face but I know it's the Prime Minister. There's a woman next to him. Blonde. She flicks her hair and laughs.

Flirt.

I freeze between the two flights of stairs.

They can't see me here.

Don't move, Martha, I tell myself.

'Living quarters are on the third floor, this floor is the day-to-day running, staff meeting rooms, offices and such.'

'It's divine,' the woman drawls. American. 'So much history.'

'Quite,' he says. 'And an honour to be part of that.'

'And you have your portrait on the wall!' she says, and she laughs. 'What an incredible likeness.'

Their shoes click on the tiles.

'I commissioned it myself.'

With public money, I think.

'And what's up these stairs?'

Shit. Shit!

I edge back up one step, two . . . quietly . . . quietly . . .

My heart pounds.

'Let me take you this way first,' he says. I peer through the banister. I can't see their faces, but I can see his hand resting on her back. 'It's cosier.'

Creep.

I breathe again, wait as the door closes behind him, then hurry downstairs and head through the door to the left, the opposite direction to the PM.

This corridor's much like all the others. Narrow, the top half of the walls painted lemon with paintings on, the bottom white panelled wood, carpet so thick my feet sink in.

And doors.

So many doors.

How the hell are you supposed to remember what's behind each one?

I rest a hand on the nearest one, lean in and put an ear to it. Can't hear anything. I take a breath, hold it, push the door. My head spinning with a million excuses and stories for whoever's sitting behind it.

But there's nobody.

An automatic light flickers on over rows and rows of chairs, a lectern at the front with the lion-and-unicorn coat of arms. God and my right, I think, yeah, that's a bloody laugh. I recognise this room – this is where he gives press conferences. I've seen it on the TV.

I shut the door; there won't be anything in there.

I walk to the next door – there are two close to each other. Swallow hard, push the first one.

Big wooden desk, a phone, computer, bookshelves, nothing else, not even any files.

I breathe again, close that door, move to the next.

At least it seems like I'm in the right area, but how the hell I'm going to find anything in here I've no clue.

I would've put it in a safe.

I put my hand on the next door and push it open.

A strange blue light shines out even before I've got the door all the way open.

Electronic light. Flickering.

I step inside, and my mouth drops open.

The door shuts behind me with a sucking noise.

Silence.

The blue, the flickering, flashes on my eyeballs, on my skin. It's . . . *mesmerising.*

I step forward, towards a whole wall taken up with screens. A big one in the middle, smaller ones around the outside. A long desk underneath. Two leather chairs.

I slump into one, staring up at the visions of the City in front of me. My hands rest on the desktop and I touch some kind of control panel and a box comes up on the centre screen.

'Name', it says.

My hand flies over my mouth.

I know where I am. This is where he follows everyone.

My fingers hover over the keys.

I don't know if I dare.

God, my heart's pounding.

The longer you take . . . the voice in my head says.

I know, I know, I tell it.

'M' I type, 'A . . . R . . . T . . . H . . . A.'

Jeez, it's weird seeing my name there.

My breath stutters out. Even my fingers are sweating.

'HONEYDEW'.

I hit enter.

The circle thing spins for a second.

'No result found,' it says.

I hit enter again to check, but it tells me the same.

No GPS then; they're not following me.

For a second I close my eyes and let a long breath out.

Then I stare back at the screen.

The power beneath my fingers.

Quickly I type.

'ISAAC PAIGE.'

'No result found.'

Thank God.

'THOMAS CICERO.'

'No result found.'

'JOSHUA DECKER.'

Same again.

'GUS EVANS.'

And again. The relief is phenomenal. Like air from a balloon.

'MAX STANTON.'

A red dot appears and the screen shifts across and zooms in. I don't know where that is, somewhere in the City. Kensington? Posh area.

What . . . ?

Why . . . ?

I hit enter again, need to check, but it doesn't shift.

'What *are* you doing, Max?' I whisper.

I wish I knew how to use this properly. Wish I could find out whose house that is. My fingers hover over the keys.

Something creaks behind me.

Hell.

I turn to look. The door handle's down. There are voices.

Shit.

I pound the delete button. Stand up. Scurry out the chair.

Fuck, there's nowhere to hide!

What do I . . . ?

I spin round on the spot.

There's *nowhere*!

The door opens fully.

What the . . . ?

There's nowhere for me to go.

10.30 a.m. *Death is Justice Morning Chat Show*

Lights flash over the glitzy studio and a heartbeat theme tune plays. Kristina, wearing a tight red top and pencil skirt, sits on a sofa. Opposite her, on another sofa, sits DI Hart, his legs splayed and his chest puffed. As the lights pause over Kristina and the theme tune fades, she smiles at the audience.

KRISTINA: Good morning, ladies and gentlemen and welcome to the *Death is Justice Morning Chat Show*. We have lots of exciting things for you this morning, including an interview with the engineer of the electric chair used on death row, and a live phone-in with death row inmate turned Christian minister on his remarkable journey from the dark side to the light and how the threat of death made him appreciate life. But first –

She turns sideways towards a massive screen on the right side of the stage. The eye logo slides to the bottom left corner and the screen is filled with the smiling face of Gerome.

KRISTINA: We're going across to the new death row to speak live to our intrepid reporter Gerome Sharp. Good morning, Gerome, and how are you today? You appear to have escaped the breakfast show!

Gerome smiles wide. His skin, his hair, his teeth, are perfect, and his clothes and demeanour ooze professionalism as he nods gently to camera.

GEROME: Good morning, and what a pleasure it is to join you in the studio. Well, let me tell you I have many hats at the moment, and I'm certain I'll have my breakfast-show one back on soon. But, let me tell you, Kristina, you really have pulled the short straw being stuck in there!

He laughs gently and she joins in.

GEROME: Because here in the new death row, this place oozing with history and character, we are plunging ourselves headlong into the lives of these *wanton* criminals. Yes, for those of you who've been watching through the night, you'll have seen our regular coverage of the cells, peeking in to watch the sleeping bodies twitch with guilt, see the bloodshot insomniac eyes of those who know that guilt will not only follow them to the chair but chase them through the afterlife, and watch the tears fall of those who know their horrific actions have been engrained into history and will never be forgiven or forgotten.

He pauses. Back in the studio, Kristina nods.

KRISTINA: It sounds like a truly *electric* atmosphere there, Gerome.

GEROME (laughing): Very funny, Kristina! It seems your talents don't lie only in presenting! But, that aside, come with me.

He beckons to the camera. It follows him as he walks down a corridor and stops outside a doorway with the words 'Cell 3' emblazoned above it.

GEROME: If you *have* been with us through the night, then you'll have noticed the absence of one particular inmate. And that's because we've been saving her for a special for you.

His eyebrows lift and he nods towards Eve's cell. The camera follows him inside.

Adjusting to different light, it focuses on Eve, sitting on the mattress. Her shaven head is clean and her face seems bare of make-up, but there are no bags under her eyes and her skin glows. On the floor next to the mattress is a tin mug half full of coffee. Eve picks it up as Gerome and the camera come in, and as she stands she offers a hand to Gerome and gives a thin smile.

GEROME: Good morning, Mrs Stanton, and thank you for allowing us into your cell.

EVE (quietly): You're welcome.

GEROME: Tell us how you're doing. You look very well.

The chains around her wrists clank as she lifts a hand and brushes it across her stubbly scalp. Her eyes drop and the camera zooms in as she bites her lip and cradles the mug of coffee to her chest. The bruises on her wrists have been covered with make-up.

EVE: Well, it's hard, Gerome, but –

Interrupting her, he laughs and glances to the camera behind him.

GEROME (winking): It certainly *looks* hard, doesn't it? I mean –

Suddenly he flinches, coffee in his face, and he stumbles backwards. The camera jerks around, back and forth, focusing on the floor, the ceiling, the door, and back again.

GEROME: Help! Get –

He gasps and falls quiet. The camera steadies, moves sideways, zooms in on Gerome. Behind him is Eve. The chain from her wrists is wrapped around his neck as she pulls him towards her. His face is red, and coffee drips down it and off his nose and chin. His hair is wet. His fingers claw at the chains, scratching at his neck.

EVE (shouting): Shut up!

Her saliva spatters his face. His eyes wide, his mouth open, he pants.

EVE (to camera): Keep the camera on me. And if you let anyone in that door, he's dead. OK?

GEROME: Do as she says! Do as she says!

EVE (to Gerome): Shut UP!

EVE (to camera): I don't want to kill him, but I will. I'm going to die in four days anyway, so that may as well be for two as for one. Keep that camera on me and listen, and don't you DARE cut transmission. I know that red light means we're live, so just keep filming.

The camera shakes slightly but it holds on her.

EVE: I'm not going to bleat on about this unfair system. I'm not going to go on about how I had no choice but to kill that man. Nor am I going to tell you about my wonderful husband who sacrificed his life so I could raise our son. You all know that and you didn't listen anyway. No, this message is for Max.

Her face slackens. Next to her, Gerome's eyes dart around the cell, his fingers cling to the chain around his neck, but he doesn't struggle any more.

EVE: Max, Max, where do I start?

Her eyes fill with tears.

EVE: With the truth. I did kill him. I hit him over the head with a metal bar. He was attacking me. I didn't do it because I didn't want to die. I did it because I couldn't bear the thought of you growing up without a mother at your side. I couldn't stand the idea of you crying and me not being there to comfort you. Or you saying my name and me not hearing it. Or you coming out of the school gates and me not being there to smile at you and ask you about your day. Or you waking up in the night from a bad dream and not being able to find me. In those fractions of seconds when I thought I would die, the only thing I could think about was you. *You*. And when Jim, my husband, your dad, told the police he did it, I opened my mouth to argue, but he shook his head at me. He took the blame willingly. He took it despite my arguing. He took it because he loved me and he loved you. And I love you, Max. I love you, I love you, I love you. And I am forever sorry for not telling you. *Forever*. Please, please, find space in your heart to forgive me. If I die, let me know you forgive me.

She stops and takes a breath. Slackens the chain slightly around Gerome's neck. He doesn't move.

EVE: I could stand here and tell you a million times how sorry I am, and how I wish I'd told you before, but it'll never be enough, and it'll never change things for you. Please don't remember me like this. Remember me holding your hand as we went over the stepping stones in the park, remember when we stood under the garden shelter and watched the storm above us as we drank hot chocolate, remember the reindeer hoof marks I made in the hallway at Christmas, the experiment with vinegar we did that went wrong, the jokes we shared, the time I painted your toenails. All those things. Remember our time, and that if your dad, your wonderful, wonderful dad, hadn't –

Without warning there's a static crackle, a flash of light and she falls to the ground. Gerome stumbles, gasping for air.

GEROME: Paramedic! For me, not her.

The camera moves from Gerome to a security guard on his left, a Taser gun in his outstretched hands, and then to Eve, sprawled on the floor, two small darts piercing her overalls. Then back to Gerome; he fiddles with a cable and tucks an earpiece back in place.

GEROME (breathless): Don't . . . Don't say we . . . never bring you any . . . excitement. Let's go back . . . back to the studio . . . Kristina?

The feed fades to black. In the studio the camera focuses on Kristina sitting upright on the sofa.

KRISTINA: My, my. That was *quite* a shock, wasn't it? What do we make of that? I think our Gerome deserves a hot drink and a sit-down. It's certainly not the behaviour you would expect from an upstanding member of society, and begs the question – would we, the public, be safe with her on the streets? Let's take a look at the latest stats on her case.

On the screen, two large columns appear. 'Guilty' at the top of one, 'Not guilty' at the top of the other. Red lights run up and down them both and stop with a bang. Kristina exhales loudly.

KRISTINA: Well, ladies and gentlemen, 72% guilty, 28% not guilty. Although the guilty votes have a majority right now, I, for one, wouldn't want to risk that dropping. A change of a mere 23% would see Eve Stanton being released in four days' time. Is that a risk you want to take? If not, then get those dialling fingers busy while we go to a break.

The lights dance and the screen fades.

Martha

She doesn't even flinch.

She shoves a zipped-up leather file into my chest.

'I presume this is what you're looking for?'

I can't answer.

'Whole pile of evidence. Photographs, memory stick, even a ledger of bribes.'

'How . . . ?'

'You never would've found it.'

'How did you know what I was looking for?'

'I'm not stupid,' she says. 'Why else would you be here?'

'Then why didn't you just bring it to the Rises for me?'

'You think I'm going to risk being caught with that?' she hisses at me. 'My career would be over.'

'You risked . . .' I start, but think better of it. Maybe not taking me to the prison was less of a risk. I don't know. I'm not sure I understand her.

I look around this room. If only I could show folks this.

'Thank you,' I whisper.

'It's a miracle you managed to get all the way down here. I should have a word with security.' She gives a bitter laugh.

'This place,' I say, pointing behind me, 'this room . . .' I don't have the words. 'Who knows about this? Everyone who works here?'

She shakes her head. 'You have to go,' she says. 'Now. Come on.'

'But this,' I say, 'if I had evidence of this, if folks knew they were being followed – their *every* move, inside their own houses and everywhere – they'd be . . .'

'I have to get you out of here before you're seen. Come on.'

'But *this*! *This*.'

'Martha!' she hisses.

She grabs hold of my sleeve, but I pull away and run back to the desk, shoving the chairs into her path. Quickly I type 'ALBERT DELONZO' and in seconds the red dot appears.

'They're coming, Martha!'

'OK, OK,' I say. She's right. I can hear voices.

She pulls me out of the room and down the corridor, and I recognise that voice coming from somewhere, that laugh echoing down the corridor.

The Prime Minister.

She drags me around a corner and we stand still, her finger to her lips.

'Let me show you the power and influence I have,' he says to the blonde American, and I hear the door open.

'*Don't* do that again,' Sofia mouths to me, and as the door to that room closes she takes me past it and leads me away.

Eve

Desperate times call for desperate measures.

During my time as counsellor I met so many people who had been pushed to the edge and who acted, in these extreme circumstances, completely out of character.

I have never, wouldn't usually ever, threaten anyone, let alone hold a chain around a person's neck.

I wouldn't have killed him; that wasn't my intention.

I regret frightening him.

I regret hurting him.

But I don't regret doing it.

When that man, all those years ago, attacked me and Jim and I lifted that metal bar to hit him with it, I had no intention of killing him. My only thought was to stop him.

I regret that he died, but I don't regret what I did.

A female prisoner once said to me, 'I never thought I was capable of taking a life.'

I thought about that many times, and before she was committed to that chair I said to her that I believe everyone is capable of taking a life. Everyone.

And I still believe that. In the right – or the wrong – situation.

I said the same thing to another prisoner, a quiet young man who had been caught up in a gang drug situation, but he disagreed with me.

I explained my argument to him; that, for example, if someone was threatening to kill my child and I had a gun in my hand, and I knew for certain that my child would die if I didn't shoot that person, then I would pull that trigger without hesitation.

'You must love your family very much,' the prisoner said.

'No more than any other parent does,' I replied.

He laughed and shook his head. 'If that was my mum,' he said, 'she'd be trying to sell the gun in her hand to buy crack instead.'

I could've cried for him.

Three days later I went to his execution. His mother was there – she'd sold her story to the *National News* and was surrounded by paparazzi. Less than a week later she died from a drug overdose.

There are so many people I've met who I hope, if it comes to it in four days' time, will be waiting on the other side to welcome me.

I'll smile and shake their hands, and I'll make my way through to find Jim.

Martha

I memorised every turn and every staircase as she took me back to the kitchen.

'Tell them you're sick,' she said. 'I'll back you up.'

I sat in the caterer's van for a while, but someone felt sorry for me, or was worried I was going to throw up everywhere, so they drove me back again.

'You can drop me here,' I said as we headed through Kensington. 'I can get the tube from here.'

They didn't even bother to ask if I was sure, probably desperate to get rid of someone who might puke all over the seats.

I waited until they disappeared around the corner and grabbed a quick look at one of those 'You are here' maps, remembering where that red dot told me DeLonzo is, and trying to figure out how to get there. Then I nipped down an alleyway, stuffed the stupid wig that was making my head sweat into a pocket and pulled my hoodie and jacket back on.

I slump down the street now, not one of them any more; my head's down, long attractive hair gone, hood up – I'm the kind of person folk keep away from, not smile at.

I turn the corner and see him straight away. Lucky. I recognise him from off the TV, all his chat show appearances, spouting his opinion on some news programme, his face plastered on the front page of his own newspaper, shouting his own rhetoric, manipulating a whole society with his grin and charm offensive.

He scares me.

I'm so nervous my veins feel like they've got ants in them.

Folks seem to think I'm this bolshy, attitude-y teenager, but that's because I don't let them see what's going on inside.

It's an act.

A show.

And here we go again.

'Mr DeLonzo?' I say, sidling up to him.

'Why?' he says. 'Are you going to tell me you have a story for me?'

'Yes,' I reply.

He laughs. 'How did I guess? Everyone has a story. Contact reception, tell them what it is, they'll put you through to the right person.'

'You're the right person.'

'Young . . .' he pauses and I feel his eyes running up and down me, '. . . lady? Is it? I have people to deal with this kind of thing for me. Contact them.'

'I don't think you'd want them to see what I have.'

Come on, I think, take the bait.

'Do you know how many people try this sort of thing on me. Just fuck off, will you?' He strides away. I let him get a little ahead.

'Is it illegal to hire prostitutes?' I shout after him. 'I've never quite understood the law. Is it illegal for them or you or both?'

He stops walking.

'I suppose if it's not illegal it doesn't really matter, but folks

175

are funny about that sort of thing, don't you think? Especially family. Wives, girlfriends, whatever. Or teenagers at school – y'know they can be real cruel to kids whose parents . . .'

He turns around.

'. . . whose parents . . . hire . . .' I pause for effect, looking over his face, '. . . prostitutes.'

I can't help but smile.

There's a look to his face. What is that? Fear? Resignation? Anger?

He walks back, rubbing his hand across the styled fuzz on his chin.

'Who are you?' he says.

'Doesn't matter,' I reply. He's stepping closer and closer. I move backwards but can't go anywhere, suddenly I'm against a wall.

Shit, shit.

'I think it does,' he says, his voice calm and measured. 'Especially if you're trying to blackmail me.'

'I'm not,' I mutter, my voice trembling. Hell, I need to be brave, strong. I take a breath.

'Speak up!' he says. 'I can't hear you under that hood. Why don't you take it down?'

'I'm not trying to blackmail you!' I shout. I flick a look at him and he's frowning, clocking me. 'Not like that. I don't want to tell folk what you did. I want . . .' Oh fucking hell. '. . . want . . .' Shit, I can't do this. '. . . your . . . *help*.' God, that hurt.

I look up at him and he reaches out and pulls down my hood.

'Martha Honeydew,' he says. 'Who would've thought it?'

DECEMBER 4TH

Death is Justice: The Breakfast Show

Gerome stands behind the counter of a TV studio kitchen. To one side of him is a shiny kettle, while in front is a plate with a slice of toast with jam, and next to that is a newspaper.

GEROME: Good morning, viewers! And welcome to *Death is Justice: The Breakfast Show*! It's great to be here again! I seem to be getting all the best gigs at the moment and all the interesting and fascinating gossip to tell you. 'What's going on today?' I hear you ask. Well, boy, do we have news for you! I hope you're sitting down. It's shocked me so much I can barely manage my morning toast!

He laughs into camera.

GEROME: But this is no laughing matter. No, because last night workers at the *National News* looked on in *horror* as eccentric owner and editor-in-chief, Albert DeLonzo, took the unprecedented step of suspending printing of all today's newspapers! Stating he had 'important and vital news' to reveal, he then, according to insiders, substituted the main stories, taking away the lead headline, which was following the ongoing tribulations of the City versus the Rises, and replaced it with what is surely going to rock society.

He lifts the newspaper from the counter and holds it up to the camera. Huge red words blare out.

GEROME: The controversial headline reads: 'In Who Do We Trust?' – and the article goes on to detail multiple cases of high-profile public bodies and officials who have not only *broken* the law, but have used their significant influence to pervert the course of justice. The charges include murder, rape, extortion, kidnap and paedophilia, with names such as DI Hart, footballer Rik Midona, and murdered celebrity millionaire Jackson Paige himself. DeLonzo claims that the evidence was collected by Paige and his wife Patty, in order to manipulate their way into influential social circles and blackmail the perpetrators after their own fortunes took a downturn.

He puts the newspaper down and leans towards the camera.

GEROME (quietly): A source close to this programme stated that Martha Honeydew and Jackson Paige's son, Isaac – both previous death row inmates and members of the terrorist organisation the Rises 7 – tried to inform the public about these revelations, but the matter was never investigated. With Isaac Paige's body as yet unrecovered from the wreckage, detectives are currently negotiating an interview with Honeydew who, following her bomb attack on death row, is being held in prison after a guilty verdict on *Buzz for Justice*. Viewers should be reminded that if Isaac Paige's body is found, or if Patty Paige, still on life support following the explosion, doesn't recover, then Honeydew will again be committed to death row. The front-page story also claims Detective Inspector Hart covered up crimes carried out by his *own* police force in return for cash payments and that drugs taken off the street were then sold on by police officers, or used for their own recreational purposes. Albert DeLonzo also hints at further revelations he may divulge later this week. While that in itself is shocking, DeLonzo further states that the Prime Minister, Stephen Renard, is a key player in covering up what he calls 'institutionalised corruption' and 'an extreme level of government-sanctioned usage of fear to control a nation'. Stay tuned, ladies and gentlemen, as we keep you up to date with all the gossip in this juicy story.

Martha

DeLonzo clicks the TV off and looks at me.

'That's a real can of worms you've made me open. They're going to come after me with everything now.'

'There isn't anything left on you,' I tell him. 'What I gave you yesterday was the last, and we burned that.'

'How do I know I can trust you?'

'I don't know,' I say to him. 'But I could ask you the same. I'm sitting here in your living room – everyone else thinks I'm in prison. You could ring the police and tell them you've found a wanted terrorist.'

'So how did you get out?' he asks.

I look at him: grey hair, bags under his eyes, not as glam or as young as he looks on TV. No airbrushing in real life, I suppose. And I look around the flat too; photos of his kids, but no kids here, just a 'world's best dad' mug that's chipped and stained. Last night he cooked us two 'meals for one' from his freezer and struggled to find a drink for me that wasn't coffee or alcohol. I said I'd have alcohol but he refused.

Strange, isn't it? What you see isn't what you get. I didn't even know he's divorced.

'I can't tell you,' I say. I want to trust him, but I daren't.

He doesn't push it. He just nods.

'What will you do now?' I ask.

He stares at the newspaper lying on the glass coffee table in front of us both, the headlines blaring.

'You could be the man who brought down a corrupt government.'

'I could be the man found at the bottom of a lake,' he replies.

We sit in silence. Rain hammers on the window outside. A dark London sky full of threats of storm.

'You're serious, aren't you?' he says at last.

I nod.

He picks up the leather folder I gave him last night, zips it open and leafs through all the documents.

'I read it all,' he says. 'I'm certain there's enough here to bring down some key players. Patty, if she wakes from her coma, couple of celebrities, Hart won't go down without a fight and he fights dirty, some politicians, but Stephen Renard –' he shakes his head – 'that'll be tough.'

'The justice system,' I say to him. 'That's what I want to change.'

He blows his cheeks out. 'Well you won't change that without destroying Renard and his reputation, and to do that . . .' He stops, thinks, scratches his head.

'We'd need to turn the public against him,' I say.

He laughs. 'Good luck with that. The public adore him.'

I don't laugh. 'I can get something that'll do it,' I tell him. 'And if you help me, I can get you it before the end of the day.'

He leans back on the sofa and looks at me. The hint of a smile to his face. 'OK, Martha Honeydew,' he says. 'You get me that, and if it's any good –'

'It will be.'

'If *I* think it's any good, we'll run with it, but on one condition, no, two conditions.'

'What?'

'That if it works, I take the credit, and *you* give me an exclusive interview for my paper.'

'Deal,' I say, and we shake hands.

The Prime Minister – Stephen Renard

Sofia opens the front door of Number 10 and the PM marches out.

His shoulders are square, his back straight and his face is stone.

He strides to the lectern, looking out at the sea of journalists filling the pavement opposite.

Sofia takes her usual place at his left.

'This will be brief,' he says. 'And no questions. Following today's attempt by the *National News*, its shareholders, workers, owners and staff, to destabilise the very fabric of our society with unsubstantiated accusations of organised crime, corruption, cover-ups and bribery, I am reluctantly forced to take action.

'This wanton disregard of the need for truth and justice to be dealt with in a democratic manner forces us to instigate a new law to alleviate the fears of our upstanding members of society regarding their safety and security.

'As such, from 9 o'clock this morning, any action deemed to be against the safety of our nation, or definable as such, will lead to immediate incarceration on death row.

'This will deter any persons or groups from carrying out such crimes, and will therefore result in safer streets, safer society and a respectful and honourable nation.

'I promise you, that when you voted for me and put your faith in me to make our society a good place to live, that you did the right thing. I will do anything and everything possible to ensure your safety and that of your families.

'Thank you.'

DI Hart

Hart throws the newspaper across the table to Max.

'This has got your girlfriend written all over it,' he spits, his stomach pulling at the buttons of his shirt, and his thighs stretching the material of his trousers.

'She's not my girlfriend.'

Hart smirks at him. 'One phone call and I could see that all the votes for your mother are guilty ones.'

'You promised me.'

'You've not delivered. You've been here, sponging off me like some Rises filth, promising every day you're going to ring her and then spending all the hours God sends watching *Death is Justice*! How many times have you used my phone to vote your mother innocent?'

'I haven't,' he replies.

'Good, because it won't make any difference.'

'Why do you say that? Because she said she did it?'

Hart huffs, lifts his eyes to the roof and sneers. 'That makes no difference. Haven't you figured out how it works? There is no democracy – it's a fallacy. The government, us the police – we decide the important cases. The rest is manipulation to get people voting more, but it doesn't make any difference. I thought you and your girlfriend –'

'She's not –'

'– and that numbskull who threw his future away, Isaac, had worked that out. The only ones people *really* get to vote on are those who nobody cares about.'

'Like my mum?'

'Most certainly not like your mum. She's dead. She needs to be made an example of. Unless you play ball, that is.'

Max turns the newspaper over and scans the front page. 'And this, saying you're involved in all this corruption, what's stopping them coming to get you?'

'Some two-bit journalist with delusions of grandeur.'

'DeLonzo?'

'A bitter, lonely man with nothing better to do with his time.'

Max makes a show of looking around the room. 'I don't see any wife here, partner, significant other, kids. Or did they find out what you did and then up and leave?'

The slap across Max's face echoes off the walls. 'Shut your mouth.'

Max steadies his chair. 'Truth hurts, doesn't it?'

'I warned you – one phone call and I could have her moved to Cell 7 and dead before midnight. I want Honeydew before tonight's papers go to print, and her face on them in the morning. If not . . .' His voice trails away.

Eve

There's a mouse who comes in here when it's dark and quiet. He didn't venture very close to me at first, but slowly he's becoming braver.

Last night they brought me lukewarm soup and a stale bread roll, so I kept some of the roll back to feed the mouse.

I didn't do it because I wasn't hungry, but rather because I felt sorry for him, and feeding him reminded me what it is to be human.

He's come back now, but I have nothing to give.

The worst thing about being in here isn't the cold, or the hunger, it's being completely cut off from the world.

I want to know what's happening. How Martha's doing in prison, what's happened to Cicero, and how Max is. I worry about what they said about arresting him.

Missing him physically hurts. It's as if ropes are fastened to my insides and are being pulled away from me, but I have no way of moving with them.

It would be easier not to have these images of him in my mind, but they come unbidden and all the time.

I've let him down so much.

If I hadn't gone along with Jim's suggestion, if I hadn't let him take the blame for killing that man, then Max would have a father now, and still have a parent in three days . . .

three years . . . thirty years . . . who knows?

Instead, in three days' time, he'll be alone.

An orphan.

And if my wishes for him to live with Cicero aren't followed, then he'll be an orphan consigned to living in a care institution.

My heart shudders with fear for him and his future.

Three days left, but what can I do?

Nothing but wait.

Martha

It's a dull day; the streetlights are on at noon.

And the Christmas lights.

I'm walking away from Regent Street and people are carrying bags probably filled with Christmas presents that nobody really wants.

Music's being piped from shops.

We wish you a merry Christmas . . .

Yeah, right.

I daren't even think about it.

What do you want for Christmas, Martha?

Isaac awake.

Eve alive.

All of us free.

And if that works, then all I want is to be with them, and be warm and dry.

The rain's stopped at least, but my feet are wet.

I cut between crowds of folk, across roads. I'm not even thinking about the stupidity of what I'm about to do.

Just do it, Honeydew, my head says.

'Cleaners,' Sofia told me when I rang.

'Is it really this easy?' I asked her.

'If you don't know someone like me, it's impossible,' she said.

Glad I kept the wig.

'I won't ask why,' DeLonzo said, when I pulled it over my head.

'Good,' I replied.

'They'll give you a uniform,' Sofia told me.

'Good,' I replied to that as well.

Two folks in my corner today.

I hope.

You've done it once, Martha, I say to myself, you can do it again.

I pull the phone out as I walk, type in the number.

'Judge,' I say as he answers.

There's a sigh on the other end. 'Thank God you're all right. The headlines . . . it's . . . Was that something to do with you?'

'How is he?' I ask. I don't want to get into everything else right now, I'm too busy thinking about what I'm about to do. Yesterday all I had to do was get in and get out.

Today . . .

My brain's nearly exploding with the worry of it.

And if I'm caught, that's it.

Game over.

I force myself to focus back on the phone call, and I'm so preoccupied that I walk straight into the road without looking. A car horn blares as it whips past me.

'The same,' he says.

I sigh. Not sure if I'm relieved or disappointed.

'His eyes were flickering. Novak was non-committal about what it meant, but it seemed good to me.'

'You will ring me, won't you, if anything . . . *anything* –'

'Of course I will,' he replies.

In the distance Big Ben begins to strike.

Twelve o'clock, I think to myself.

'I hope you're safe,' he says.

Safe? When was I *safe*?

'I've got to go,' I say.

'Listen, Martha, Max rang. He wanted to speak to you. I told him you weren't here and he asked where you were.'

'What did you tell him?'

'The truth. That I didn't know. But I gave him your phone number. I hope that's OK with you.'

'Of course,' I reply. 'Was he all right?'

In my head I can see Cicero sucking the ends of his moustache as he thinks. 'Difficult to tell,' he says at last.

Big Ben finishes striking.

'Take care, Martha. Ring me before you head back. Things here are a little . . . worrisome.'

I nod, but don't answer and I click the phone off.

I'm coming up to Horse Guards Parade, near where Sofia told me I'd find the cleaners' van. I'm practising in my head what I'm supposed to say, and I'm not looking where I'm going.

But there's a shout ahead and I stop. Fear and self-preservation holding me back.

Something's going on.

A riot van screams past me, sirens blaring, lights flashing.

Then another.

And another.

What the . . . ?

I know I shouldn't, but I break into a run. I want to see what's happening.

People are streaming in the opposite direction though, pushing past and away from me. There's fear in their faces. Mums clenching hands of children and pulling them along, or shoving pushchairs through gaps, suited men with elbows wide to push others out the way, old folk shuffling as fast as they can.

'What's going on?' I shout.

Nobody stops.

Nobody says a word.

There's another shout in the distance.

A bang of a gun and everyone ducks.

Screams fill the air.

'What's happening?' I hiss to the woman crouched next to me, but she just shakes her head.

I do what I probably shouldn't.

I stand up, and I walk between the bodies crouched small in fear.

Nobody tells me not to, or grabs at my legs or urges me to sit down.

They don't even look at me.

Not far away are a dozen or so people standing, not shouting or screaming, just standing, completely still. I can't tell how old exactly, older than me, twenty-ish by the way they're dressed.

And in their hands are placards.

I step closer to see what they say.

Another riot van screams past.

I step closer still.

'JUSTICE FOR ALL' one of the placards reads.

Then there's one with photos of Hart and the PM pasted to it. 'CRIMINALS' is written across in red.

'THE RISES 7 WERE FRAMED' another says.

I freeze. Shivers go up my back.

Why would people say that?

Then there's one with a photo of Eve. 'VICTIM' it says across her.

I prickle, blink tears away that I don't want.

Why would anyone do that?

I move forward again, but the vans open their doors and police stream out of them. I don't how many, ten, twelve maybe, and they plough towards these unarmed, peaceful protestors with batons up and stun guns aimed.

I hear the thuds, the screams, and I feel so useless.

Go on, Martha! my head shouts. *Save them. Help them.*

How?

One of the riot police turns around and spots me. He points a gun at my chest. Nobody around me says or does anything.

'Where are you taking them?' I shout.

The officer ignores me and turns away.

My chest goes hot, so angry it's like I'm burning.

'I said,' I shout and I'm marching forward now, 'where are you taking them?' He turns back, gun lifted again. I freeze.

'Death row,' he says. 'For crimes against the safety of our nation.'

There's no trace of emotion on his face.

'Come on,' I say to the people around me. 'We can stop this. How many of us are there? Look around. There's loads of us. And there's . . . how many of them? Twenty at the very most? Come on.'

Nobody meets my eye.

'For fuck's sake!' I plead. 'They're going to kill them! And they haven't done anything. Come on!'

One man turns to me, chubby and bald, older. 'They're sympathisers,' he says. 'They're endangering our safety.'

'That's bollocks and you know it. Those people are going to die for sticking up for others. All they've done is wave some bits of cardboard in the air. How is that *endangering safety*? Don't you think they have the right to do that?'

Nobody answers.

'They're going to die!' I say.

'Yes,' the same man says. 'But we're not.'

I stare at him, shocked at the selfishness.

'Then I'll do it myself,' I reply.

'Then you'll die too,' he says.

Selfishness or self-preservation? I don't know. But I do know that if all these people acted together we could stop it.

'Excuse me.' There's a small, gentle voice behind me. I spin around, angry tears in my eyes and my whole body shaking. 'Did Sofia Nachant send you? Are you here for the cleaning job?' A tiny, fragile-looking woman with a clipboard and a beret is staring at me.

Madness, I think. Sheer fucking madness.

I glance back to the demo, the folks being dragged away and stuffed in a van, the pain on their faces, their pleas for us to help them.

And I look to the folks around me, desperate to save themselves.

And I look to this tiny woman.

Choices, Martha. Make the right one.

'Is it you?' she asks again.

Shouting starts coming from the crowds but I turn away.

'Yes,' I reply.

'Good,' she says. 'Then come this way.'

Am I part of the problem or part of the solution?

Isaac

Beep.

Beep.

Warm.

Soft.

Still.

Beep.

Music, quiet.

Whistling, close by.

A tune.

Dark, but bright lights.

Throat's sore.

Beep.

Legs hurt.

Breathing . . . in . . . out . . . that's hard.

Arms heavy.

'Would you like a cup of tea, Dr Novak?'

Novak?

What?

'That I would, Judge.'

Judge?

Footsteps.

Aftershave?

Move my fingers, toes.

Eyelids are heavy.

It's bright.

Blurred.

A face.

Bald. Eyebrows. Wide eyes.

Another.

Moustache. Glasses. Smile.

'Hello, young man.'

Cicero.

'Welcome back.'

Martha

I can remember the route through the woods to the far side where the best tree for climbing always was.

I can remember the short cut through the school grounds that avoids the caretaker's office so you don't get caught when you're late.

And I can remember the way from the kitchens to that room in Number 10, as if I've known it just as long as both of those.

That nobody stops me is a bloody miracle I don't understand.

Don't I look a bit like that teenager Martha Honeydew who caused all those problems and then supposedly blew up death row and tried to kill loads of folks and is a terrorist?

No?

A wig on my head, a uniform on and the fact that I'm supposed to be in prison, not walking around the corridors of one of the most heavily guarded buildings in the world, seems enough to stop anyone asking questions.

Folks only see what they want to see.

'Twelve thirty,' she said, 'and there'll be nobody in there.'

Jeez, so much that could go wrong, and part of that because I'm so crap at technology.

I walk down the corridors carrying some weird basket-thing full of cleaning stuff.

'You must be here for the toilets,' some guy says to me. 'At least they didn't make us wait until the end of the day like they usually do.'

I smile at him. 'It's a shitty job,' I say, the words falling out before I can stop them.

He laughs at me, striding off down the corridor 'Well, it's appreciated,' he calls over his shoulder. 'Some people in here have no manners or decency. Everyone is in a meeting or at lunch right now,' he continues, 'but if you could make sure you're gone before they return at twenty to one. It's not the done thing for the cleaner to be here during normal working hours, but like I said, it's appreciated.'

I wait until he disappears around the corner.

Twenty to one?

She said I had half an hour. That gives me . . . ten minutes. Shit.

Here we go then, I say to myself, let's be quick, and I push open the door.

It's empty as Sofia promised.

The strange blue light flickers around the room.

Time to crack on, I tell myself.

I scrabble around in my pocket and take out a small device. I click it on, then take my phone out and log on to the internet, clicking on the link DeLonzo's already set up. I wait a second, then there it is – live feed from this tiny little camera.

Next I pull one of the leather chairs over to the door and, praying nobody barges in, I stand on it and stick the camera to the wall just above the door frame, then I angle it till it points at the bank of video screens.

My hands are covered in sweat; I wipe them down my trousers.

Time on my phone says 12.34.

That went quick.

I double check the camera's stuck on. Yeah, that's not going anywhere.

Jesus, I'm nervous.

I push the chair back, sit on it, and type in 'DI HART'. The red dot appears, the screen zooms, and I give it a second so folks can see it's following him.

Check the time again.

12.35.

Another minute gone.

How time-conscious are these folk?

Are they going to walk back in bang on 12.40?

Doubt it.

Then I type in the first celebrity that comes to mind, and another dot appears in a different part of the City.

Next I type in a film star.

Then a singer.

Good job this system's quick. Better internet than we ever had in the Rises, that's for sure.

12.37.

Come on, Martha.

Last couple. Some ordinary folk.

I type in a shopkeeper's name I found out.

Then a schoolteacher.

Some guy I met who works in a fast-food place.

A childminder.

I could go on, but I think they'll get the point.

Then I move around the room, snapping photos.

I'm going as fast as I can, but time's zooming past. I check my phone, 12.39.

Oh hell!

Come on, come on, come on, Martha.

I'm not leaving yet. Not till I've finished.

I take a selfie of me in the leather chair, the screens behind me, thumbs up, and I wave to the camera which should be live now.

Live? I think. Live?

Holy fuck.

Oh, I think I hear voices.

Hell, Martha, you were going to do the photos first, then the video, I tell myself. Start the video just before you left. This way . . . oh shit . . . this way . . . it's been live for nearly ten minutes. What if someone's already realised where it is? What if that gets back to folk who work here? What if . . . ?

Oh shit.

I need to get out of here now.

God, Martha, you're so stupid sometimes.

I look at the time again.

Bloody hell, that's it. Time's up.

I shove my phone in my pocket, straighten the chair so folks – hopefully – don't realise too quickly that I've been in here and I dash to the door.

I pause, fingers on handle, thinking . . . listening . . .

As if people are going to be that specific about time, I think.

I hope.

I can't hear anyone . . . or anything . . .

I ease the door open.

Still can't hear anything.

And I step out of the room.

Breathe, Martha.

And I take one pace, two paces down the corridor.

'All done?'

Oh shit, that man again. I jump a mile.

I nod and smile.

'Crappy job, hey?' he says.

'Yes,' I reply. I'm past him now. Keep walking . . . keep going.

Nearly at the end.

My phone blares into the silence.

I nearly jump out of my skin, shove my hand in my pocket and grab it. In the panic I drop it, then kick it to the side. I scrabble around on the floor.

Down the corridor I hear a door open.

Shit, shit, shit.

And close again.

The phone's still ringing.

'No phones,' Sofia told me. 'They don't let cleaning staff bring phones in. Security measure. They don't want anyone filming anything.'

Bugger.

I grab it.

Hear a door open again.

'Hey, you!' That guy. 'This toilet hasn't been done. What are you playing at?' He stares at the phone in my hand. 'You're not allowed that in here? What are you doing?'

Oh fuck!

The display says it's Cicero.

Cicero? What . . . ? Isaac?!

My stomach tips, and for a second my head spins. I go to rub the sweat off my forehead and knock the wig sideways.

Holy crap!

'I said . . .' His voice is louder, he's coming towards me. Then he pauses. 'Are you wearing a wig? Don't I recognise you from somewhere?'

'What is it?' I whisper down the phone.

'Put that down and come here!' He's shouting now. This isn't good.

'Martha,' Cicero says.

The man tries to grab the phone from me. I cling to it.

Don't let go, don't break it.

But he's strong. And angry.

'Martha, can you talk?' Cicero. 'It's Isaac.'

'Let go!' the man shouts.

'Fuck you!' I shout back, and I spit in his face.

He lets go of the phone, slaps me across the face and my wig falls to the floor. I stand there, frozen, scared.

Another door opens.

'It would be better –' The voice stops, but I already recognise it. I turn as if in slow motion.

His eyes bore into me.

'Martha Honeydew?' the PM hisses. 'What . . . ?'

I don't wait to hear any more. I turn and I run down the corridor. I know the way, I know where I'm going, but suddenly alarms are blaring everywhere.

Fuck, fuck, fuck.

I run, up and along, then down. Put the phone back to my face. 'Cicero,' I shout over the alarms, 'give me a second.' I can't get bad news like this.

I look around, somebody behind me.

Turn down another corridor quickly. Then another. Look around and can't see anyone. Turn again and there's the door in front of me.

It opens – Sofia. Her finger goes to her lips.

I run through as fast as I can and she gives me a thumbs up and I step into the kitchen.

'People!' she shouts across the room. 'The emergency alarm has sounded. This is not a drill. All housekeeping staff who have checked in with me are free to go, everyone else must remain.'

I don't catch her eye, I just step outside with the rest of them, and as soon as I'm out of sight of any of the security people I put the phone to my ear again.

'Are you still there?' I whisper, as I walk with the crowd.

Nothing.

'Cicero?' I hiss. 'Are you there?' But there's no answer.

My heart sinks.

The line goes dead.

I keep close to them all, safety in numbers, and I click the phone again, ring back but it's engaged, so I click it off again and wait.

He'll ring back, won't he?

We're outside now and folks are separating. A few hanging around for a cigarette, some crashing on a bench. I walk across the road, heading to St James's Park, away from the noise and crowds. As my feet hit the path on the other side, my phone rings again.

'Cicero?' I hiss down the phone. 'What's happening?'

Silence.

'Cicero . . . ?'

'No, it's me, Max.'

'Max? What? Where are you? What do you want? Are you back in Daffodil House?'

I'm jabbering now, trying to keep calm, my feet pounding across damp grass as I try to find somewhere quiet and private to sit.

'No,' he replies.

'Then why . . . ? Look, I've got to go. I need –'

'No. You need to stay on the line and you need to listen to me.'

'Max –'

'You owe me.'

'I *owe* you? What? What the hell are you going on about?'

'I need you to meet me. You're in the City, aren't you? Meet me at the front of the Old Bailey in half an hour.'

'Max, I can't. I've got to . . .' *Hang on, Martha,* that voice in my head says. 'Cicero, he just . . .'

No, Martha.

Something's stopping me.

'It won't take long,' he says. 'Please.' His voice softens. 'I need to see you.'

Jesus Christ, what do I do?

The phone beeps in my ear.

What is that? A message? Another call?

I move it from my ear and squint at the screen.

Low battery!

Jesus.

Think, Martha. Quickly.

'Max, I've got to go, my battery's nearly flat. I'll ring you again later, OK?'

'No. I need to speak to you now. It's urgent. Meet me and I'll bring you a charger.'

My head spins, trying to work everything out.

'OK, OK,' I say. 'Half an hour at the Old Bailey. But I can't stay long.'

'It won't take long,' he replies, and the line goes dead.

1 p.m. *Death is Justice*

Overhead lights dance and jive across the audience and studio. On the right of the stage the eye logo fills the screen, the small padlock of Cyber Secure in the bottom corner.

Kristina trots out from backstage, a white dress with plunging neckline, gold belt pulling in her waist and gold peep-toe high-heeled sandals. A long gold necklace dangles into her cleavage.

KRISTINA: Hello, ladies and gentlemen, and welcome to this special afternoon episode of *Death is Justice*!

The audience whoop and applaud. A couple of wolf whistles.

KRISTINA: Well, ladies and gentlemen, we've had quite the development since the announcement from our Prime Minister, Stephen Renard. I must say though, anything that keeps our streets safer gets my vote. Anyone endangering the lives of our children and our vulnerable should feel the full force of the law, as I'm sure you'll agree. But what an effect it's had on our death row! And personally I find it terrifying that so many members of society have been threatening the safety and security of others and I, for one, feel reassured that the PM is taking such a strong stand.

A murmur of agreement breaks out into applause, growing louder until the audience are all on their feet.

KRISTINA: But away from such seriousness, let's get on with the entertainment! For your pleasure today we will have Gerome reporting live from the cells, showing us the full impact of this new law, we will have the final stats and possible execution of drunk driver Shellie Du Bec, we'll be asking your opinion on possible multiple executions as numbers on death row more than double, but first we have the latest on Eve Stanton. Gerome, I believe you are with Stanton at the moment, aren't you?

The eye logo moves to the corner of the screen, Gerome's smiling face filling it instead. Behind him are the flaking walls of the cells.

GEROME: Good afternoon, Kristina! And welcome to this veritable den of iniquity! Who would've thought that so many people were planning on destabilising our country? I'm shocked, I tell you. But it does make tremendous entertainment, and

I've enjoyed the last few hours in here more than the whole rest of the week. Let me walk you through.

The camera follows him along a narrow corridor.

GEROME: We're actually moving backwards along Dead Man's Walk right now. Behind me, at the end of the corridor, is the execution room, as you know. These white crumbling bricks and ever decreasing archways were the last thing prisoners in history would've seen, and they are again now. How reassuring it is to see the country finally brought back to a high standard of both preventative justice and punishment. We're now entering the beginning of the cells. The boxed lights above the doors illuminate if the cell is occupied, and as you can see by the row of lights leading down this incredibly bleak corridor, every cell is occupied. Cell 1 isn't just *occupied* though, ladies and gentlemen; no, it is *full*. Such has been the success of the PM's new law. Which leads me to our exciting news of the day. Kristina, shall I do the honours or would you like to?

Back in the studio, Kristina smiles at the screen.

KRISTINA: I think, Gerome, that the audience and viewers

at home would be really excited to see you break the news to the occupant. I'm on tenterhooks here waiting for their reaction.

On the screen, Gerome smiles and winks.

GEROME: Precisely what I was thinking, Kristina. Here we go then.

The camera follows him as he enters the cell next to him. Propped against the wall in the far corner is Eve. Her skin is pale and drawn in around her cheekbones and eye sockets.

GEROME: Eve, what a pleasure to see you again.

He squats down, holding the microphone out to her, but keeping a safe distance.

GEROME: How are you?

She stares at him, eyes glassy and bloodshot.

GEROME (quietly): I have some news for you, Eve. News I think you'll welcome and that will stop this pain for you.

Her eyes focus and she sits up straighter.

GEROME: You won't be up to date with news, and it's

not especially relevant to you, but the PM has brought in a new law making any crimes deemed to be against, or risking the safety and security of, our nation punishable by death. As you can imagine, we've had a sudden influx here on death row!

He smiles wide, his teeth white against the gloom of the cell.

GEROME: Tell me, Eve, when you changed cells early today, they led you out blindfolded, didn't they?

EVE (hoarse and quiet): They always do.

GEROME: Of course, but to clarify for our viewers. And then they put you into the next cell?

She nods.

GEROME: Or did they?

He pauses, glances to camera with raised eyebrows, then back to Eve again.

GEROME: In fact, do you know which cell you're in right now?

The camera zooms in on her face, for once the lines around her eyes and the bags underneath clearly visible.

EVE (shakily, quiet): It's day four, so this is Cell 4. I know it is.

She reaches her arm out. The camera zooms in on four distinct scratches across her arm.

GEROME: Well, Eve, you are right that it is your *day* four, but this is not *Cell* 4. You see, with the sudden increase of prisoners, we've had to make some changes. And, as there was only one person on the row before you, who's now in Cell 7, we had two empty cells between you both.

Eve's face drops. Her lip quivers. She shakes her head from side to side.

EVE (whispering): No, no . . .

GEROME: It was the most sensible option. And, Eve, you can thank your fellow criminals and Rises sympathisers for this, because you have been spared two days of pain. Yes, you have advanced directly into Cell 6! Tomorrow will be your judgement day!

Eve jumps to her feet, the camera shaking as it follows her, and she lunges out, the chains tightening as she fights against them, rattling throughout the room and down the row.

EVE (shouting): NO! NO! That's not right, that's not fair!

GEROME: I'm afraid you forfeited right and fair when you committed the crime that landed you here. You did commit the crime after all, didn't you, Eve? You did kill that man?

EVE: He was going to kill me or Jim! Or both of us! I couldn't leave Max an orphan!

GEROME: Yet he will be now, won't he? In just over thirty-one hours in fact. Probably.

The chains clang as she bucks against them.

EVE: You despicable man! This atrocious system. I hope you all rot in hell for the pain and suffering you've caused innocent people!

GEROME: Strong words, Eve, yet I think you'll be the one rotting in hell for the pain and suffering *you've* caused.

EVE: I demand to speak to someone!

GEROME (laughing): Eve, darling, you're speaking to the whole world right now! They're all watching your little outburst, and they all heard you say once again that you killed that man. And, quite honestly, I thought you'd be pleased. This whole unpleasant episode will be over two whole days before you thought it would be. In two days' time your son will be able to get on with his life again!

The camera focuses on Eve's face, zooming close as it crumbles into tears.

GEROME (off-screen): If he hasn't been arrested by then, but that's another story, hey, viewers?

EVE: What?

Back on Gerome, the camera follows him out of the cell and into the corridor.

GEROME: Well, Kristina, there you have it! I think it's safe to say, she did *not* see that coming.

EVE (shouting in the background): Why would Max be arrested? What's happening?

GEROME (to camera, ignoring Eve): But, frankly, it makes sense, and what use would another two days serve anyway? She's admitted to it. There is no doubt. What more do we need to know? Kristina, it's over to you.

KRISTINA: My, my, Gerome, what drama! And what a reaction from Eve Stanton there, who you'd think would be better at controlling her emotions. It seems she can't keep the tears in, even for the good of her son. But let's see if what Gerome's saying is true. Have the public made up their minds on Mrs Stanton? Is there anything left to debate or would another two days have been a simple waste of time, and if so, could the justice system be streamlined further? Let's answer the first of those questions now.

In the studio, Gerome's face is replaced by two columns; Guilty and Not guilty.

KRISTINA: Computer, give us the stats!

A loud ticking sounds over the audience as lights in the columns move up and down.

KRISTINA: I cannot *wait* to see this!

They stop with a bang.

KRISTINA: And there we have it. Not guilty at 18.6%, guilty at 81.4%. Not the landslide I was expecting, but pretty cut and dried in my opinion. Will another day make any difference? Keep voting, and join us tomorrow to find out! In the meantime, if you can't wait for an execution, then don't go away – because after the break we'll be checking the stats of that drunk driver!

As jaunty music fills the air, the eye logo returns to the screen, the padlock of Cyber Secure in the corner fastening around a fluffy white cloud.

Daffodil House

Cicero sighs and turns the television off.

'I don't think it was a good idea for you to watch that,' he says to Isaac.

'I needed to,' he replies, his voice low and croaky.

Dr Novak fusses around him, whistling as he removes the blood-pressure sleeve from his arm. 'You seem fine.'

Isaac nods. 'I have a headache, but that's it. Where's Martha?'

Cicero looks down at the phone in his hand. 'I can't get through,' he says. 'She's probably on her way back here.'

Isaac shuffles in the bed, sitting himself upright. 'I need to do something. This –' he indicates to the TV – 'this has got worse.'

'You're not to do anything!' Dr Novak says, throwing a blanket around Isaac's shoulders. 'You need to rest and keep warm.'

'I've been resting for days,' Isaac replies. 'I need to –'

Cicero shakes his head. 'Wait for Martha,' he urges. 'Then we'll sort things out. I'll keep trying her.'

The Prime Minister – Stephen Renard

'How?' says the Prime Minister, the leather chair in the Blue Room creaking as he shuffles back.

Sofia leans forward and tips whisky into a glass in front of the PM. 'I'll have it thoroughly investigated,' she says.

'And why didn't the prison tell me? And what was she doing here of all places? Why would she risk it?'

'No disrespect, sir, but it was definitely her, wasn't it? There's no way you could've been mistaken?'

'Definitely.' He knocks the drink back. 'I wasn't the only one who saw her.'

'Do you think we should keep this quiet?' she asks, standing up and strolling towards the door, the camera still stuck tight to the wall above it. She flicks on a switch to a coffee machine nearby.

'Of course we should keep this quiet!' the PM shouts, spinning around to face her. 'How would it make us look if the public knew Honeydew was out?'

'I understand,' Sofia mutters, and she pours a drink into a mug.

'That wretched girl,' he says. 'If only Patty had got rid of her like I told her too. How is Patty anyway? Do we have any news?'

Sofia sips at her drink. 'She died last night. A result of her injuries.'

The PM grabs the whisky bottle and pours himself another. 'No great loss,' he says. 'The woman was a waste of space. She always thought she was controlling things, but she never was. Not even her husband. If she'd got him under control, he would've blasted that Honeydew girl away when we had the chance. We'd have none of this now.'

Sofia throws a quick glance to the camera and strolls back to the desk.

'Do you know the main problem with being a leader, Sofia?'

'No, sir, what would that be?'

'People.'

Martha

Bloody phone's dead.

I go to a phone box but then I remember I don't know Cicero's number, or anyone's, and we haven't had a home phone for years.

God, my head's pounding, I feel sick.

Why was he ringing?

Good news or bad?

What did his voice sound like?

I'm running now.

Maybe if I get to the Old Bailey sooner, Max will already be there, I can get the battery pack off him, ring Cicero, find out.

And what the bloody hell does Max want?

Is he still angry?

Jesus, this is bloody torture!

It's downhill on this stretch after St Paul's. Only a bit, but enough to get my breath back a little.

God, I'm sweating. Air's cold though.

I trot along the street, in and out of crowds, onto the road to avoid folk and back up on the path. People frown at me.

It's bloody London, I want to say to them, everyone's in a rush. Fuck off.

Jesus, I'm bad-tempered.

Who wouldn't be?

Here we go, round the corner.

Presume he'll be at the front.

Odd place to meet, not very secluded. All open roads.

I slow to a walk.

Can't see him.

I stand still, look back and forth.

There's a few cars parked close by. Must be government cars, officials or such, because nobody else is allowed to park here.

Getting my breath back now.

I take the phone out as if by some miracle it'll suddenly have battery again, but it doesn't.

'Martha.'

I spin around. There's Max right in front of me. I didn't see him walking up.

'Max,' I reply, and I go to hug him. However angry he is with me right now, he still saved my life, he's still my friend. But he steps back. 'Max, I'm sorry. Let's not fall out; we should be working to help each other. And your mum.'

'I've been helping you for ages. It's your turn now.'

'Course,' I reply. 'You know I will. But first, do you have that battery pack? Cicero tried to –'

'Back to yourself again?'

'What?'

'Thinking of yourself again. Screw me and what I need.'

'It's not like that, Max. Cicero –'

'You know, I was starting to feel sorry for you. Wondering if I should be doing this, but Hart was right –'

'What?'

'He said you're nothing but a spoilt, selfish, self-obsessed little shit and you've just proved it.'

My stomach flips. Everything spins. Needles over my skin.

'What's Hart got to do with this?'

'He promised me, you see. He made me a deal.'

I stare at him. I feel dizzy.

'You, for Mum.'

'What?' I say.

He laughs at me. 'Are you stupid? I give him you, he gives me Mum. You for Mum.'

'What?' I repeat. I can't get my head around the words he's saying.

'Is that all you can say? *What?* I said –' he's talking slowly now, treating me as if I'm some idiot – 'I made a deal with him: he promised to release my mum if I led him to you.'

'Max,' I say, trying so hard not to shout at him, still struggling to understand the level of stupidity here, 'are you a moron? There's no way he can do that.'

'He's a detective inspector, he's got contacts; he can do whatever he likes.'

'No, he's not in charge. He might *think* he is . . . but . . . Max, even if he could, there's no way he's going to do that! He won't do anything for you! You can't trust him!'

'Yeah, he told me you'd say that.'

'Because it's true!' I shout.

He grabs hold of my arm, trying to pull me down the road.

'Let go!' I shout, and I try to pull away from him, but he's strong and my feet are stuttering along the path.

'Everything's always been about *you*. That's going to change.

224

I'm not doing this for me, Martha, it's for my mum, and I know you'll understand that. You owe her that.'

I'm still trying to pull away from him, but I can't get my balance, my feet are running away from me. He yanks me towards a black car parked at the side of the road. A door opens, legs swing out of it.

Fat legs.

'Max, don't do this. Max, please.'

God, I'm nearly crying. Begging him. Can't believe this is happening.

'Max, he's lying to you. He's not going to let your mum out.'

'Yeah, right. I've had it with listening to you – look where that's got us.'

'Max, let me go. Please.'

Hart looms out of the car. People are gathering around, slowing down to watch. A few taking phones out.

To film, or ring the police?

Film probably.

Jesus Christ, Martha, think. What can you do? He gets you in the car, it's all over.

'Please.' I'm crying now. 'Please.'

'Beg all you want to,' Max says. 'I'm not changing my mind.'

Only one choice.

'I'm sorry, Max,' I sob.

'So you should be.'

'I'm sorry, but I've got to do this.'

'Do what?'

And I'm sorry, Eve. But what choice do I have?

I grab out at him, yank down the hood of his jacket.

People are watching, and that's good.

'Max Stanton!' I shout at the top of my voice. 'Help! It's Max Stanton. Rises 7 terrorist.'

He lets go of me, his face falling as he gawps at me. The whole street stops. People staring at him. Phones out and pointed.

'It's Max Stanton!' I shout again. 'Get the police, quick!'

I look up. Hart's standing there. Aghast.

'DI Hart!' I shout. 'Thank God. Quick, it's Max Stanton from the Rises 7. He might have a bomb!' I hear myself shout and feel ashamed of what I'm doing, but I need to stop them turning on me. Unmasking me.

People scream, some run, some still film. The media excelled at controlling them through fear and I've just played into their hands. They're looking to Hart to keep them safe. What choice does he have now?

Max stares at me with such hatred I'm surprised I don't drop down dead.

'I'm sorry,' I say quietly to him, and I really am, 'but he played you. He'll never let your mum out.'

'You bitch,' he says.

Right now, I think I am.

'Run,' I say, but he shakes his head.

'He'll not do me any harm,' he says. 'He's on my side.'

Hart's walking up behind him. People are screaming, shouting, pointing at Max.

'Let go of her!' a man shouts, running forward and pulling Max's hands from me. 'Get yourself to safety,' he urges. 'Quickly. Save yourself.'

I can't argue with Max any more.

I have no choice.
I have to go.

The rain starts.
The sky's heavy, grey, miserable.
My mood.
I walk alongside the railway, thinking how all this could end if I just took a couple of steps in the wrong direction.
I pass phone boxes but can't ring Cicero, and even if I did have his number, I can't handle bad news right now.
The rain soaks through me; life is shit.
I should've let Hart take me.
Shouldn't have betrayed Max. That's not what friends do.

I trudge through the streets, lights reflecting in the puddles gathering in gutters, rubbish floating on top like abandoned ships. I walk past shops with Christmas lights promising happiness and family, memories to cherish.
Loneliness to live by.
I catch my reflection in one of the shop windows.
I stop, pull my hood down and stare into the eyes of the stranger staring back at me.
I recognise my eyes, my nose, the shape of my head that I've got used to now. I recognise the pain, but not how much it drips from me.
What do I do, Mum?
Mrs B?
Can I come to you?
Will you hold me, hug me, comfort me and welcome me?

'Pick yourself up, girl, you are strong. You can do this.' That's what Mrs B would say.

'What is the alternative to coping, Martha?' Mum would say. 'You cope because you have to, because if not, you go under. You fight until you have won.'

How long for? When do you accept defeat?

Do you ever?

A crowd of women are approaching. I pull my hood back up.

'It's got to be a good thing, surely,' one of them says. 'In the newspaper they said it'll make the country safer. No more bombs in our city. No random attacks.'

'Eve Stanton never hurt anyone,' another replies.

'She killed that man!'

Their footsteps stop. I don't move.

'If someone attacked you down an alleyway, and he was going to kill you, what would you do? Wouldn't you defend yourself? She never meant to kill him. She hit him over the head to save herself and her husband. Wouldn't you do that?'

'I wouldn't put myself in a dangerous situation.'

'Walking home at night? She wasn't even alone.'

'Which is why this new law is a good thing. It'll make the streets safer. If it had been like that before, then Eve Stanton would never have been hurt.'

Before I even think, I spin around to them. 'What new law?' I ask.

They both put their hands on their bags and take a step away from me.

'Sorry, I didn't mean to make you jump,' I say. 'But what new law?'

'The one the PM passed this morning,' the first one says. 'Death row for anyone committing any crime deemed to be against the safety and security of our nation.'

The hairs stand up on the back of my neck.

'Even without having killed anyone?'

'Yes,' she says, nodding.

Shit.

I run away from them. Run like my own life depends on it. What the fuck have I done to Max?

Jesus fucking Christ. I run and I run, with my lungs screaming at me and my legs shouting, over bridges, through alleys, across roads. I run and run and run.

The rain pounds but I don't care.

Thunder rumbles.

Cars zoom down streets splashing me, but I don't give a damn.

I run into someone, knock them over, but carry on and on.

I throw the gate open, launch myself down the driveway and pound on his front door.

No answer.

I pound again and again. On and on.

A light goes on in the hallway.

I keep banging.

The door opens and I barge in.

'What the hell, Martha?' DeLonzo says.

'You know what's happening?'

He closes the door, puts his hands on his hips and nods.

'How can you be so calm?'

He sucks air in through his teeth. 'Honestly, Martha, this

has just speeded things up. I think the end result is inevitable. Considering the public's opinion of her at the moment, it's highly, *highly* unlikely the vote would be lower even if she did still have two days.'

I frown at him. 'What the fuck are you talking about?'

He winces. 'Clearly not what you're talking about.'

'What's going on?' I say.

He sighs. 'Eve,' he replies. 'They moved her forward into Cell 6. Tomorrow will be her execution day.'

I don't see the floor coming up to me, but I bloody feel it as I hit it.

DECEMBER 5TH

Martha

'Martha.'

I think I hear my name.

'Martha?'

Louder.

'Martha?'

Someone's touching my arm.

I open my eyes. There's a dim light. I blink, blink again, try to remember.

I'm dry, warm.

Things come into focus.

There's DeLonzo looking at me, a mug in his hands, half a smile on his face.

I scrabble to sit up.

'Where am I?' I ask.

'My living room,' he replies, his voice is calm and quiet.

I lift the duvet, move my feet. 'My clothes?' I ask. I'm wearing someone's else's pyjamas.

'My housekeeper undressed you,' he replies. 'You were soaked. Don't worry, she's discreet. I was going to let you have my bed, but she thought it might freak you out if you woke up there in the middle of the night.'

'What happened?' I ask.

'You passed out. You came round again after a minute or so,

but you were incoherent. Overtired. Stressed. Lack of food. All of them. Who knows?'

I swing my legs off the sofa. 'We need to move,' I say. 'I put the camera in, but then this thing happened with Hart and . . . and . . .' The room spins. 'Whoa.' I put one hand on my head, steady myself with the other.

'Take it easy,' he says. 'Stay here, have some lunch.'

'Lunch? What time is it?'

'Nearly eleven,' he says. 'You've been asleep for nearly twenty-four hours. You must have needed it.'

'Jesus! I don't have time to take it easy.' I close my eyes, willing the dizziness to pass.

'You do,' he says. He stands up. 'I woke you because I wanted you to see something.'

He flicks the TV on.

'Watch and listen.'

The music for the headlines fades.

'We're breaking with our normal scheduling today to bring you the ongoing news regarding the scandal at Downing Street,' the newsreader says.

My blood runs cold.

'Overnight, live footage was released from a camera hidden within a room at Number 10 . . .'

Instinctively my hand goes over my mouth.

'. . . showing an invasive and intrusive system of national, and perhaps international, surveillance, allowing individuals to be followed, even around their own houses, and their whereabouts to be known at all times.

'While some think this level of surveillance could help

promote safety, some members of the public, and indeed some high-ranking officials, are questioning whether this system, apparently linked to mobile phones, contravenes human rights. Many claim Renard has set this up without anyone else's knowledge and are calling for his resignation.'

Sickness lurches through my stomach.

'This clip taken from the internet shows the system being used to its full effect.'

I watch as the TV screen fills with a face hidden within a hood which I know is mine. It moves away from the camera and the whole of the room can be seen, the large screen in the middle, smaller ones around the outside. Thank God I got it pointing at the right angle. It shows the person, me, sit down at the leather chairs, it shows the names I type, and it shows the red dots on the screen and the system following them as they move through the streets.

It shows me, who nobody will realise is me, leaving the room.

There's no audio, so no one hears the alarms set off after the PM finds me.

But after it's fast-forwarded – the timer on the corner counting fast – it does show the PM entering the room.

At first he's only visible from the back, but as he sits at the chair he glances over his shoulder and his face is clear.

Then it shows his fingers on the keys as he types in my name. MARTHA HONEYDEW.

And it shows the message on the screen: 'No results found'.

And it shows him slam his fist on the desk, him getting up, him pacing the floor, and then him stopping. A smile stretches across his face and he stands up straighter.

The American woman I saw there yesterday comes onto the screen, and he leans forward to kiss her on the cheek.

Both of them say something, and then they laugh.

And then they sit down at the leather chairs together.

Then the PM says something to her, and he types in the name of the American president.

The system, the central screen, seems to slow for a second, then it pans left across the world. The words 'Washington DC' appear as it zooms in on them, then the red dot is in the White House.

Holy fuck.

Who knew that?

The TV goes back to the newsreader. 'Who placed the camera in the room is as yet unknown and we are still waiting for a statement from Renard.'

'I had no idea,' I whisper.

'Neither had I,' DeLonzo replies.

'But,' I say, 'you must've . . . you must've got this up as soon as I set the camera.'

'As soon as you pressed the on button,' he agrees.

'Oh my God,' I say. 'Oh my fucking God.' I leap up and hug him, but as I do I remember his name in those documents and I feel vulnerable.

I pull away from him.

'Don't make assumptions,' he says, and he looks away.

'Oh shit,' I say. 'Eve.' And memories leak back. 'Max. Oh fuck, Cicero.'

Eve

Cell 7.

But not day seven.

I hope for a miracle and I pray for one too.

And I think of Max.

All

the

time.

If he hasn't been arrested, that awful man Gerome said.

Why would they arrest Max?

What are they accusing him of?

What will they do to him?

Put him in here?

Execute him?

I wish I could bargain with them, tell them I'll gladly die if they let him live and leave him alone. I question if, in getting involved in this as deeply as I have, I have sacrificed my son, but then I wonder if it would've happened at some point anyway, and if they were holding on to that information on me to release whenever they saw fit.

Perhaps this didn't start with Martha; perhaps it was the day I picked up that metal bar. If only Jim and I hadn't gone out that evening. If only it had been torrential rain and we'd taken a taxi instead.

If only.

I remember all the times I've heard 'if only' from those I've counselled, and I try to tell myself what I would tell them.

'The choice to attack was the perpetrator's; you didn't cause them to do it. It was not your fault.'

But my reasoning shouts back at me and I cannot escape the conviction that I *should* have, *could* have done something differently, and if I had then this would not be happening now and my son would be safe.

My head is filled with a thousand things. From Max, to Cicero, to Martha, to my friends, and to those I counselled who faced death with dignity and honour, as well as those I watched cry and scream through the whole process.

Someone once asked me, 'How do people face death? Do they accept it? Do they suddenly find God?' But there isn't one definitive answer. They face it in their own way.

What is my way? I don't know.

'The time is: . . .'

Oh, here we go. The countdown.

'11 a.m. You have: ten hours until your possible execution. The current stats are: 72% in favour of execution, 28% against. We will update you in: one hour.'

Ten hours.

I'm starting to shake; my brain feels thick.

I'm frightened.

Max

'You promised me.'

'You didn't deliver. You're lucky you weren't actually arrested or you'd be on death row right now. The only reason I didn't take you to the police station was because then I'd have too much explaining to do. Your friend *Honeydew* probably thinks you're in Cell 1 now though. Imagine doing that to a friend.' He tuts. 'To someone who saved your life as well. I told you she's a bitch.'

'I don't care about her. I care about my mum and you promised me –'

'And I told you – you didn't deliver! Do you want to spend the day going around in circles, or do you want to watch your mother's last few hours of life?' He throws the remote at Max, but he dodges and it hits the TV screen and cracks it.

'Wanker,' Max spits at him.

Hart turns to him, shirt buttons straining at his stomach and face red. 'Get out,' he says. 'Fuck off back to the Rises. You've got half an hour before I make a call and tell them you've been seen around this neighbourhood. Got it?'

Grabbing his bag off the back of a chair, Max storms out of the house.

Martha

Sometimes folks don't turn out how you expect.

Sometimes they do.

S'pose life's like that.

DeLonzo surprised me.

'Do you think I should go to death row?' I asked him. 'Start a campaign outside or something? Try and get folk to vote her innocent? We've done it before.'

He unlocks the car, holds the door open for me. 'You did it before because you managed to break into the system. Two things there. First, you're not good with technology – Max is – so that's not going to work. Secondly, each time he's broken into the system, they've made it stronger. He wouldn't get in now. They're wise to him.'

'What then?'

'If this had been two days ago, or if she had two more days, then we might stand a chance of changing the public's opinion on her. Media's a powerful tool.'

'Don't I know it?' I mumble. 'But folk *are* calling for the PM to stand down.'

'Relatively few. And that alone is not going to change the justice system in less than –' he looks at his watch – 'ten hours.'

I climb in the car, wait until he's in the driver's seat.

'You're telling me it's hopeless?'

240

'Yes,' he whispers.

'But . . .'

He starts the engine. 'For Eve, but not for those who come after her.'

'Why not for Eve?'

He pulls away into the flow of traffic. '"God grant me serenity to accept the things I cannot change . . ."?'

'I know that saying,' I reply. 'And the rest of it – "Courage to change the things I can."'

He sighs and shakes his head. '"Wisdom to know the difference."'

'But I don't believe in God anyway. Or stupid sayings. While I can fight, I should fight.'

'Courage is knowing when to save your strength for the next battle.'

'Bollocks to whoever made that one up as well,' I say.

He nearly smiles. 'Me,' he says.

He pauses, checking traffic at a junction.

'I'll drive you up to the gates of the Rises.'

'Take me to the Old Bailey instead.'

He sighs, flicks the indicator the other way and pulls across the rows of traffic. 'If I refuse, what will you do?' he asks.

'You don't need to ask me that, do you?' I fold my arms across my chest, watching the streets of London around me.

'If you go back, you can find out what Cicero wanted.'

Huh, I forgot I'd told him about that.

'It might not be bad news.'

I don't reply.

'I understand you're scared but –'

'Leave it,' I snap.

'Patty's dead,' he says out the blue.

My blood runs cold.

'You know what that means?'

I nod. 'That if they catch me, I'm back on death row.'

He doesn't reply.

'To be honest, I think they'd be taking me there anyway.'

He nods and I turn away from him, staring through the passenger window.

The silence holds us for a while.

I don't know how I feel about Patty. I hope she didn't suffer.

The streets are quiet. It's odd. There's hardly any folk around. The ones there are walk close to walls, keep their heads down, scuttling along, no eye contact, no smiles.

All the vendors usually selling tourist tat are gone.

There's no homeless on corners or in doorways.

Not even any bloody taxis!

We drive past the *National News* building.

'Where've all the demonstrators gone?' I ask.

'They left when the new law came in and the arrests began.'

'Why aren't there even any police on the streets?'

I glance at him and he's frowning now. 'I don't know,' he replies.

There's no traffic jams.

We slide down the roads.

'It's like we're in some zombie apocalypse,' I mumble.

He turns again, no traffic, no folks walking, no cyclists or delivery vans.

Nothing.

He pulls up at the side of the road, the arches of the Old Bailey next to us. He doesn't say a word.

'This is weird.' I say, staring out of the window.

'Yes,' he replies. 'Very.'

I take a breath and step out of the car.

'I'll wait for ten minutes,' he says. 'Just in case.'

In case what? I want to ask, but I don't think he knows either.

I close the door behind me, and the sound echoes off the walls.

The engine cuts out and silence falls.

Silence but for my bloody heart pounding against my ribs. Shit, this is scary.

I step past the arches, the doorway on my left. The road with no cars on my right, the shops, estate agents, solicitors on the other side with no customers, no staff.

Did everyone die in the night?

Is there some kind of airborne virus?

I turn left, walk along the front of the building.

There is nobody. Nobody at all.

The wind blows, a crisp packet scuttles across the tarmac and into the gutter. There's an empty drink can and I kick it. The sound could wake the bloody dead.

Last week, when Isaac was on death row, this place was heaving. What's happened?

'Testing . . . testing . . .' A voice booms out and I jump out of my skin and spin around.

There's the huge screen, still there, fizzing into life.

The eye logo appears on it.

Massive.

The words 'An Eye For An Eye For' spin around the pupil, the ice blue of the iris shimmering.

'Testing . . . testing . . .'

I freeze, watching it. It flickers, changes, and there instead is that Gerome guy looking all swanky and charming, holding a microphone to his face, the walls of death row behind him. He walks up to a door, stops and puts a finger to his ear.

'Can you hear me?' he says. 'Hello . . . hello . . . testing . . . This is going to work, right? This is going to be on the outside screen for everyone to see?'

I look around at the empty space around me. Erm, yeah, right.

'Excellent. Is my nose shining? Can you get make-up here?'

You dumb fuck, I want to say to him. More flickering, and the eye logo's back.

For a moment I stop, carefully look up around me.

There's a camera on top of that lamp post, another on the corner of that shop. There's one on a different lamp post too, one on the edge of the screen. I walk towards the Old Bailey and I see one above the entrance as well.

I look back to the first one as I move and it follows me. I'm surrounded. Who's watching me? The police? No. Renard? He must've found the camera I put in and taken it down, surely?

I could sit here and be a one-person demo against the death penalty and against Eve being executed, but that's not going to do anything.

What then?

I walk to the front doors, bold as brass, face still hidden though. I take a deep breath, push on the doors and step inside.

Jesus, look at this place!

Marble floors, massive portraits, domed ceilings . . . Wow . . . it's stunning.

My shoes, still wet, squelch along the tiled floor. I glance behind and there's a trail of footprints. A small rebellion. I smile.

'Stay right where you are!' There's the click of a gun being cocked. I freeze.

'What are you doing here?'

Oh shit. Think, Martha, think.

'I . . . erm . . .'

There's the click of another gun. I slowly put my hands in the air. I try and look around, but daren't move. There's someone halfway up the stairs, someone else stepping out from behind a massive pillar, both dressed in black, both pointing guns at me.

'Thought this was where the audience go now,' I manage to say.

'Have you got a ticket?'

'Errr . . .' My God, this is weird. 'I was hoping to buy one.'

'You're in the wrong place. Ticket sales are at the entrance on Newgate Street.'

'Th-thank you,' I stutter, and I start to edge backwards. 'Who are you guys?' I ask. 'Police?' I keep my hands in the air.

One of them snorts. 'We're above the police. We're government.'

'I don't understand,' I say.

'You will,' he says. 'Now get out of here.'

I'm out the doors, hear them being locked behind me.

I run across the front of the building, but then I pause.

Something's going on. Something in the air, on the wind, coming. I can feel the excitement and the threat of it.

Standing in the middle of the road, hidden under my hood, I take a careful sideways glance to the camera.

Then I lift my right hand, and give them the finger.

Eve

I remember all their names.

I remember if they said they were guilty or innocent and I remember if they lived or died.

I remember their tears of guilt, of sorrow, of frustration or fear.

I remember their silences.

I remember a man who'd committed the most terrible murder, who showed no remorse, who asked me if I thought he should live or die. I didn't know my answer then and I still don't know it now.

I remember a young woman who fell carrying her baby and it died. A tragic accident; every day she begged to live. *Dying is too easy*, she said to me. *I should suffer a lifetime of pain for what I've done.*

She sobbed before they executed her.

I didn't know whether to feel glad for her release from the torture she'd put herself in, or sad at the sheer waste of a good person.

Of those who lived, I wonder who will be watching my final judgement, and I wonder what they will think of me now, to know I'm guilty and I'm a hypocrite.

Mostly I worry about Max and what he thinks of me.

And I wonder about his future that I most likely won't see.

I wonder what he'll do when he leaves school.

If he'll go to university.

If he'll meet someone to love and what they'll be like.

If he'll have children one day.

And I wonder what he'll tell them about me.

'The time is: 4 p.m.'

My stomach turns over.

'You have: five hours until your possible execution. The current stats are: . . .'

I close my eyes while I wait. I never, *never* understood what this was like, the torture without physical pain. The strain.

'. . . 81% in favour, 19% against. We will update you in: one hour.'

Why is it *in favour* of execution and not *in favour* of the accused? Because it's biased from the very beginning and execution is what they want?

A lightness comes over my head.

The votes swing one way, then the other, and I can't make sense of it. At eleven o'clock it was seventy-two percent in favour of execution and it felt hopeless; by one in the afternoon it was sixty-three percent and my spirits soared at the possibility of going home and holding my son in my arms again. Another hour and I fell to the ground when it said eighty-nine – all hope lost – only for it to have lurched back down to sixty-nine percent by 3 p.m. And now up again.

It is a strange form of torture that plays with that most powerful of things: hope.

I want to give up trying to work it out, but I cannot let go of that possibility that I just might go home.

Home.

Where the heart is, said Pliny the Elder.

Where love begins, said Mother Teresa.

Where our feet may leave but not our hearts, said Oliver Wendell Holmes.

And where I was fortunate enough to share the lives of so many wonderful people.

I have only five hours to go.

Only five hours.

Five hours.

Five.

Wait for me, Jim.

Daffodil House

Isaac stands at the window looking out over the Rises to the wall holding them in.

'Where do you think she is?' he asks.

'In the City, doing something brave,' Joshua replies.

'Or foolish,' Isaac says. 'I thought you said there were crowds of people outside the wall?'

'I did,' Joshua replies. 'And there were. All with banners and placards, hating everyone in here and calling for their blood.'

'There's nobody there now.'

'Nobody?'

'Just a couple of guards.'

'Strange. You should sit down and rest.'

Isaac turns around slowly. 'I've spent enough time sitting and resting,' he replies, and he paces the length of the room and back again.

Cicero stumbles in, his eyes red and bloodshot and his face blotchy. 'Has anyone seen my jacket?' he asks, his voice barely a whisper.

Joshua stands up. 'Why, where are you going?'

'The Old Bailey,' he says. 'I have to be there for her.' He rubs his forehead. 'I need to be in the audience.'

Joshua and Isaac exchange glances.

'They're not letting people out any more,' Joshua says, his voice calm and gentle.

'I don't care. I have to try.'

'And even if they did, there aren't any tickets left.'

'Someone will sell me one. If I pay enough money. I know they will.' He strides into the hallway, pulling open the cupboard and rummaging through. 'It's not here.'

'Maybe in the bedroom?' Joshua says.

Cicero's footsteps stomp through the flat. 'No!' he shouts. 'It's not there either.' He appears back in the doorway.

'Thomas,' Joshua says, 'I don't think it's a good idea.'

'It doesn't MATTER if it's a good idea or not!' Cicero shouts. 'I have to be there! Don't you understand that? She's going to look out at the audience and there won't be anyone, *anyone*, she knows there, and they'll all hate her. I owe her this. I have to be there for her.' He stands with his hands on his hips, his face taut and his head shaking. 'Screw the jacket,' he says, and he storms out.

The door slams behind him.

Isaac glances to the clock on the wall. 'Less than five hours,' he says. 'We should do something too.'

'There's nothing we *can* do. Nobody can get out of here any more. They won't let us. We're prisoners.'

He stops at the window again. 'Cicero thinks he can get out. I can only see two guards,' he says.

'Two guards, both with guns,' Joshua replies. 'And even if we could . . .'

Isaac slumps down on the sofa. 'This is useless,' he says, and he turns the television on, flicking between stations.

'. . . fear has caused many people to stay away.' A reporter stands in the middle of an empty Piccadilly Circus, the neon lights flashing across his skin. 'It's truly an unprecedented experience. Bus drivers, shopkeepers, business owners, all staying off work in fear of being arrested following the revelations of the level of surveillance of the public. While many insist this represents no threat to those who have nothing to hide, some argue it breaches the civil liberties the government claim to uphold, or that innocent people could be caught up in an attempt to reduce crime stats. A statement released by the police only minutes ago states they will be taking action *against* this system and potentially against the PM himself, saying surveillance on this level is an affront to their professionalism and could lead to serious loss of jobs and a decline in the skills of the force.'

Isaac glances to Joshua and raises his eyebrows.

'Interesting,' Joshua says.

Martha

Bloody glad DeLonzo waited for me.

I could've walked to the Rises, but it's scary.

No folks around, no cars, no police, and it's getting dark already.

Without all that, you see the City differently; its soul's gone.

The wall around the Rises looms in the distance.

If I get in there, I'm not sure I'll be able to get out again.

I'm frightened.

And I'm worried.

I'm trying not to think of what Cicero's going to say to me. The expressions likely to be on their faces when I open the door.

The empty bed.

And Eve.

Oh God, Eve.

What she must be going through now.

'There must be something we can do for Eve,' I whisper. 'We can't give up.'

'What would you like to do?' DeLonzo asks. His voice is soft and kind, so unlike all the times I've seen him on TV. I can't balance this man with that man, and with what I know he's done.

'I know you said we can't hack the system, but what if we went on TV and spoke to voters, got them to vote her innocent?'

I hear him suck breath in. 'I could go on our news station, yes, I could do that. They'd let me. But you do know how the voting works, don't you? Max managed to get past it, but it's like a living thing; they programme in what they want the end result to be and the computer gets it there, but in a believable way. They add in some variation for jeopardy and excitement of course, but if they want it to be guilty, then it will be guilty. Even if you have a thousand people every second voting her innocent, the computer will fight against it.'

'How can they get away with that?'

He laughs. 'Two things. First, that they do it with actual votes, so if somebody goes in to check, they'll see a phone number attached to each vote. Second, it's the government.'

'Omniscient and omnipotent?' I say.

He looks at me, eyebrows raised, as if saying, How can some orphan girl from the Rises know such clever words?

'Just because I come from the Rises, doesn't mean I'm stupid,' I tell him.

'Quite,' he replies. 'But you don't know everything; yet they do, and they control everything. They're . . .' He taps his fingers on the steering wheel, searching for the right word.

'Machiavellian,' I reply.

'You should come and work for me when this is all over,' he says, smiling. 'You're better than half my staff.'

I'm not used to compliments, not sure how to react.

'This'll never be over,' I mutter, staring at the wall running alongside us now. 'And once I'm in there, there'll be no coming out.'

He pulls up at the side of the road, the gates a little ahead of us.

'You didn't plant that bomb, did you?' he says.

I look at him and shake my head.

'This will be over one day,' he says. 'I'm certain of it.' He reaches into his inside pocket and passes me a business card. 'Call me when it is,' he says, 'and we'll arrange for you to tell your story to the masses.'

I stick it in my pocket, open the door and step out.

'And, Martha?' he calls after me. 'I am sorry about Eve, but in a battle there are always casualties.'

'There've already been too many,' I reply, and I close the door, watch him drive away and suddenly feel very alone.

I walk towards the gate with my hands shaking. Daffodil House almost blends into the dark sky, but I know it's there, with its news waiting for me.

They don't question my pass. 'Get in and stay in,' they say, and I feel like I'm entering a prison complex.

As I walk through the turnstile I see blood on the ground. Fresh, glistening in the moonlight. I step over it without saying a word, but I could cry.

I walk through the underpass, past the boarded-up shops and onto the scrubby grass. I think about visiting Mrs B's grave, but I can't face that right now.

The park looms ahead. It's dark now and the broken bench, the one swing and the metal poles sticking up that used to be a climbing frame look like bones of something that died years ago. Some girl's walking towards me.

'Got any food?' she says.

I shake my head. 'Sorry,' I say. 'No point going that way though,' I tell her. 'Shops are shut.'

'There's nothing in them anyways,' she shouts back. 'Oh well, I'll go see the guards. See what they've got for favours.'

For favours? What the hell? Is that what I think it is?

Are things that bad already?

'There hasn't been food in for days. Folks panic-bought the lot of it, only we didn't have any money. Could murder a Twix.'

I open my mouth to argue with her, but I have no clue what to say.

Maybe there'll be posters sent out soon, like the war propaganda posters they showed us at school.

We'll be told to 'Farm for Food', with pictures of smiling kids with carrots or such. 'Dig for Victory', 'Sew for Warmth'.

Huh, yeah, and 'Get your pants off for a Twix.'

Urghh. I shudder. Doesn't bear thinking about.

Perhaps they'll give us some name supposed to make us feel we're getting a good deal and we're special – the *Rises Independent* maybe?

Should be more like – *The Rises Fuck Off Cos You're On Your Own, Pal*.

I realise my feet have stopped me at the park, if you can call it that; must've been the shock of that girl.

Remember, being here with Isaac? Him twisting you round on that swing, leaning back and looking at the stars?

Our stars in the sky we shared?

Daffodil House stares at me, the lights in the windows like eyes.

I'm sorry, I tell it in my head, *but I can't come in right now. I'm not ready.*

As soon as I go inside, climb the steps or take the lift, walk down the corridor and open my door, there will be those looks of pity and those soft shakes of their heads and I'll have to stop pretending.

I'm not ready for that.

I sit on the one solitary swing, wrap my arms around the chains and lean backwards.

Our stars, Isaac.

Are you up there, looking down at me?

Daffodil House

'Stars are bright tonight,' Isaac says. 'No clouds. There'll be a frost in the morning.' He looks out of the window while Joshua's thumbs tap at his phone. 'And there's someone sitting on the swing in the park,' he adds. 'That's only the third person I've seen out there all day.'

'People are scared,' Joshua says. 'And when they're scared, they stay within their own four walls.'

'Apart from someone like Cicero.'

'Quite.'

'Do you think that's where Pete is now? At home? Your home.'

Joshua sighs. 'I hope he's at work. That would explain why he's not answering my calls and texts. If there's some emergency at the hospital.'

'He's a doctor?'

Joshua nods. 'Have you tried Martha's phone again?'

Isaac steps towards the table, takes his phone and dials the number.

He shakes his head. 'The number you have dialled is currently unavailable,' he says in a mocking voice.

'Maybe her battery's dead.'

'Or she is,' Isaac mutters.

The door creaks open and then slams shut, the whole flat rattling with it.

Isaac and Joshua exchange a look.

Footsteps shuffle down the hallway, then stop at the living room.

'You were right,' Cicero says from the doorway, swaying from one foot to the other, his face bloodied and swollen; a cut under his left eye.

Blood drips from his nose and down the front of his shirt, mixing with the dirt and boot prints. His glasses are missing, and his lip is split. 'They're not letting anyone out.'

'Oh my,' Joshua says, jumping out of his seat and grabbing hold of Cicero. 'They did that to you?' He holds Cicero around his arm and steers him into the chair. 'Isaac, would you get some warm water and a flannel?'

'I'll have the whisky in the kitchen cupboard too,' Cicero adds.

Joshua grabs tissues from the box and passes them to him.

Cicero dabs at his face and nose. 'We're prisoners,' he says.

Joshua nods. 'I'm sorry,' he whispers.

Cicero closes his eyes and tears pour down his face. He gulps and suddenly his body is wracked with sobs.

Joshua takes him in his arms and holds him.

'I've never told her I love her,' Cicero sobs.

'She knows,' Joshua whispers in reply. 'In her heart, she knows.'

Eve

'The time is: 8.30 p.m. You have: thirty minutes until your possible execution. The current stats are: . . .'

Every time that voice comes on I think I'm going to faint. I'm struggling to hold it together.

'. . . 78% in favour, 22% against. We will update you in: ten minutes.'

It's gone down. Not enough though. Will it carry on going down? Is this all part of the entertainment game to keep people voting right up until the last second?

Thirty minutes to go.

Everyone I've spoken to who survived this said they thought they would lose their minds in that last half an hour.

This could be the last thirty minutes of my life.

I hear big, heavy footsteps and a guard appears in my doorway.

'Time to go,' he says. 'Come on.'

'Where to?' I ask.

'The execution room.'

'But –'

'You'll get your final stats there.'

'Why? Why is it different? What's going on?'

He shrugs. 'Something to do with expecting more people. Best way to control it all apparently. Everyone in here; one at a time through to there.'

He grabs the chains around my wrists.

'I'll drag you if I have to,' he says.

I stagger along behind him like a dog on a lead, but without the promise of treats, out of the doorway and into a corridor.

'This way,' he says.

'Dead woman walking,' he shouts. 'Dead woman walking.' My head spins.

We follow the old white bricks, chipped and dirty, under an archway and carry on.

'Dead woman walking,' he shouts again.

Another archway, but smaller.

All I can see ahead is darkness.

Another archway, smaller still, and the guard ducks to get through.

I know what this is – it's Dead Man's Walk – where criminals in the past were taken from Newgate Prison and out to the execution yard.

We go through another, still smaller, archway and turn.

Cold air wafts down and shouting booms from above.

'DIE, DIE, DIE.'

I look up, and angry faces are leering down at me. Something hits me in the face – some kind of rotten fruit.

'They're pissed off,' the guard says. 'Couldn't get tickets to watch you fry, so they've all gone up there with their rotten fruit and veg. Pissed off myself cos I don't want to get pelted with it.'

'I'm perfectly capable of walking through,' I tell him. 'I don't need an escort.'

'Sure,' he says. 'But I've got a switch to flip down there!' He laughs at me.

'Dead woman walking!' he shouts again, and above us the crowd jeer.

'DIE. DIE. DIE.'

At the end of the corridor he pushes the door open and pulls me into the execution room.

As it slams behind us, I'm struck by the silence.

I was expecting a torrent of noise, shouting and laughing, but there isn't anything.

He leads me across a scuffed wooden floor and he unchains my wrists. The feeling of relief is incredible.

'Make yourself at home,' he laughs as he disappears behind another door. I'm left alone.

In the middle of the floor is a chair. Not *the* chair because that was destroyed. This one looks like something they found in a museum, a high-backed wooden, slatted chair, with leather straps to go around your wrists and ankles and one to go around your chest.

My chest.

There's a metal dish of sorts on the top, lowered on a swivel and tightened with an over-sized bolt, and red and yellow wires run from that to a small room behind.

The guard will be in there, waiting next to what I imagine is a heavy-duty switch ready to be thrown, and next to that will be an old-fashioned power meter that will light up when the electricity ripples through.

Maybe they're deliberately going for the medieval look to add to the feel of the prison cells and the history of this place. Reminders of the prisoners they've held here – Daniel Defoe, Casanova and William Penn.

I wonder what they thought while within these walls?

If I'm freed, the first thing I'll do is hug my son and tell him I'm sorry.

The second thing will be to tell Cicero I love him; I should've done that a long time ago.

I'd hoped they'd keep some of the rituals from the old death row, but fear of it all going wrong again seems to have caused them to change things. Now there is no victim speech and no time allowed for me to speak.

In moments of madness I imagine I'm telepathic and I can seep into the brains of those I love and whisper my messages of reassurance and receive theirs in return.

Does it hurt, having two thousand volts of electricity passed through your body?

How long will it take me to die?

I am a miserable soul. Right now all hope I had for survival is draining from me.

'The time is: 8.40 p.m. You have: twenty minutes until your possible execution. The current stats are . . .'

How quickly ten minutes pass.

My head pounds. I think I'm going to collapse.

'. . . 71% in favour, 29% against. We will update you in . . .'

Silence. It's gone down. I don't know if I dare be hopeful.

The voices from Dead Man's Walk still echo in my ears – DIE, DIE, DIE.

'. . . ten minutes.'

Daffodil House

Isaac sits on the edge of his makeshift hospital bed with Joshua.

On the other side of the room Cicero is sprawled on the chair with the bottle of whisky on the table next to him and a glass in his hand. The bottle is nearly empty now.

'I'm sorry,' Dr Novak says, standing up from the other chair and leaving the room. 'I can't watch. It makes me feel complicit. I shall go to the other room and pray.'

Joshua nods, but nobody says a word.

The light from the television flickers on their faces. The smiling face of Kristina leering at them as she struts across the studio floor.

Cicero pours another drink and downs it in one. His face is cleaner but swollen, and his right eye is black.

'Do you want to pray?' Joshua whispers.

'I don't believe in God,' Cicero slurs.

'Neither do I,' Joshua replies. 'But –'

'God can't hack the voting system,' Isaac mutters.

'I have to do something,' Joshua says.

'Did you used to pray when you were presenter of this godforsaken shambles?' Cicero asks.

Joshua turns slowly to him. 'Every time,' he whispers.

8.45 p.m. *Death is Justice*

The camera zooms over the applauding audience and rests on a smiling Kristina, in fitted blue trouser suit, platform heels and hair piled on top of her head. She flicks loose strands out of her face.

KRISTINA: Welcome back, ladies and gentlemen, to this extended episode of *Death is Justice*. With so many people on death row we have a mountain of garish gossip and sensational secrets to share with you. Not only that, but exciting outbursts of prisoner angst as they are forced into sharing cells! My, have we seen some fisticuffs! But on with today.

She steps towards the screen. The eye logo fades, replaced with live feed from Cell 7.

KRISTINA: Yes, An Eye For An Eye Productions are always the innovators, and this week's episodes have seen some high-energy, fast-moving justice brought to you. Possibly the most exciting is the culmination of what has been the most fascinating sequence of judicial events and votes we have ever seen.

First we had the first ever teen on death row –
Martha Honeydew – and the scandal we saw there
as she was rescued by her one true love, Isaac
Paige, on her final day. It soon turned out that
she had manipulated the poor, defenceless boy
into killing his own father, a crime for which we,
the voting public, had no choice but to vote him
guilty. That in turn would have seen our first teen
execution on death row, but, as you are all aware,
we suffered the shocking attack by the terrorist
organisation commonly known as the Rises 7, led
by the errant Honeydew, and death row was razed
to the ground by the bomb she planted. You would
think that would be enough, but no, it seems
the Honeydew drama was far from over, as we
discovered not only that ex-designated counsellor
Eve Stanton had seen fit to hide the missing teen,
but that it was she herself who killed her attacker
some fourteen years ago, not her husband, who
was executed for it. And that is where we are now.
With the rapid influx of prisoners, Stanton has
had her execution brought forward. A welcome
relief? Many say so. And an end, we hope, to this
unsavoury sequence of events.

Next to her the two columns fill the left-hand side of the
screen – 'Guilty' at the top of one, 'Not guilty' at the top of
the other – while on the right is the live feed of Eve from
the execution room.

KRISTINA: The last few hours have seen the stats move up and down at an alarming rate, but can it fall below that magical 50 percent in the last ten minutes? Well, ladies and gentlemen, viewers at home, I'm certain that time will fly by!

On the screen Eve can be seen pacing back and forth in front of the chair. Then she stops, her head lifting and her watery blue eyes flicking around.

The camera zooms in on her face, vacant and scared.

KRISTINA: Will she live? Will she die? Who can tell? Quite frankly, as we know for certain that she did in fact kill her attacker, I'll be surprised if that guilty stat doesn't reach one hundred. Why people would risk freeing a killer is beyond me.

She strides back to her desk.

KRISTINA: Join us again after this short message from our sponsor. Don't go anywhere, viewers – with the stats this close, anything could happen.

Martha

The wind howls and whips around me. Sings through the chains and the bars like a banshee.

I prefer it at Bracken Woods – the peace, the calm, the animals too. Maybe I'll go there in a minute. Memories are thick there too. Maybe I can pretend he's still with me.

Can't hide forever, that voice in my head says.

Supposing I can? I ask it.

I've got nothing to go back for.

I've failed.

Think wider, it says. *Think what's happening with the PM. What will tomorrow bring?*

Without Isaac, without Eve, I don't give a damn.

What's with the police? The quiet streets?

Who cares?

You do.

I kick my legs and swing up high.

Wish I didn't care. It'd be a whole lot easier.

I tip back, watch the sky and the stars moving as I swing. It makes me dizzy.

I skid my feet on the concrete and stop. Look at my watch. If it's right, there's six minutes until Eve's last update.

Oh, Eve, I'm so sorry. So damn bloody fucking bastard sorry.

I scream and stand up. Swipe and kick at the swing, miss it, pick the seat up and throw it against its own chains.

Goddamn, I'm angry.

Bastard angry.

I scream again, grab the swing, yank it and yank it and yank it. One chain snaps and I pull it again and the other chain – God, they must be old and rusty – breaks off. I lob the seat away, kick at it.

And I stand there and sob and sob and sob until there is nothing left.

Then I lie down on the scruffy, dirty, chipped horrible concrete and stare up at the dark and beautiful sky.

And I'll stay here, Eve, for as long as I can, and think of you.

Eve

'The time is: 8.50 p.m. You have: ten minutes until your possible execution. The current stats are . . .'

My head swims. I turn around and throw up on the floor. I thought I'd be calm, collected and dignified, but I'm a mess.

'. . . 85% in favour, 15% against. We will update you in: five minutes with the final count.'

I'm scared of dying, of pain, of the unknown.

I'm scared for my son, with no one to take care of him.

I'm sorry for everything.

They call this the execution room but it isn't really a room; it's more a space. It's like a stage. It reminds me of going to the Globe Theatre with Max – wooden floor, sky above. Some of the audience are standing below me, but not as close as at the Globe, and instead of it being open, there are metal railings.

It dawns on me: I'm like an animal at a zoo. I'm solitary and isolated but observed and scrutinised. I'm vulnerable, surviving only because they choose to let me. Or not.

Beyond what I suppose you would call the stalls are what must be the more expensive seats. They are covered, should the rain come, and I imagine they must have cushions for comfort too.

It rained when me and Max went to the Globe, but it was summer rain and we smiled as it drenched us and kept eating our ice creams regardless.

I step towards the railings and peer out. There are ice-cream vendors here too, and burger bars, popcorn, hotdogs, chips; it all smells divine and it takes me back to memories that are too painful to think about.

I thought I was incapable of feeling any more pain, but it seems not.

The crowd are here, but they're quiet, which surprises me; I was expecting food and insults to be hurled.

'The time is 8.55 p.m. and the lines are now closed. The final stats are –'

I'm standing. Wobbling, but standing.

I don't know how that went so quickly.

The pause is interminable.

'– 90% in favour of execution, 10% against. Your execution will take place in: five minutes.'

My legs go, and I fall to the floor.

What?

What?

What?!

Oh Jesus, oh God . . .

I'm going to die.

I'm going to die.

I'm going to die.

Oh God, please no, please no, please . . .

Max.

Max.

Oh God, Max, I'm sorry.

There are hands on me, pulling me.

I can't see.

I'm dizzy, everything's blurred.

Oh God, no.

Max, I'm sorry, I'm so, so sorry.

They drag me up.

I want to buck against them, fight and fight, but I can't.

I sob.

Try to breathe.

Please no.

They shove me in the chair.

I scream at the top of my lungs. My throat burns.

I kick out.

Kick and scream.

Heavy hands grab my ankles.

Hold them still.

Something goes around them, pulls tight and I can't move my legs.

I can't move my legs!

I scream again.

I should be dignified. Face death with some self-respect.

Fuck that.

This is crazy.

This is wrong.

This should be stopped.

Not just because it's me.

'No!' I shout out. 'No! No . . . !'

I hit something, but my hands are grabbed.

I buck against them but something goes around my chest. Pulls in tight.

I can't breathe.

Oh, Max.

Jim.

I don't . . . don't . . .

Be there for me, Jim. Be with me. Stay with me.

Help me. Hold me. Comfort me.

I can't move my hands, not my body either now.

Am I such a bad person that I shouldn't be allowed to live?

Am I worse than the people doing this to me?

Or those who have voted to have me die?

I'm strapped in the chair.

This is it.

This is it.

The last time Max will see me.

Compose yourself, take a breath, come on.

'Look,' a voice says. 'Look at the people, Mrs Stanton.'

I don't know who says it or if I imagined it, but there's kindness there, and that is like the slap I need to calm down.

I take a breath and I look.

Everyone is standing.

I glance at the clock. Two minutes left.

They're standing and they're silent. And their hands are on their hearts.

My eyes fill with tears.

That's not hatred from them; that's respect and sympathy and honour.

One and a half minutes left.

I smile. I actually smile.

And then I think of my son. My wonderful, kind, caring, honest son, that I have had the joy of raising for the last sixteen years, and the pleasure of his company.

'I love you, Max,' I say out loud.

I know he can't hear me, but I hope and I pray that someone somewhere will lip-read and will tell him, or in years to come he will find out.

'I love you, Max,' I say again, and I say it slowly and clearly. And I smile again.

Because I might have done one terrible thing in my life – killed that man and allowed Jim to take the blame – but I have not done anything else wrong. I have worked for good, I have helped people, I have been a decent person and I have raised the most wonderful human being, who will go on to be someone and do something that matters.

'I love you, Max,' I say again.

'I love you, Max.'

I'm crying, but I feel calm now.

I am scared, but it will be over soon.

One minute on the counter.

A guard plunges a sponge into water and puts it on my head. It runs down my face but it feels cool and refreshing.

'I love you, Max,' I say again, and I'm sobbing and sobbing, but I feel the strength of those people below with their hands on their hearts, and I watch as the timer goes down to thirty seconds and their heads bow in respect.

I catch the eye of the guard. 'He knows,' he whispers in my ear, and I realise it was his voice before, 'but I'll find him and tell him for you.'

'Tell Cicero too,' I say before I can change my mind. 'Tell Cicero I love him too.'

There are tears on the man's face. 'You're a good woman, Eve Stanton, and a sad loss to this world. You'll be missed.'

I see him turn to the window of the room behind me and nod to whoever is at the controls.

'I love you, Max,' I say for the last time.

And I close my eyes.

Daffodil House

The whisky bottle's empty, knocked to its side.

The room is silent, the television muted.

It's dark but for the flicker from the screen.

Cicero reaches out the remote control and turns it off, and the room is plunged into darkness.

They sit, not a word shared.

Cicero pulls himself to standing and stumbles from the room; a second later the bedroom door slams.

'I hope Max is OK,' Joshua whispers eventually.

Isaac says nothing, just walks to the window and stares out.

'Still quiet out there?' Joshua asks after a few minutes.

'Very,' Isaac replies. 'There's still someone down at the swings though.'

The silence presses on them, nothing even from the flats around them, as if a blanket of respect has been spread over the whole area.

'But whoever it is is lying on the floor,' Isaac adds. 'It looks like the swing's broken too.'

Another couple of minutes pass.

'There was a scream earlier,' Joshua whispers. 'Did you hear it? A while ago. Before . . .' His voice trails off.

'What are you thinking?'

Joshua shrugs. 'I don't know. Probably nothing.'

Isaac continues staring out of the window. The wind howls through the gaps.

He sighs and folds his arms over his chest. 'I'll go and check,' he says.

'You should stay inside; you're still injured.'

'I'm fine. And I need to get out of here,' he mumbles, and he limps from the room.

Max

Crowds pour silently out and around the Old Bailey, and above them the streetlights peer through the frosty darkness and throw puddles of white on the pavements.

Hands are shoved in pockets, shoulders are hunched and tear-stained faces stare down.

Nobody notices the boy in black hidden in a doorway.

As the crowd thins Max steps out and falls in next to a woman straggling at the back.

She glances his way. 'I could cry for a week,' she whispers.

'Sorry?' Max says.

'Eve Stanton. That . . .' She shakes her head. 'Just awful. Were you in there?'

'No,' he mutters. 'I wanted to be, but the tickets were all gone.'

'They sold out in two minutes flat,' the woman says.

Max snorts. 'You people, desperate to watch someone suffer and die.' He sneers at her. 'Like rubber-necking at a car crash. You should be ashamed of yourself.'

She stops walking and puts her hands on her hips. '*You* should be ashamed of yourself,' she says. She pauses, glances down the road and then steps closer to Max. 'We organised buying up all the tickets,' she hisses at him. 'We put our savings in –'

'That makes it fucking worse!'

'Shut up!' she says. 'And listen! We put our savings in, we raised money, people donated for Christ's sake because they felt so strongly about it. And do you know why? Do you?'

'Cos you're all sick.'

'Because we wanted the last faces she saw to be people who respected her and who cared. We stood in silence, with our hands on our hearts, and we stayed with her while she died, and she saw us doing that.

'*That's* why we did it.' She jabs him in the chest as she speaks and he backs away. 'We didn't want people in there who were going to shout and insult her. We're all friends and family of people who have been there, and we made sure her final minutes were as peaceful and as respected as they could be.'

She stares at him but he looks away. 'Why did *you* want a ticket?'

He doesn't say a word.

'Are you going to answer me or are you feeling ashamed now? Why did *you* want a ticket?'

'I . . . I . . .' he stutters, 'I wanted to tell her that I'm sorry,' he says, and he pulls down his hood. 'And that I'm proud to be her son.'

As she stares at him, and his eyes fill with tears, the woman steps forward and wraps her arms around him.

Martha

I close my eyes.

It's so quiet.

A dog barks in the distance.

An owl hoots.

The odd car rumbles, but not many.

No sirens.

No alarms.

How odd is that?

Usually out here there's folks shouting. Engines revving, trains spluttering on the line, folks' phones ringing, motorbikes tearing past, TVs blaring, stereos. All sorts of noise.

But not tonight.

Nor today.

Weird.

I haven't seen anyone while I've been here. Everyone's stayed inside, and that's odd too.

I open my eyes again.

The sky's lovely tonight.

Deep blue velvet with pinpricks of stars.

Someone at school once told me that when you die you become a star. Just as likely to become a woodlouse, I told them. They didn't like that.

I like the sky though. The calm, the thought of all those

millions of miles and not knowing what's at the end, or even if there is an end, makes me feel kind of tiny down here, and insignificant.

Which is a good thing.

Makes me wonder how much all this shit matters.

Isaac.

Eve.

There's questions in my head that I don't want to find out the answers to. I wish I could stay ignorant forever, but I know I can't.

I'll bloody freeze to death down here and catch pneumonia or something.

It's *cold*.

Come on, Martha, my head tells me. *Time to go.*

I take a final deep breath in and slowly push it out, watching it disperse in the air above me.

Suddenly a face looms above me and I jump.

It stares at me, as I stare at it.

We both blink.

We both stare.

What the . . . ?

Shivers run down me, goosebumps, needles.

My mouth falls open.

So does his.

'Martha?' it says.

He says.

He says.

'Isaac?! Oh my God, Isaac, really? Really?'

I sit up, reach out to him, pull off his hat. 'Isaac!'

He smiles at me, touches my face, reaches into my hood and nudges it down, his fingers feeling all over my face and my head. 'It is you, isn't it? Isn't it? Martha?'

'Yes!' I say, and I'm crying, but with happiness. I touch him. His face, his head, his shoulders, hold his hands. He's crying now. We both are.

'I thought you were dead,' I splutter. 'I thought that was why Cicero rang me. I thought you must have died. I couldn't face coming back and you not being there.'

'I'm fine,' he says.

'I didn't plant that bomb.'

'I know,' he replies. 'Of course you didn't.'

We're staring at each other, wanting to believe but not quite daring to.

'It is you, and you are alive,' I say.

We grab each other, hug each other and the relief is incredible.

'I love you,' I tell him.

On our knees in the middle of this clapped-out broken-down park, we hold each other and stare into each other's eyes.

'I love you too,' he says.

We smile.

We laugh with relief.

And we kiss.

DECEMBER 6TH

Martha

I swing from happy to sad and back all night and into the morning.

Guilt for feeling happy.

Guilt for feeling sad.

When we got back to the flat, Cicero hugged me, gave me a bit of a smile and went off to bed. Joshua made me some food.

I feel grateful to have these people in my life.

I feel grateful to have a life.

The sun's lifting now, straining desperately through the fog hanging in the air.

I'm standing at the window in my bedroom. Isaac's behind me, still sleeping.

I woke early and I lay there watching him, taking it in that he's still alive and I am too and that we finally, finally are together.

I thought about staying there forever, or accepting this as the life we could have together – behind a wall holding us prisoner.

And stuff wandered into my head – Max, Eve, Patty even, and Sofia.

How did society get to this point?

Did it take a wrong turn?

Or did circumstance just lead us this way?

We have a corrupt government, a justice system that only serves those with money and media that manipulate the public to think what they want us to. Why didn't someone see what was happening and put the brakes on?

They didn't in Nazi Germany, did they? my head tells me.

Face it, Martha, politicians manipulate.

But surely not all?

And the world is about money.

And apathy is everywhere.

Is it apathy? I wonder. Or is it just that folks are so busy trying to look after themselves and their own?

Who was it who said, 'You either have to be part of the solution, or you're going to be part of the problem'?

I don't remember.

He said, 'There is no more neutrality in the world,' too.

I can't just sit here then, can I?

We can't leave this undone.

Or Eve's death, and mum's, Ollie and Mrs B's, meant nothing.

The Prime Minister – Stephen Renard

In the safety and security of the blue room, the PM and Sofia sit on the leather swivel chairs in front of the screens.

On the central screen, red dots move in different directions, some areas are filled with dots, but more are empty.

'There are fewer and fewer,' she says. 'People are learning how to disable the GPS.'

She moves the cursor and the screen slowly changes to show various parts of the City and the surrounding Avenues. She pans towards the Rises.

'Deny, deny, deny,' the PM says. 'The evidence against me is flimsy.'

Sofia nods. 'True,' she agrees. 'And some people simply won't care that you took money or gifts in exchange for jobs in the government. Some don't care that you've got this room, or they think it's a good thing.'

'I still don't understand how that Honeydew girl got in here.'

'I'm launching a full inquiry, sir; don't you worry about that. I still think it's best not to tell the public it was her though. We don't want them losing faith in the justice system right now.'

'I agree,' he says. 'Do you think I should come clean about anything else though?'

Sofia leans back from the screen and looks at the PM. 'People say they like honesty,' she says, 'but I doubt they would if they really knew what goes on in the world. Perhaps *selective* honesty would be the better way to go.'

He nods. 'I like that. Selective honesty. I admit I've made some mistakes in the past but I've learned from them. I understand the pressures of temptation, blah, blah . . . try and tap into something that affects them.'

'Speak to them on their level. Be one of the people.'

'Do you think I should tell them about the houses too?'

'What houses?' she asks.

His face screws up. 'The celebrity footballer, what's his name? Can't remember now. The one who was here the other evening. He gave me a house in the south of France for making him a sir.'

'I didn't know that.'

'It's nobody's business anyway.' He stares off into the distance as he thinks.

With one eye on him, Sofia types 'MAX STANTON' on the keyboard. 'Where is he and what is he doing?' she mutters to herself.

'No result found', flashes up on the screen.

'Gone to ground again?' she whispers.

'I wonder if they've found out about the others or if I can risk keeping quiet about them,' the PM says.

'Others? Did you give anyone honours, just for, well, because they'd done something honourable?'

'I have more important things to remember than lists of people I've given honours to.'

'Sir, I think you should do whatever your conscience is most comfortable with.'

'Screw my conscience,' he says. 'I'll say anything that will keep me in power. Or do anything.'

'Anything?' Sofia asks.

'Of course,' he replies without hesitating.

Death is Justice: The Breakfast Show

Gerome sits on a red boxy sofa. To his left is Albert DeLonzo, and to his right is Police Commissioner Gordon Ruhier.

GEROME: Good morning, and welcome to what we're sure will be an enlightening programme today. Joining us are *National News* editor-in-chief Albert DeLonzo and Police Commissioner Gordon Ruhier. Commissioner Ruhier, last night you issued a statement calling for a vote of no confidence in Prime Minister Stephen Renard, and since then your men have called for strike action across the City. This is an unprecedented move on the part of the police, isn't it?

RUHIER: My officers are deeply concerned with the manner in which they've been treated and what this new system of Renard's will mean for their futures. We've also received instructions from Renard's office to step down from significant duties, such as the security at death row and the Old Bailey, and have since found out that government-paid guards are now stationed there. As they work for the government, there's some doubt as to whether they have to follow the same strict guidelines and code of conduct that the police force are subject to. That's before we even consider the fact that the level of surveillance he's instigated violates human rights.

GEROME: Many are saying that only those with something to hide would have any issue with this surveillance system. And doesn't it make crimes easier to solve, seeing as you'd be able to locate people, *and* follow them?

RUHIER: There are many issues here. While it's true that CCTV is not a new thing, this level of surveillance is. It contravenes Article 8 of the Human Rights Act, which states that everyone has a right to respect for private and family life. We don't know if this system is foolproof; what if identities were mistaken? Could it be used to frame innocent people? We the police force need clarification which we are not being given. The public are not happy, and understandably so, and many of my officers are concerned this could lead to people protesting against the invasion of their privacy, and potentially rioting in the streets. We are also of the view that it is an affront to our investigative skills.

GEROME: But surely the most important thing here is the safety of the public. Since the instigation of the

PM's law stating crimes against the safety and security of our city are now punishable by death, the streets have been very quiet, haven't they? Don't you think this is a direct consequence of this law?

RUHIER: The streets aren't quiet; they're deserted. I joined the police force to protect the public, both physically and in terms of their rights. Those rights are being destroyed by the very people who should be protecting them. That is why today my officers are voting on whether to take strike action.

GEROME: That's a serious threat from your officers. But why haven't you spoken out before? Previously you've allowed DI Hart to take the lead on all media involvement.

RUHIER: Which, given the recent claims against Hart, is no longer possible or acceptable. Plus, I'd like to make clear, things have now reached a point where my conscience and my beliefs are more important than my career.

GEROME: Are you saying your career would have been in danger if you'd spoken out?

Ruhier shakes his head and takes a breath.

RUHIER: Speaking your mind has been a dangerous thing for many for quite some time. This must be stopped.

Gerome turns to DeLonzo.

GEROME: Mr DeLonzo, if I can come to you, you broke this story, you've seen the impact on the streets, and you've heard Mr Ruhier's thoughts just now. What is your opinion?'

DELONZO: Before I answer that question I'd like to ask Mr Ruhier why he and his men haven't acted on the story when clearly there is enough evidence to back up the claims? Why are people such as DI Hart, for example, still walking the streets?

RUHIER: I'm not at liberty to discuss that.

DELONZO: Does that mean someone higher up than you – the PM, for example – has ordered you not to?

Ruhier squirms in his seat, wipes his brow and shakes his head.

DELONZO (shouting): A minute ago you said your conscience is more important than your career. Answer my question. Has the PM, Stephen Renard, ordered you not to arrest Hart or anyone else named in the story broken by my newspaper?

RUHIER: The people have been ruled by two things – apathy and fear. Fear has paralysed them while their rights are being abused under the guise of protection and the overwhelming apathy this results in is –

DeLonzo stands up and leers over Ruhier, jabbing at him with his finger.

DELONZO (shouting): Which are you ruled by, Ruhier? Apathy or fear? We have the evidence, we passed it to the police. When will these people who've committed manslaughter, rape, kidnapping, bribery, all under a cloak of power, when will they be brought to justice?

He turns to camera.

DELONZO: You, the public out there, are powerful when you move together, you need to stand up now and demand justice. Murderers do not get away with their crimes. Demand that those who've protected their own positions by holding the secrets of others over their heads are stopped! Demand fair and proper justice!'

Behind him, Ruhier squirms in his seat.

DELONZO: This is your chance. You either act now, or you never act. And if you don't, then things will never change.

Off-screen one person claps. Then another. And another. DeLonzo nods slowly.

The Prime Minister – Stephen Renard

'It's the right thing to do, sir,' Sofia says to the PM.

'I'll play the game, Sofia,' he says, 'but that doesn't mean I think I'm wrong.'

She adjusts his tie. 'The public just need to believe you're taking control of this. They'll see your humanity and your determination. They'll be reassured by that.'

'I don't see why the police are taking the high ground on this; it makes their job easier. I'm sure it must only be the corrupt ones who don't like it. They don't want to be observed and found out.'

'Prime Minister?' Gino the intern steps into the room. 'They're ready for you.'

'At last. Why has it taken so long?' the PM asks.

'Apologies, but there's such interest in what you have to say that we decided to set up a screen at the end of the road so the masses can hear you while being kept a safe distance away.'

The PM smooths his hair down. 'Good idea.'

As Renard steps out of the room, Gino turns to Sofia. 'I don't know what you're thinking. The press will eat him alive. He should've just released a statement.'

Sofia ignores him and follows the PM.

Martha

I turn the television off and look around the room.

Cicero hasn't said a word to anyone all day. He's hardly moved.

'What are you thinking?' Isaac asks me.

'We go into the City with as many folk from the Rises as we can. Head to Downing Street.'

'The guards at the gate have guns,' Joshua says.

'Do you think they'll use them?' Isaac asks. 'If there are enough of us.'

'What else can we do?' I reply.

'It's a hell of a risk,' Isaac says.

'Yeah, though folks have risked more,' I point out.

'But you're asking others to risk their lives,' Isaac replies.

'Enough people have died,' Joshua says.

'But this is the only chance,' I say.

'I don't know, Martha,' Isaac argues. 'We've only just . . . me and you . . .'

'That's selfish,' I reply, but I get him.

The front door bangs and we all stop and look at each other, listening to the footsteps down the hall.

Max appears in the doorway. Clothes dishevelled, face dirty and streaked, hair all over the place.

So Hart didn't have him arrested then.

He walks straight over to me and I flinch, waiting for the onslaught, deserving it.

'She's dead,' he whispers.

I stand up, least I can do, and I force myself to look at his face. 'I'm sorry,' I say. 'For everything.'

He stares at me.

'Did you go?' I whisper.

He shakes his head. 'Tickets were all gone.'

'I'm sorry,' I say again.

'I saw the audience coming out. They weren't cheering and hyper like I've seen other crowds. They were quiet and subdued. Some of them were crying.' He pauses and I can see he's steadying himself. 'They were all people she'd counselled, or their families. Or friends. This one woman, she said they'd bought them all, that they wanted the last people Mum saw to be people who respected her and cared.' He stops again, sucks in a massive shuddering breath and wipes his hand across his face. 'Do you know what she did then?'

'No,' I whisper.

'She hugged me for a long time. Then she bought me a hot drink and we sat for ages. She asked if I know anything about Sofia. I said I didn't, and she said nobody does. Then she asked me if I know anything about Cyber Secure, or if any of us do, and I said no again. Do you know anything about them?'

I realise I'm frowning. Sofia? Cyber Secure?

'No,' I reply, shaking my head. 'What's that got to do with anything?'

He shrugs. 'I don't know. But then she told me change is coming. She said the people are ready to act.'

The room falls into silence, the only sound the ticking of the electric fire as it heats up.

'Kind words, but I didn't believe her. How many times have we heard in the last few weeks that things are going to change? People talk bullshit.

'So this morning I went to hand myself in,' he says this quickly, then looks away from us, staring at the floor and then out the window. 'I didn't think there was much point in anything, so I went to the police station and told them who I was.'

He lets the words hang; suddenly I have visions of police or government goons rushing in from the hallway with guns pointing, ready to arrest us all and take us to death row.

I snatch a glance at Cicero. His eyes tell me he's thinking the same.

'But they weren't interested,' Max says, and he lifts his hands in desperation. 'Not even when I told them I'm one of the Rises 7. They just said that they have *bigger fish to fry* and that we're *yesterday's news*.'

Now Cicero looks at Max.

'They laughed at me! Laughed! Said the press love nicknames for people or groups to grab readers and make them buy newspapers. Something catchy like *Jack the Ripper* or *The Boston Strangler*. They said the media thought the "Rises 7" had a good ring to it. I told them I wouldn't leave until they arrested me and took me to death row because that's what I deserved, and they laughed even harder and asked me if I knew how many nutters they get a week claiming they've done something or asking to be arrested for the night so they've got somewhere warm to sleep.

'I told them I wasn't lying and that I hacked into the voting system too. Then one of them came up and stared at me. He said that if I really am Max Stanton then he has a message for me. I thought he was going to punch me or something, but he passed me this piece of paper, and he told me one of the guards from death row brought it in, said he didn't know how to get it to me, but he knew there was a warrant out for my arrest. He said he had been about to pass it to the *National News* for them to make a story of.'

Max holds up a folded piece of paper, no bigger than his palm, grey and crumpled, edges torn. He opens it.

'Max. My name's Al. I work on death row. I have to put the straps around the prisoners so they don't escape. I don't like it, but I can't find another job. I had to put the straps around your . . .'

Max's voice breaks. He sucks in a deep breath, lets it out slowly.

'. . . your mum. She was crying a lot and it made me sad. She was a nice lady. I remember her from when she was a counsellor. She was kind. I wish I could've let her go but I couldn't. I'm sorry. She kept saying the same thing over and over, and I told her I would tell you. Then she smiled. I think it made her feel better. She said lots of times, "I love you, Max."'

He wipes his face.

'And she said . . .'

Max pauses and looks to Cicero.

'. . . she said, "Tell Cicero I love him too."'

The air in the room stops.

Everything stops.

We're all watching Cicero.

I can hardly see for tears, but I blink them away.

Cicero is staring at Max like the words are taking ages to sink in.

His mouth's open.

Then his face crumbles, smiles and cries, shakes his head. 'She . . .' he manages to get out. 'She said that?' There are tears running down his face now.

Max nods and passes him the piece of paper.

Cicero sniffs, his hands shaking as he reads it for himself.

'Thank you,' he whispers to Max. 'Thank you.'

Max takes the paper from him and puts it in his pocket. Then he looks around the room, nodding acknowledgement to Isaac. 'When are we heading into the City then?' he asks. 'There are things to do.'

How do you convince a load of people to walk past two guards with guns and risk being shot?

Turns out they didn't take that much convincing.

Turns out Gus had been on the case all morning.

We walked out of Daffodil House and they were already gathering.

Not all of them, that's for sure.

As I've come to realise, some folks are fickle, some don't want the hassle, some blame us for all this, some want to bury their heads in the sand and some think the wall protects *us* from *them*.

Perhaps the wall is more like a mirror.

We're not marching, not clutching iron bars or guns or knives or anything. Our hands are empty and we walk, stroll, wander up to the gates and the turnstile.

Me, Cicero, Joshua, Isaac and Gus.

Max stayed back in the end. Said he had *computer stuff* to do, whatever that means.

We are not the Rises 7 and we are not the terrorists they say we are.

In spirit we will always be seven, but we are from everywhere and we will fight for everyone.

I've heard the phrase 'One man's terrorist is another man's freedom fighter', but I don't agree; a freedom fighter does not target innocent folk.

The air sparkles with frost after the clear skies last night and our feet crunch. The wall is dappled in white, the bar at the gate is covered in silver.

One guard stands just behind the bar, to the left of the turnstile. His nose and his cheeks are bright red, his collar's turned up and he's wearing a woolly hat. He's dressed all in black; not police, but from some kind of private security firm. Like the men in the Old Bailey – they weren't police either.

The other one's in his little kiosk thing. I can see him holding a mug to his face and blowing across it.

If they've been out here all night they must be bloody freezing.

As we get closer, he puts his mug down and I see him stretch his arms out and pick up his gun.

Cold and achy and stiff, I think. I bet they'd like to go home.

The first one puts his right hand on his gun and takes a step closer to the turnstile.

'Nobody's allowed through,' he says. 'On the government's authority.'

We all slow down.

'It's for your own safety,' he says.

The masses behind us are slowly bumbling to a halt, but the sheer number of people is forcing us against the barrier.

'Why?' I ask.

His finger taps on the side of the gun near the trigger and his eyes flick over the crowd of us. The other guard steps out of the kiosk.

'Errr ... because ...' The first one loses it before he can think and takes a couple of small steps backwards. But the second strides forward, lifting his gun up and pointing it towards us.

'The people who live in the City and the Avenues don't want you there, and they're threatening to kill any of you who go there.'

'I've been watching the news and haven't heard anything about that,' I say.

'They don't put everything on the news.'

'I think we'll take our chances anyway,' I say. 'Shall we all go through the turnstile, or would you lift the barrier?'

'We've been instructed not to let you through. Not even if you have jobs to go to.'

'You're not the police though?' I ask.

'No. We answer to the government.'

'Then we're going through,' I say.

'Then I'll be forced to shoot you,' he replies.

He cocks the gun and the sound of it echoes over our heads. There's an intake of breath, a mumble of worry and some folk step back.

But I step forward.

'If you shoot me,' I say, loud and clear so every one of those behind me who've put their trust in us can hear me, 'then as you're not police, you'll end up on death row.'

'Self-defence,' he says, a smirk on his face. 'I'd only be following orders.'

'That doesn't wash,' I tell him, and I lower my hood so he can see who I am. Isaac steps forward with me. 'Didn't wash for me, nor Isaac, not Max's mum either – Eve Stanton. Did you see her die yesterday? She acted in self-defence.'

His face falls. I glance to his hands and can see his finger moving away from the trigger.

'We've been there, and it's not nice. There's no concession for self-defence or *orders*, but I think you know that. You're bluffing. But . . . you want to die by electric chair, then have a crack at me, because I'm done. I've got nothing to lose, y'see. You've got . . . what? Family? Wife? Kids?'

He glances to the other guard.

'We don't want to argue, or fight; we just want to pass through peacefully. We'd like you to let us pass, please.'

Nobody moves.

Nobody says a word.

Not even a whisper.

Then, very slowly, he lowers his gun, walks to the gate and presses the button for the bar to lift and we walk through.

'Thank you,' I say to him.

We walk quietly.

Isaac squeezes my hand and I smile at him.

I'm bloody scared, but he's at my side.

And at my other are Cicero, Gus and Joshua, and behind me are people who care and who need this to change.

Good people.

As we walk I phone DeLonzo.

'This better not be a trick,' I say down the phone.

'I'll hold my side of the bargain,' he says.

'We'll be there soon.'

'And so will more,' he replies.

And I ring Sofia, twice before she answers.

'I'm busy right now,' she says, quick and efficient and I guess who's with her. 'But I can see you later.'

'And Hart?' I ask.

'Yes, all as planned.'

Jesus Christ, I think as I put the phone back in my pocket. If this is a trick then we're done for. And it'll be all my fault.

'OK?' Isaac asks, and I nod.

'Promise me,' I whisper, 'if it goes to hell, get these folks out as quick as you can.'

He doesn't try to tell me it'll be fine, because we both know how easily this could all go wrong. He just nods.

The roads and streets all the way into the City are quiet.

We see no buses, no taxis. Some shops are open, but most are shut.

The closer we get, the more folks are around.

Some nod at us, some walk with us.

It seems the woman Max spoke to after Eve's execution was right.

There's a tension in the air too.

And fear.

Fear of each other is what tore this city apart.

Fear for each other is bringing us together.

We get to Whitehall and the crowds are growing. The Rises folk with me start to disperse, mixing with the folk from the City and Avenues who are out now as well.

Me, Cicero, Isaac, Joshua and Gus walk on, stopping in front of the tall railings at the end of Downing Street.

On the other side are half a dozen guards, dressed in plain black, just like the others.

'Private security again,' Cicero whispers. 'Hired by the government.'

The crowd are buzzing.

Isaac squeezes my hand and I turn around.

Up ahead, to the right of the railings, is a large screen. 'National News', it says across it, and past that, on the other side of the railings, is Albert DeLonzo, standing outside Number 10, a microphone in his hands, pointing to the black, shiny door behind him as it opens.

The Prime Minister – Stephen Renard

Cameras flash as the PM steps from the door of Number 10 and strides to the lectern set up halfway across the road. He looks around, his chest out and his chin up, but he acknowledges none of the press waiting for him.

Sofia stays in the background, her eyes flickering to Gino on the PM's right, scanning the audience like he's looking for threats.

She rolls her eyes and lets out a long sigh.

Shouts echo from the crowds down the road on Whitehall.

'Ladies and gentlemen,' the PM begins, and his voice carries over the noise with ease, 'it's with a heavy heart that I address you this afternoon, but one also filled with hope, determination and a solid sense of justice and fairness.'

The crowd on Whitehall quietens.

'Unsubstantiated claims have been launched against this government and against many of those who have the privilege of holding senior positions within our national authorities. As leader of this country, it is my responsibility to thoroughly investigate all these accusations and ensure justice is done and that punishment is rightly imposed on any wrongdoers. You have my word that while I am in power and in a position to do so, I will see anyone, and *everyone*, who is guilty of a crime appropriately punished.

'I believe wholeheartedly that I am the best person to do this, and so while these claims are under investigation I will continue to lead this country –'

A roar of sound surges from the end of the street. Banging and clattering against the iron railings holding back the crowd.

'TRAITOR!'

'LIAR!'

'– will continue to lead this country!' He stands taller, puffs his chest out further, his voice ringing out with confidence over the heads of the press. Cameras flash and microphones are thrust at him for questions.

'You covered up for murderers!' It's DeLonzo's voice. 'And paedophiles.'

The PM falters, his lip judders as he presses his mouth closed and his Adam's apple trembles as he swallows. 'A country which is built on a foundation of morals –'

'Not your morals!' a different journalist shouts.

'– and which I will guide out of these stormy waters with a compass of right and honour.'

He lifts a hand and wipes his brow. A video camera captures the quiver of it.

Sofia steps forward.

'Sir, it might be best to wind it up,' she whispers.

Almost imperceptibly, he nods.

Martha

More people plough in.

The mood shifts; smiles drop.

It's so packed that the air is filled with hot breath and sweat.

I cling to Isaac's hand, desperate to keep him safe, worried this is all too much for him and too soon.

'There's a lot of people,' I say. 'You reckon they're all here because they want the PM to stand down?'

'I hope they're here because they know things need to change,' Isaac says. 'Because they realise things took a wrong turn somewhere and they let it happen. And because they trust we, the people, can do something.'

I hope he's right.

As more and more folks push in, I lose sight of Cicero and Joshua.

Folks squash up to each other more and more, and they start talking, asking each other why they're here.

I listen.

And I hear stories of folks' kids being turned down for school places because someone else had more influence, or knew the right person, or could make a donation to the school.

I hear someone say she knew she was better experienced and qualified for a job, but this guy got it because his dad played golf with some high-up person in the company.

Someone says that a guy got medical treatment before her mum because he went to uni with the doctor.

Someone else that their kid wasn't allowed to play with the others because his mum originally came from the Rises.

Sucks.

Stories everywhere, seeping out. Like tiny holes in a dam, drop of water here, drop there. How much will it take?

Folks are pissed off.

And the more they talk, the more others do, and the more stories come out of the woodwork.

'It's always been who you know, not what you know,' some guy says, 'but never like this. Not to get people off murder charges or kiddie fiddling. It's sick.'

His mate shrugs. 'Dunno. P'raps it always has been but we never knew.'

'We need someone in charge who can sort this, not that fucking joke of a Prime Minister who's only worried about trying to impress celebrities. He's a disgrace.'

His mate frowns, stares off behind him. 'Would you look at that?' he says.

I turn and follow where he's looking; there's a guy climbing the railings into Downing Street!

The crowds are cheering him. Arms lifting and supporting him, ready to catch him if he falls and relaunch him back on his way.

Cheers go up as he reaches the top.

'That's what we all should be doing,' the guy near me says.

On the other side of the railings, the guards lift their guns and aim them at the man climbing over.

I look around to point it out to Isaac, but he's already grabbing out for me.

'It's Cicero,' he says.

The Prime Minister – Stephen Renard

'People are calling for your resignation, and in light of the accusations being made against you, many argue that you have lost all credibility as a leader. How do you respond to that?' DeLonzo's voice is strong and loud over the crowds.

'I say this: that in the face of adversity we must turn to our laws to protect us and give continuity . . .'

He glances down to the speech and the list of prepared answers written for him by Sofia.

'. . . strength and power –'

'How does it give *us* strength and power?' DeLonzo shouts again. 'It might give *you* strength and power, but not the people. Not –' He pauses.

Silence falls.

The press turn. So does the PM.

Calmly and slowly, Cicero is walking along Downing Street from the railings at Whitehall.

Suit and overcoat on, tie neatly knotted, hair barely moving in the breeze. His arms hang relaxed at his side, his palms out in peace.

Cameras and phones point at him.

The guards at the railings behind him stand and watch, their weapons lowered. Whatever Cicero has said to them has, if nothing else, stopped them from shooting him.

But from the other side of Downing Street, three other armed guards tighten their grip on their guns and raise them as Cicero moves towards the PM.

'I come in peace,' Cicero says, a smile flickering beneath his long moustache. 'I come as a man of justice. I come on behalf of the people.'

'You're a wanted man and a terrorist,' the PM retorts. Without taking his eyes off Cicero, he calls out, 'Arrest him!'

'What did I do?' Cicero asks.

The guards pause.

'What is your evidence against me?'

'I don't need evidence. I'm the Prime Minister for God's sake.' He turns to the guards behind him. 'Arrest him now!' He looks to the guards in front of him. 'I'm telling you to arrest him!'

'These are your own security guards, aren't they? They're not police. Do they have the authority to arrest *anyone*?'

'They do as I say.'

'Presumably you brought them in because the police have called for a vote of no confidence in your government and are refusing to take direct orders from you.'

'I'm the leader of the goddamned country for Christ's sake, and whether police or security guards, they will do what I say! Now arrest him!'

The guards' eyes flick to each other but nobody moves.

Sofia steps further into the background.

'I'm not a terrorist,' Cicero states calmly. 'I had no involvement in the blowing up of death row. You have no evidence against me, or reasonable grounds to suspect me.'

'Screw evidence or *reasonable grounds*. This is my country and I will do as I like!'

'You cannot do that,' Cicero continues. 'For too long you've been acting outside of the law and that is not acceptable. You are accountable to the people! You should lead by example, yet instead you have allowed corruption to thrive and people to get away with the most horrendous crimes, all to serve your own power! You have allowed a system of surveillance to monitor people in the streets and even in their homes, which is in direct violation of human rights.'

The PM launches himself towards Cicero, his arm rising in the air and a finger jabbing at Cicero's chest.

'This is my country. I was elected by the people. They put their trust in me –'

'AND YOU BETRAYED IT!'

'– and I will rule this country as I see fit!'

'Even if that means breaking the very laws you force everyone else to live by?'

Martha

The cameras are fixed on Cicero and the PM.

I stare at their faces on the screen, then through the gates.

'Let me through!' I shout, rattling at the gates, but the guards on the other side ignore me.

What the hell, Cicero?

'Cicero,' I shout through the gates, but he can't hear me.

I rattle the gates some more. Isaac joins me, Joshua and Gus too, but there is no way on this earth they're going to move.

Folks press forward, crowding in, pushing and shoving, desperate to peer along Downing Street.

'We're going to get crushed!' I shout to the guards. 'You *have* to open the gates.'

But they ignore me.

Bodies are squashed up against the railings. They clatter as folks' breath is squeezed out of them, and cries go up into the air.

'You,' I gasp, grabbing air into my lungs as I'm pushed hard into the gates, 'are going to be responsible for these people dying if you don't let us through!'

But the guards don't even acknowledge us.

No choice, I think, and I launch myself at the gate. If Cicero can do it, then I bloody can too.

'Martha!' Isaac shouts to me.

315

But I'm up, over the top and coming down the other side.

The guards do nothing – shocked maybe, or just not prepared to lift a gun on a teenage girl and face the death penalty.

For the second time today, it plays in my favour.

I walk up to the one in charge, stare him in the face and unclip the keys from his belt.

'Thank you,' I say, and I run back to Isaac and pass them through the gate.

'I'm going to Cicero,' I tell him, and quickly I squeeze his hand.

I hear his voice as I run away. 'Please! Be calm!' he shouts at the crowd. 'Be patient, please, and we'll get through.'

The Prime Minister – Stephen Renard

'Arrest him!' the PM shouts.

'I'm not doing anything.' Cicero shrugs.

'I don't give a fuck if he hasn't done anything. Arrest him for . . . public order offences!'

Cicero looks behind him. Martha is running towards him. Behind her the gates are easing open slowly.

'Your people are coming,' he says calmly.

'If you don't arrest him, I will!' the Prime Minister shouts. 'And stop those people!' Then he stares down the road. 'Honeydew?!' he hisses. 'Martha fucking Honeydew? I should've known this would have something to do with her. Arrest her too!'

'You don't have the power to arrest anyone,' Cicero says.

The PM's face glows red. 'I have all the power in this country!' he shouts. 'You will *not* get anything over me.'

'I think I already have. As far as I can see, it's you who should be arrested and tried. How many deaths are you responsible for?'

'I haven't killed –'

'But you've *allowed* them to be killed. And after all, everything is black and white, no grey allowed. No defence. No witnesses. No evidence. You allowed them to be killed, so you're complicit.'

Renard shakes his head, his eyes screwed up and his hands in fists. 'This is ridiculous. This can't happen.'

'It can, and it will.'

Martha is nearly upon them now.

'That wretched girl,' he hisses. 'If it wasn't for her . . .' His eyes flick from one to another, to another. A rabbit in headlights. A mouse in a trap.

But then they rest on the guard's waist.

In a split second Cicero sees what Martha doesn't.

The PM lunges forward and grabs the gun from the guard's holster, turns on the spot, and aims it at Martha just as Cicero throws himself towards her.

The *BANG* tears the air apart.

Cicero and Martha fall to the ground.

Silence swallows everything.

Martha

I don't know what's happening around me.

There must be folk everywhere, but I don't see any.

There must be noise too, but I don't hear any.

We're in a bubble.

Me and Cicero.

I don't take my eyes off his.

I will not be pulled away.

I will not leave him.

I will not let another of my friends die.

I pull down his tie and yank open his shirt. It's soaked with blood and my hands turn scarlet.

Not again, not again, please not again . . .

Suddenly other hands are near me, someone thrusting a scarf towards me. I wipe at Cicero's chest and see the hole.

'Pressure.' I hear someone, recognise the voice, but I don't turn.

I nod. I know this. Come on, Martha, get on with it.

Holding the scarf over the wound, I press down hard.

He flinches. Blinks but it's too slow.

'You saved my life. Again,' I say.

His face is paling, clammy.

'Stay awake. You need to stay with me.'

His eyes do this nodding, blinking thing that I know means yes.

'You're crazy, y'know,' I say to him. 'Fancy climbing over

those railings at your age. And then leaping in front of a gun. You should know better.'

The corners of his mouth lift a little.

'How did you get over?' he croaks.

'Me? I climbed like you did. Then I got the key and gave it to Isaac. Perhaps you should've done the same!'

'No,' he says. 'Worked better my way.'

He coughs. Spit flies out of his mouth.

It looks pink to me.

He closes his eyes.

'Keep looking at me!' I shout, and I pat his face.

His eyes stutter open.

'Are they taking him? Has he . . . ?' he splutters again. Red this time. '. . . arrested?'

'Don't talk,' I say to his eyes. 'Save your strength.'

I keep my hands on his chest, but I look around.

Suddenly I'm back in reality again and there are people, legs, arms, bodies jostling and shuffling everywhere. But nothing makes sense.

Sirens wail.

Blue lights flash.

Not again, I think. I can never escape. Please not again.

Sirens blare louder.

Lights flash brighter.

A path forms between the people.

Here they come, I think. I know the routine. An ambulance for Cicero. A police car for me.

My eyes blur with tears, and the lights, the people, the uniforms, everything melts into one bright, moving mess.

I blink and tears fall down my face.

And then my vision clears.

I blink again. I want to see what comes next, I need to.

A solitary policeman is walking towards the PM. He's reaching for his handcuffs, I'm sure he is.

I hope he is.

I want to laugh but I daren't. Not yet, not till I hear those words. I glance left and Isaac is with me; a look on his face that I can't understand. Disbelief? Shock? Fear for Cicero.

'I think you did it,' I breathe. 'Cicero, I think you did it.'

Blue lights flash on his pale skin.

He smiles at me, a glorious, happy smile. 'You finish it, Martha,' he rasps.

'No,' I tell him. '*We'll* finish it,'

He squeezes my hand and his eyes close.

6.25 p.m. *Death is Justice*

Wearing a red figure-hugging 1940s dress and holding a clipboard, Kristina is perched on the edge of the desk, smiling to camera.

KRISTINA: Ladies and gentlemen, I am shocked and awed! What a day it has been and what an incredible show we have for you this evening. Never would I have envisaged events panning out as they have. If you've not tuned into any news or current affairs programmes yet today, then, boy, is this going to be an eye-opener and an evening full of entertainment for you! Grab a bottle of wine, a flask of coffee, or a whole flagon of beer, and order that pizza, because I'm telling you, when our programme begins in five minutes' time, you will *not* want to move from that seat!

Martha

Suddenly there are people everywhere and I've lost where the PM is.

Folks from Whitehall pour in and the security men drop back; too many for them to deal with. Isaac's with me, kneeling next to Cicero, the leg of his trousers soaked in blood.

Paramedics run up, gently push us aside. They check Cicero's breathing, touch the bullet hole, moving quickly, efficiently. It's getting dark, there's drizzle in the air, lights flashing, and I can't make out enough of anything to figure out what's happening.

'He'll be all right,' Isaac whispers, wrapping his arms around me.

I'm aware of cameras in my face, watching, filming my every move.

What will the public demand of me now?

More police arrive, and are gently holding people back, but folks see what's happening and stop.

In all the mayhem a tall skinny man in a police uniform appears. Not in the riot vests like the others are wearing, but in a smart dark jacket with a chain across and medals with ribbons on his chest. Another officer nods at him, and Hart shoves in from the other side. He's shouting, bellowing at everyone, pointing as his fat belly wobbles and he blusters. He's out of breath, ordering folks left, right and all over the place.

But they ignore him. All but the tall skinny officer, who strides up to Hart and pulls his badge off his chest. He's shaking his head as he puts his hand out flat, waiting for something, I think.

I wish I could go and spit in Hart's face. Despicable, horrible man. I don't, but I can't help smiling at his humiliated expression as he hands over his gun. The skinny man says something I wish I could hear, but as he points away to the distance and Hart shakes his head and storms off, I can kind of guess.

I hope that's not the end of it though.

Cicero's on a stretcher now, an oxygen mask on his face, a bag of fluid attached to his arm. They're lifting the stretcher.

'Where are you taking him?' I shout. 'What are you doing with him? Can I come with you?'

The paramedic pushes past me. 'Central General Hospital. We need to work on him; there won't be room in the ambulance. Follow us down.'

'Is he going to be OK?' I trot alongside them, desperate to keep up.

'He's lost a lot of blood, but it looks like the bullet missed anything vital.'

'Cicero?' I say, touching his arm as they push him towards the ambulance. 'Cicero, can you hear me? Please . . . Cicero!'

His eyes flicker and my heart lifts. My hand is over my mouth and I could cry for him.

His fingers pull at the oxygen mask. 'You,' he croaks and I bend down to hear him, 'you stay here. Finish this.'

'Sir, please keep the oxygen mask on,' the paramedic tells him.

'Do it, Martha,' Cicero says, and the paramedic steps in and puts the mask back on his face.

324

I watch them go.

Watch the stretcher ease into the ambulance, the doors shut and the lights flash and hear the siren blare as it tears away from us.

Isaac touches my arm, points across to the other side of the road.

There's the PM. And there are handcuffs on him.

I wander over and it almost feels like I'm in a dream. The tall, skinny police officer is with him now.

I hold my breath, waiting, hoping for those words.

A shiver runs down my spine, and I stand there in the cold and the dark, and I listen.

'Stephen Renard, Prime Minister of the United Kingdom, I arrest you for the attempted murder of Thomas Cicero. You do not have to say anything. But it may harm your defence if you fail to mention something you later rely on. Anything you do say may be broadcast on *Death is Justice* or quoted in national newspapers or on internet sites.'

'I acted to preserve the safety of our nation, not to endanger it,' Renard says. 'I wanted to kill that trouble-causer Honeydew, not Cicero, you idiots! And there's nothing wrong with that. This is all her fault – people have died because of her, and she needs getting rid of. You –' he tries to lift his hands to point to the police – 'are playing into the hands of sympathisers and do-gooders. In this country we uphold the strictest and most stringent laws and have among the lowest crime rates in the world. Killing her is in the best interests of the safety and security of this country.'

Is he right?

Have I caused all this?

'Death row!' someone shouts. 'Put the scum on death row!'

'He covered up murders of children to save his friends!'

'Lives don't matter to him, money does. Let's see him fry!'

Folks are angry, but not with me any more.

I see the fear in the PM's face. I know it, I recognise it, I've lived with it. For years that fear has hung over folks I know like a storm cloud waiting for lightning to strike. And now it's poised over the man who caused it.

I should be happy, shouldn't I?

Should be smiling, shouldn't I?

Isaac's arm goes around my shoulder.

'He'll be executed,' he says.

'I know,' I whisper. 'I know.'

6.30 p.m. *Death is Justice*

Lights flash across the set and the audience, and the theme music blares. Kristina steps from backstage and up to her desk. She pauses, waves to the camera. The music dies and the camera spins over the audience and onto her. She smiles wide.

KRISTINA: Hello again and welcome.

The audience cheer.

KRISTINA: Welcome to what I can assure you is the most exciting show I've ever had the privilege to present. Not only do we have a round-up of the ongoing votes of those incarcerated on death row, and details of their crimes, but it seems we may well have a live, late-night addition to death row, and, boy, will that be someone you are definitely not expecting! Yes, ladies and gentlemen, often during my time hosting this show, and indeed during my limited time on *Buzz for Justice*, I have been shocked to the core, but nothing has prepared me for this. So pull up a seat, grab a drink, and prepare for what may well shake your world, as we take you live to the action. I must warn you, though, that this report contains flashing images and scenes of a violent nature.

Kristina sits down at the desk. To her right the eye logo on the large screen moves to the left corner, and static in the middle slowly clears to reveal the scene at Downing Street.

MALE VOICEOVER: Earlier today, Great Britain was shaken to the core. Shocking actions were taken by desperate men and women. Desperate for their voices to be heard, desperate for the plight of the innocent to be revealed, desperate to see the guilty brought to justice.

The screen shows Cicero walking along Downing Street. The footage pauses as the PM takes the guard's gun. The camera freezes on the PM's oversized, distorted face.

MALE VOICEOVER: Fearing for the lives of those gathering in Whitehall, and desperate to see justice finally served, former Justice Thomas Cicero, a wanted member of the Rises 7, scaled the railings and went to speak with the Prime Minister, Stephen Renard, about his concerns.

The screen changes, a slow-motion shot of the PM's finger squeezing the trigger, a flash of white from the gun.

MALE VOICEOVER: Although Justice Cicero was clearly unarmed and presented no threat to anyone, Renard ignored orders from his own police force and took matters into his own hands.

The feed returns to normal speed. The bang of the gun jolts the audience, a few shouting out in surprise. On the screen Cicero lies on the ground, Martha leaning over him. She moves his clothes and it zooms in, pausing for a moment as blood seeps out.

The camera returns to Kristina. She dabs her eyes. Crocodile tears.

KRISTINA: That all took place barely half an hour ago. We now take you live to the scene.

The screen changes again. Gerome appears, overcoat on, collar turned up and fuzzy microphone held to his mouth. In the background sirens blare, blue lights flash and people rush around.

GEROME: Good evening, Kristina. As you can see around me, things are a little chaotic still. In fact, if you look to my right, you can just see the ambulance transporting Justice Cicero to hospital disappearing into the distance. Running alongside him as he was rushed into the ambulance and as paramedics fought for his life was none other than Martha Honeydew. What we're unable to tell you at the moment is exactly why Honeydew isn't in prison, as I'm sure you realise, following last week's *Buzz for Justice* decision, she should be. And also why, on her appearance today, she wasn't instantly re-arrested. Indeed, at this precise moment, she is still on the scene, as is previously missing and presumed dead Isaac Paige. I'm hearing rumours that the other surviving members of the Rises 7 are also here, but we've yet to confirm that. However, what I think viewers will find more interesting is if we step over here.

The camera follows him as he pushes through crowds. He pauses near a row of other journalists, cameras poised, microphones in hands, serious faces. In front of them is Police Commissioner Gordon Ruhier and, with handcuffs around his wrists, the PM. Some distance to the side, and away from the hubbub, is Sofia.

GEROME: In the moments following the near-fatal shooting, Stephen Renard was arrested by Police Commissioner Gordon Ruhier and charged with the attempted murder of Justice Cicero. Up until a week ago, the PM would not have been placed on death row unless Justice Cicero doesn't survive, but in accordance with the new laws he himself brought in – that any crime deemed to be against the safety and security of our nation is punishable by death – he is about to be transported there.

The camera follows Ruhier as he drags the PM past and towards the waiting police cars.

GEROME: Prime Minister! Mr Renard! A quote, please. For the viewers. What do you have to say to your public? Did you mean to kill Justice Cicero?

Renard stumbles as Ruhier pushes him towards the camera.

RENARD: No! Of course not. I only ever acted with the best of intentions. I did not mean to kill Cicero. My objective was to apprehend the errant Martha Honeydew by any means necessary. Seeing her running towards not only myself but the journalists and other innocent people around, I acted with courage and honour and, in grabbing the security guard's gun, sought to do what I could to take her down and protect the lives of those around us. It was unfortunate that Cicero leaped in front of the gun.

GEROME: But what about the other claims? What about the police calling for a vote of no confidence in you? This must surely be the end of your career.

RENARD: A leader is not an adequate leader unless he takes risks for his people. Allegations that I covered up crimes by public officials, high-profile individuals and celebrities and millionaires in return for cash

331

or rewards of some kind are completely false. These did not in any way affect the safety or security of the nation, as at no time was any criminal left at large, unchallenged or not prosecuted for their actions. Any claims that this was the case and that I then risked the safety of our public are completely false, and the calls for me to be held accountable for these crimes are utterly unsubstantiated.

Ruhier pulls him away as the camera focuses back on Gerome.

GEROME: I think we can all read between the lines there, Kristina. Did you *count* the number of times he said *safety, security*? And I wonder if the phrase *Thou dost protest too much* might be apt here.

Back in the studio, Kristina stands next to the screen and the oversized image of Gerome.

KRISTINA: I think you may indeed be right, Gerome! I cannot understand how anyone could think him innocent here, even if Justice Cicero lives!

GEROME: Well, Kristina, our esteemed Prime Minister is now being put into a police car to be driven to the Old Bailey. If I were you, I'd get your running shoes on and be the first to interview him over there!

KRISTINA: What a coup that would be!

The camera zooms in on Kristina.

KRISTINA: And what a treat that would be for you, viewers! Join us after the break when we will be live at the Old Bailey, feeding back to you as the PM is prepared for death row! Don't go anywhere!

Martha

They take him away.

The guards of whatever that security operation was have disappeared. Scared for their own skins, I reckon, and the police seem to be taking action again.

'Who's in charge now?' someone shouts. 'Who's the leader?'

'What's going to happen to us?'

'What about the wall?'

It started as murmurs; it's getting louder now.

Folks are getting nervous.

If no one's in charge, then . . .

They look around, one to another to another.

Then I hear the clicking of heels on tarmac and I turn.

Sofia's standing at the lectern.

'Please,' she says, 'please stay calm. Stephen Renard, the man who's manipulated this situation and you, the people, has gone. He can no longer be Prime Minister. For the foreseeable future I will stand in his place and I promise you I will lead fairly, openly and honestly. Change will be necessary, but cautious change, and change for the better and for the people. I'm proud to hold this office, and I'm proud to be the youngest-ever leader of the country. Under my leadership injustice will be fought, tolerance of others will be promoted and poverty will be destroyed.

'I will lead this country to a prosperous and just future.

'And I promise that the streets of our city and our *country* will be safer than they've ever been.'

A few folk clap.

Some cheer.

But I don't.

Something about all this doesn't sit right with me.

I want to see Cicero. I turn to walk away, but I spot something.

A police officer nodding to someone, reaching for his handcuffs, walking towards me.

My stomach lurches.

My blood runs cold.

Prickles over my skin.

I spin to Isaac, standing to the side. Still with his hat on, face hidden, surrounded by different folk and blending in with them.

Me?

I'm alone, in the middle of the road, my hood down, face for all to see.

The TV cameras are trained on me; everyone knows who I am.

I see DeLonzo in the crowd of journalists; he's talking into a microphone, pointing my way, then to the police officer.

I catch Isaac's eye, he looks from me to the officer, everything is slow motion.

Then realisation creeps over his face, his eyes widen.

Next to him, Joshua and Gus look from him, to me, to the officer, back to me.

'No,' I mouth. 'No!'

Isaac leaps forward, but Joshua and Gus grab him and pull him back into the obscurity of the crowd.

The officer reaches me.

I don't run. There's no point.

'Martha, no!' Isaac shouts, but Joshua throws a hand over his mouth and he and Gus drag him back and back.

'Martha Honeydew,' the officer says, 'I'm arresting you for the murder of Patty Paige.'

'I didn't plant that bomb! You all know I didn't! Renard manipulated the whole thing!'

The police officer doesn't look me in the eye.

'I'm sorry, miss,' he whispers so only I can hear. 'We're just following orders.'

'But . . . but . . . the police . . . you called for a vote of no confidence in . . . in –'

He looks up to me now, shaking his head. 'In Stephen Renard,' he says.

Cold runs through me like sickness.

I don't understand, but I hold my hands out.

What choice do I have?

But if they're going to play this dirty, then so am I.

7 p.m. *Death is Justice*

Kristina, tailored coat with oversized fur collar, stands outside the Old Bailey. The wind blows at her blonde hair, and she pulls strands away as they stick to her glossed lips.

KRISTINA: Welcome back, viewers! You are joining us outside the Old Bailey. Only a few moments ago the police car driving the now *ex*-Prime Minister, Stephen Renard, pulled up at this very spot, where he was escorted out, still handcuffed, and led into the building behind me. As many of you know, before entering death row the accused are placed in a holding cell where their heads are shaved, they are deloused and given prison overalls to wear.

She moves towards the doorway.

KRISTINA: But don't worry – you're not missing *all* the action! It's my absolute pleasure to inform you that *Death is Justice* has been granted exclusive access to the holding room! Let's go!

She smiles wide and turns, and the camera follows her through

337

the doors, over the marble floor, through a doorway and down a corridor. She turns at the end, goes through another doorway and down a dark, narrow stairway.

KRISTINA: It's certainly spooky and scary down here!

She stops next to an old metal door with a small panel in it. Next to it stands the guard from Eve's execution.

KRISTINA: Ladies and gentlemen, I must warn you about what may occur in this room. As I'm sure you appreciate, emotions will be running high, and as we're bringing it to you live, I can only apologise that we will be unable to censor any inappropriate behaviour or language.

A guard unlocks the door and pushes it open. Kristina steps inside.

KRISTINA: Oh my.

The camera pans around the cell.

KRISTINA: I don't know if you're seeing this, ladies and gentlemen, it's very dark, but there are . . . four . . . no, five people in here. It's very cramped. There are no beds on the floor. There's a bucket in the corner which I can only presume is for . . . for . . . *toilet issues*.

She wafts a hand in front of her face.

GUARD: We were told to put him straight in here. It's Cell
      6. He's gonna be executed tomorrow.

KRISTINA: Pardon?

GUARD: I said, he's gonna be executed tomorrow.

KRISTINA: But . . . but this would've been prime-time
      viewing for a whole week! There would have
      been enough material here to beat all previous
      records. Who's signed off on this?

GUARD: Dunno. It came from higher up than me.

KRISTINA: *Anybody* is higher up than you!

Kristina stops and checks herself, reapplies her smile and
looks back to camera.

KRISTINA: What a coup that is, ladies and gentlemen, and
      we at *Death is Justice* are the first to know! Such
      are Renard's crimes that he's to be executed
      tomorrow. Well, we will most definitely be
      bringing that to you. What an opportunity this
      is for you to cast your judgement. The power
      is in your hands. Should Renard be allowed to
      live or should he die? Does covering up those

crimes make him accountable for them? And what about his attempt to kill Justice Cicero? I know how I'll be voting, but I can't *wait* to hear whether you agree. Join us again after this short message from our sponsor.

The screen starts to change, but flickers and falters. Kristina's image pixelates, the sound is distorted.

KRISTINA (breaking up): This is fucking ludicrous. Get me the producer now.

The feed breaks up and is replaced by the fluffy cloud logo of Cyber Secure, streams of data gently flowing into it as the silver padlock flies across the screen and fastens onto the cloud.

FEMALE VOICEOVER: For all your data security needs – we keep them locked.

MALE VOICE (OFF-SCREEN): We apologise for the break in transmission. We are experiencing some technical issues, but will return to our live feed as soon as possible. We apologise for the break in transmission –

The screen changes, the cloud disappears, static fills it again, followed by the image of Kristina back outside the Old Bailey.

KRISTINA: Welcome back, viewers, and apologies for lack of signal. If you didn't hear before it was lost, then, boy, do we have a surprise for you! Not only are we seeing for the first time in many years a Prime Minister being ousted from his position, and the first time one has ever been put on death row, but in a radical and exciting development, he has been placed – I hope you're sitting down for this – straight into Cell 6! What a shocking move, and what a scoop for *Death is Justice* for us to be the ones able to share that news with you live as it broke, and straight from the venue itself. We truly are right at the hub of the gossip and the goings-on. But what does this mean for you, the viewer, the voter? Well, ladies and gentlemen, children, in this building behind me right now, technicians are working to install a camera directly into the Prime Minister's cell, another in the corridor, one along Dead Man's Walk and, as we know this is a once-in-a-lifetime opportunity and ticket demands are going to be through the roof, more cameras are also being installed in the new execution room itself. You can subscribe to this premium service, meaning close-up footage live from these new cameras will be fed directly to your screens, into your homes, or onto your media device for the bargain price of £99.99. This will give you unlimited access, from as soon as they go live tonight, right through to either Renard's execution or his release. Do not miss this offer. For those of you hoping for tickets to the live event itself, phone lines will open in half an hour, and tickets will start at £150 for back-row with restricted-view, right up to £499.99 for executive box seats. Full details are –

The camera wobbles. Blue lights flash, the siren of a police car wails.

KRISTINA: Well, we are having an exciting evening. It appears we have yet another contestant . . . I mean, *prisoner* arriving. What a treat! Let's head over and see who it is.

The camera follows Kristina along the path, stopping with her in focus as the police officer climbs out and opens the rear door. Martha steps out. Cameras flash across the dark. White mingled with blue.

KRISTINA: Oh my! We have a repeat offender! It's none other than teen killer, bomb-planter, Rises dweller, girl on the run, Martha Honeydew.

The police officer escorts Martha towards the doors. Kristina trots alongside.

KRISTINA: Honeydew! Martha! Can we have a quick word for our viewers?

Martha pauses on the steps and turns around, looking directly to camera.

MARTHA: Keep watching.

As she's led inside the feed is cut.

Cicero

The long hospital corridor is empty but for one police officer standing outside a door. The lights are bright around the nurses' desk halfway down, muted near the wards. Machines beep softly, and somewhere in the distance a phone rings.

A dark-haired doctor in blue scrubs walks down the corridor, his plastic shoes squeaking with every step and his name tag – Peter Caplan – bouncing against his chest.

As he reaches the door, the police officer steps in front of him.

'Thomas Cicero is under arrest,' he says.

'I know,' Pete replies. 'I've just operated on him, with one of you on my shoulder the whole time. Why anyone would think a heavily sedated man would be capable of evading security while having a bullet taken from his shoulder is beyond me.'

The officer stares at him.

'I need to go in,' he says. 'I need to tell my patient how the surgery went.'

Sighing, the officer moves away.

Pete walks over to Cicero, lying in the one solitary bed in the room. The light is dim and the only noise is the bleeping of a machine.

'I'm Peter Caplan, the surgeon who took the bullet from your shoulder this evening,' he says as he busies himself looking at the machines, checking the drip, adjusting a dial, not making eye contact with Cicero.

Cicero reaches across to the bedside table for his glasses. 'You're also the ex-partner of Joshua Decker.'

'You'll be pleased to know that the operation went well. We don't foresee any problems and you should heal well.'

'He misses you,' Cicero adds, the tube from the drip going into the back of his hand flapping as he puts his glasses on.

'We plan to release you in the morning.' He looks up, finally meeting Cicero's gaze. 'Unless there are any problems.'

'Such as?'

Pete stares at him. 'A high temperature isn't uncommon and can be an indicator of infection. In which case we'd be forced to keep you here.'

Cicero nods slowly. 'I see.'

Pete falters. Pauses, mouth opening but quickly closing again. With a shake of his head he turns away, shoves his hands in his pocket and heads towards the door.

But he stops, looks back at Cicero and stares.

'Where is he?' he whispers.

'Safe,' Cicero replies.

'Are you sure?'

'As sure as I can be.'

Pete's hand goes over his mouth and he shakes his head. 'I was stupid,' he whispers, stepping back to the bed.

'No,' Cicero replies. 'Scared maybe, but not stupid. Even what I just did wasn't stupid.'

'I'd beg to differ on that one,' Pete says, and there's the glimmer of a smile.

They both fall quiet for a moment.

'What can I do to help?' Pete says eventually.

Cicero smiles at him. 'I think the best thing you could do right now would be to phone Joshua and speak to him.'

Pete nods and the air of a sigh leaves his chest.

As he pulls the door open to leave, Cicero hears his voice:

'This man has a temperature, officer. It's likely he's developing an infection. He won't be going anywhere in the morning.'

Cicero closes his eyes and a smile stretches through his moustache.

Isaac, Joshua, Gus

'And then there were three,' Gus says. 'Who will be the last man standing?' He mimics a TV commentator. 'Will it be Rises dweller, ex-death row occupant, former drug addict and police informant, Gus Evans? Or will it be millionaire boy, previous teen ambassador for crime and lover to Martha Honeydew, Isaac Paige? Or could it be recent TV presenter, gay-rights activist and voted *Women Today*'s sharpest dresser, Joshua Decker?'

'Shut the fuck up,' Isaac says.

'It's more likely to be "and then there were none",' Gus whispers, low and menacing.

'You're not being helpful,' Joshua points out.

'I don't know what helpful is right now,' Gus says.

'Somewhere to stay perhaps,' Joshua says. 'We can't go back to the Rises – we'd never make it out again. Or a plan of what to do.'

'What? Plan B, because Plan A didn't work out too well yesterday?' Gus asks.

'More like Plan Z,' Isaac says.

They stroll along the deserted streets. A few takeaways are open and light from inside pours out into the darkness.

'I've got some money,' Isaac says. 'What about some chips?' He stops in front of a cafe with steamed-up windows and broken blinds, the lights above the name flickering on and off.

They nod and go inside.

The tables are covered in red gingham plastic covers, and an oversized salt shaker, a sticky vinegar bottle and a tomato-sauce bottle congealed around the lid are huddled in the middle of each.

The smell of reused oil hangs in the warm air and a TV in the corner is covered in a layer of dust. A tall, skinny man wipes his hands down his apron and looks at them – the only people in there – from behind the counter.

'Three cups of coffee, please,' Isaac says, 'and –' he looks to the others – 'chips?'

'Got soup if you prefer,' the man says. 'Roasted vegetable. Homemade.'

'That'd be good,' Joshua replies, and they take their seats at a table near the back, the TV – tuned to *Death is Justice* – in full view.

Kristina's voice rings out. The three of them stare at the screen.

'They put him straight in Cell 6,' Isaac whispers.

There's a clattering and the chef lifts the counter hatch and thuds over to them with a tray balanced across his arms.

'Voting lines are open already,' he says. 'The public are going mad for it. A minute ago they said they've already had over a million votes.'

The three shrink away from him as he places bowls and spoons on the table.

'Mostly guilty votes too,' he adds. 'They want blood.'

The door rattles open and a bell above it pings. They all jump.

A man stands in the doorway. Hat pulled down and scarf around his face.

The three look down into their soup.

'I'm closing!' the chef shouts.

'I only want a cuppa!' the man says.

'Sorry, too late. These folks are just leaving now.'

The man turns and leaves.

As the chef follows him, Isaac, Gus and Joshua look to each other and start to stand up.

'Oh no, you don't have to leave,' the chef says, flicking down the latch, and turning the sign to 'closed'. 'I thought you'd appreciate eating in peace and not having to worry.'

They don't move.

'I know who you are. I clocked you soon as you came in. I'm not going to report you.' He walks back to the counter and grabs a basket of bread rolls. 'This is all ludicrous,' he says, waving a hand to the TV. 'It should be stopped.' As he puts the basket on the table, they sit back down.

He moves over to the window and pulls down the blinds. 'It's difficult though, isn't it? We think we have democracy and freedom of speech, but we're told who is our enemy and who is our friend. Frightening times.'

He turns to the screen, the fluffy cloud of Cyber Secure filling it.

'My son's just signed up to Cyber Secure. He told me I should too, said they've got a good deal on at the minute – half-price subscription for a year. I'm forever losing things, you see. Driving licence, passport . . . He said they file digital copies of everything. Are you signed up? No, I don't imagine you are.'

'What do we owe you?' Isaac asks, reaching into his pocket.

The chef shakes his head. 'Nothing. It's my pleasure. There's some cake in the cupboard. Help yourselves. I have to go. Lock up when you leave. OK?' he says placing a key on the table. 'And drop the key through the letterbox.'

'I don't know what to say,' Joshua says, standing up to shake the man's hand.

'You don't need to say anything.'

He pulls off his apron and heads to the back of the cafe. 'That poor girl's back in there, bless her socks. Shocking it is. She didn't do that bomb.'

He glances back.

'Glad to see you're still alive too,' he says to Isaac, and with that he leaves and the sound of the back door closing echoes around them.

'Soup's good,' Gus says, slurping it from his spoon.

'So are people,' Joshua whispers.

Martha

The smell is foul. It's putrid.

And the noise!

Oh my fucking God, this place is hell.

I didn't have much hair to shave so they left me. Still covered me in that God-awful delousing crap though. It made me dissolve into a coughing fit before, eyes running and snot everywhere, but this time I remembered to shut my eyes and hold my breath.

It's bloody cold down here too.

The floor's stone.

Walls are brick, old, flaking, damp and mouldy.

My feet are bare.

They lead me through and over some kind of wooden hatch and it wobbles as I stand on it.

'Watch your step,' the guard says. 'That's the River Fleet down there. Fall in there and you'll catch hypothermia – wouldn't want that, would we?'

'They used to throw bodies down there in medieval times,' I tell him.

'Well, would you ever? A Rises girl with intelligence. Or are you just making shit up?'

'If you had any intelligence then you'd know, wouldn't you?' I smile at him, but he doesn't smile back – still working out what I've said, I think.

Dumb fuck.

He stops at a door. There's a lit-up plastic box above it with a metal cage around it. Someone's painted 'Cell 1' on it in really bad handwriting.

'What you doing?' I say to him.

He looks at me, confused.

I'm shaking my head. 'They said to put me in Cell 6.'

I can see a cloud pass over his eyes as he tries to remember. 'No one told me that,' he says.

'Suit yourself,' I reply. 'I won't be the one getting into trouble. It's not like I especially want to be in Cell 6 either.'

He grabs the chains around my wrist and yanks me further along the corridor.

We stop again.

Another door, another cell, another light box with crap writing across it – 'Cell 6'.

I don't say anything.

He undoes my chains and shoves me through the doorway.

I hold my hands up and turn around to him.

'What's going on?' I ask, but he's gone.

'There aren't enough chains to for everyone,' a voice replies, a voice I recognise. 'So they've decided we don't need them, especially considering we're being watched all the time by that hideous camera on the wall.'

I step towards the voice, and dusty shafts of moonlight from the tiny window up high are cast across the prisoner's face.

'Good evening, Prime Minister,' I say to him. 'Or do I just call you Stephen now?'

DECEMBER 7TH

7.30 a.m. *Death is Justice* trailer

No music plays. Instead there's a loud thudding heartbeat rhythm, the overhead lights pulsing to the beat. Kristina walks from backstage wearing a tight-fitting white trouser suit and crisp purple blouse with a deep neckline. Her hair is straightened. Her make-up is severe.

The lights tip to rest on her. There's no smile on her face.

KRISTINA: Ladies and gentlemen, welcome. Death is a serious business, crime is a serious business and safety is a serious business. Our current occupant of Cell 7 knew this, had known it for many years; in charge of our country, his responsibility was to lead by example, show compassion and honour, be fair and just. Yet he did none of these. Today he faces judgement by the millions he failed. Those he watched and judged with impunity, those whose loved ones his system sent to their deaths, leaving families grieving. This system he set up, a system to follow people in the streets and in their homes, to catch the guilty and protect the innocent, has done just that, caught the guilty – him. Today will see the ultimate justice served as he is voted on by the very people he has failed – you. Get voting, and join us this evening to find out how he has been judged.

Isaac, Joshua, Gus

'We should leave,' Joshua says, stretching out of one of the wooden chairs. 'I'm sure he didn't mean for us to stay the night here.'

Isaac folds the tea towel and places it on the counter. 'I've left him some money for the soup,' he says. 'And I've washed up.'

'Where we gonna go?' Gus asks, peering out the window. 'It's looking busy already.'

'Don't know,' Isaac says. 'The Old Bailey, but . . .'

'We should,' Joshua replies.

'If we want to get ourselves arrested!' Gus says.

Isaac leans forward and unplugs a phone charger from the wall. 'You've got a missed call,' he says, handing the phone to Joshua. 'Pete.'

Taking the phone, he looks at the screen. 'No message,' he mutters.

'Ring him back,' Gus says. 'We can wait.'

'Supposing it's a trap?' Joshua asks.

The others look at him.

'Then we run like hell,' Gus says with a smile.

Martha

I said nothing to Renard all night.

Can't get used to him having a proper name.

Stephen.

Steve.

Stevie.

He doesn't look like a Stephen now, with a shaved head and white prison garb on, little nicks in his scalp that've been bleeding.

I'm sitting next to him on the concrete floor.

There are five of us in here. I'm the only female.

Their eyes have been on me all night. Made me feel like a piece of meat.

I look at *Steve.*

'What did you do to get in here then?' I ask with a smirk.

The hatred pours from him as he looks at me.

'You have caused one hell of a lot of trouble,' he says.

I hear the whirr of the camera on the wall. I remember that sound, and I know when it's focusing, when it's listening in, and when it's fine-tuning so everyone else can hear and see too.

'I only reacted to what you were doing,' I tell him.

'Running a country?'

'Manipulating a nation.'

'I had an excellent team around me,' he says.

'And a whole load of dodgy documents.'

He turns to me. My God, does he look weird without hair and his posh tailored suit and his hand-stitched bloody shoes.

He looks like . . . I don't know . . . like he could be anyone and have done anything.

'I presume you're referring to the documents Paige had a copy of. The list of crimes and misdemeanours?'

'Yeah. I get why you did it – to keep yourself in power and to control folk and that – but didn't you ever feel bad about it? I mean, you were covering up some shocking stuff. Really horrible. Didn't you ever think they should be punished for that?'

'They were!' he says. 'By living under my say-so, knowing that at any time I could call it in and get them to do or say whatever I wanted. The bigger the crime, the more abhorrent it was, the more harm it could do their careers or their positions and so the better they were required to behave.'

'You really are a horrible man.'

'But am I? Really? I never hurt anyone, never caused any physical pain –'

'Mental. Psychological.'

'– or *any* sort of pain to anyone who didn't deserve it.'

'What about the victims? Or their families?'

He shuffles on the cold concrete, his face creasing in discomfort.

Yeah, be uncomfortable, I think. Suffer.

'They served a purpose. The more vocal they were, the better. It raised the stakes and made the perpetrator even more desperate to hide.'

I hear the camera whirr more.

Does he notice that? I don't think so.

'So why the need to follow everyone?'

'The GPS and the phones? That was genius, wasn't it?'

He smiles. It's unnerving. Unnatural. Weird.

Then he shakes his head and runs his hand over the stubble.

'*She* was genius.'

I open my mouth to ask another question, but he struggles to his feet, stretches his arms up in the air and starts padding around the room. If I didn't know better I'd imagine claws growing instead of toenails, and a pointed red tail dangling down.

Isaac, Joshua, Gus

They walk in silence through crowds starting to grow.

Around them people mumble and frown at screens, shaking their heads and swearing.

'It's a pile of fucking shit, man,' one voice says as they pass a group of men. 'I tell you, I reckon this whole thing is some scam, made up to control us. Anyone he doesn't like, lob them in prison, on death row, or in the Rises.'

Gus glances at Isaac and tries to smile.

'We'll never know the truth. All bloody hushed up by government, like Marilyn Monroe or JFK, and anyone who says differently is some weirdo conspiracy theorist or an enemy of the state. I don't reckon Honeydew did that bomb either, you know? Don't reckon we'll ever know who did though.'

They walk on.

Past people leering over the *National News*. A photo of DeLonzo holding up the bundle of documents, the headline – 'GOTCHA!' – bold across the top.

'The public need to stand up now,' Gus whispers.

Isaac nods, but Joshua ignores them, his face fixed as he ploughs on and on, and as he turns down a narrow street the other two follow. He turns again and leads them to the back of a building. Trucks and rubbish bins around, concrete steps leading to a door with no handle on the outside, and a covered area with industrial-sized waste units.

Gus reads the writing on one. '"Biological waste"?' he says, and he looks at a smaller one. '"Caution: sharp implements".' He turns to Joshua. 'Where the hell have you brought us?'

Joshua puts his fingers to his lips and motions to the camera above the doorway. Then, keeping directly underneath it, he pulls a bin over, clambers up to stand on it and yanks the camera from the wall.

'I did not see that coming,' Gus says.

'This is the back of the hospital,' Isaac says. 'Pete's a doctor, isn't he?'

Joshua nods, then takes his phone from his pocket and presses call. 'We're here,' he says.

'What . . . ?' Isaac starts.

'Just wait.'

Martha

'So how do you reckon this works then?' I ask Renard, following him as he stalks around the cell. 'You reckon the five of us will be kept here in Cell 7 but taken into the execution room one at a time? And they'll do the vote results one at a time? Jeez, I bloody hope they swill the chair down. Someone told me that some prisoners crap themselves. Or wet themselves. Or throw up. Sure someone told me that some guy burst into flames.'

There's sweat on his head; it's glistening. And on his upper lip too. He's pretty bloody pale as well.

'Ever thought what it's like to die?' I ask him. 'Y'know, if it's painful or whatever. I reckon electrocution's got to hurt. I mean, I accidentally got a shock off a dodgy plug once and that stung like hell. Think how many more volts there's going to be. Good job we haven't got hair or it'd frizzle!'

'Shut up,' the PM says.

I have no intention of shutting up.

'When I was in here before, I heard folks scream with the pain. Heard them cry like babies before they went in, begging to be let out.'

He storms up to me.

The camera whirrs.

His face is in mine.

'Shut the fuck up! I should've had you killed ages ago!'

There's fear in his eyes.

'This whole thing is your fault! If you hadn't taken the moral high ground, then my plan – mine and Sofia's –'

'Sofia?' I ask. 'Sofia Nachant who never took me to prison, but dropped me off in the Rises instead.'

Something flashes through his eyes.

'Yeah,' he mutters. 'That Sofia.'

'The time is: midday.'

The PM jumps at the electronic voice. His face falls. 'What's that?'

I put a finger to my lips.

'The current stats for Cell 7 are: in arrest order –'

The whole room holds its breath.

'Tommy Grant –'

Tommy must be the one with his head down. The one trembling.

'– 43% in favour of execution, 57% against.'

The air goes from him like a punctured balloon.

'Trent McIver: 51% in favour, 49% against.'

The guy in the shadows in the corner sobs.

'Amir Djily: 27% in favour, 73% against.

'Stephen Renard –'

The voice stops.

'Why do they do that?' he mutters.

'Drama,' I say to him cheerily. 'Atmosphere. You're today's entertainment, don't you know? Isn't it fun?'

'– 64% in favour of execution, 36% against.'

His head spins around to me. 'That's lower than I thought it would be.'

I look at him and I actually feel sorry for him.

'It's all a fix,' I say. 'Didn't you realise? I thought you controlled all of this. They've already decided if you're going to live or die; the rest is just manipulating the masses. Like you're so good at. People hate you – if that percentage is too low, then more people will vote to make sure you die! When it cuts to Kristina in the studio, she'll say something about *making sure you get what you deserve* and urge folks not to *miss out on this once-in-a-lifetime opportunity.*'

He stares at me.

His face is blank.

'Martha Honeydew: 54% in favour of execution, 46% against.'

I shrug at him.

'Non-committal. I imagine all the votes are going on you. Nobody really cares about me any more. I'm yesterday's news. I might get a by-line, but you're the headliner.'

'I had no –'

'The order and timing of the final stats, with potential execution five minutes later, is as follows: Tommy Grant, 8 p.m., Trent McIver, 8.15 p.m., Amir Djily, 8.30 p.m., Martha Honeydew 8.45 p.m., Stephen Renard 9 p.m.'

I glance at Stephen's terrified face.

'Oh,' I say. 'They've switched us round. Seems you're the finale.'

12.15 p.m. *Death is Justice*

A thudding heartbeat rhythm plays as lights flash over the studio. Kristina trots out from backstage, waving. The audience applaud, some stand. The lights dance over her, then come to a halt as the drumbeat stops.

KRISTINA: Hello, ladies and gentlemen, and welcome to this specially extended, day-long episode of *Death is Justice*. I'm sure you've all been glued to your screens throughout the morning, watching and listening to the incredible conversation between our Miss Honeydew and the errant PM. Oh, I mean, Stephen Renard.

The audience give an *oooh*, and Kristina laughs.

KRISTINA: And I'm sure you all just heard the stats update. I must say, I for one am surprised the PM, sorry the *ex*-PM, isn't scoring higher than that. Or is it that you haven't had a chance to log your vote yet? Don't miss out on this once-in-a-lifetime opportunity to affect the state of our nation and show just how you feel about corruption, lies and our leader being an accessory to murder.

The screen to her side is filled with the live feed from Cell 7, a close-up of Renard's face. Kristina strides to the high desk and sits down, a spare stool waiting across from her.

KRISTINA: But to help you decide how to vote and to give you a full insight into the man, we have a very special guest for you. When he let us down, she stepped in; when he lied to a nation, she told truths; and when he failed on his promises, she promised to deliver. Ladies and gents, viewers at home, it's none other than former aide to ex-PM and now death row occupant Stephen Renard, and now our youngest Prime Minister ever, Sofia Nachant.

The audience whoop and applaud. Lights dance and music blares. Sofia steps out from backstage, straight back, wide smile and a sleek wave. She stands for a moment, then strides to the desk. The two women shake hands and both take their seats.

KRISTINA: Miss Nachant – or should I refer to you as Prime Minister? – it's an absolute thrill to have you here. On behalf of all the *Death is Justice* viewers, let me thank you from the bottom of my heart for coming to allay the fears of the public and help to restore our trust in the leadership of our country.

SOFIA: The pleasure is all mine, Kristina. Thank you for extending the hand of friendship and support and allowing me this opportunity to reach out to the viewers and the voting public. It's been a tumultuous few days, and days that have shaken the public's confidence. It's vital that we reassure them that their futures, their safety and their privacy are paramount to us.

KRISTINA: I believe you've said a key word there – *privacy*. The system implemented by Renard– this, I'm not sure how best to describe it, this *intense* surveillance – has been the cause of much consternation.

SOFIA: That it has, and I think the level of surveillance, whereby it was possible to locate anyone at any time, not only impacted on human rights, but also led people to believe that we, the government, don't respect the privacy of our voters, or trust them. I want to reiterate that this is absolutely not the case.

KRISTINA: One thing I'm wondering though . . . how was this whole system instigated without anyone else's knowledge? You yourself were his aide, his secretary, his right-hand man –

SOFIA: Woman!

KRISTINA (laughing): Of course! But . . . how long had this been going on for, and why didn't anyone else know?

SOFIA: Two very difficult questions, and I hope the public are watching because this is clearly on their minds. What people have to understand is that as well as being a series of office and function rooms, Downing Street is also the Prime Minister's home, and as his, or her, home, there are parts of it that are off-limits even to staff. It was only through chance that I stumbled across this room. Of course, as soon as I did, I started trying to figure out a way to stop it and I approached Stephen directly.

KRISTINA: That was very brave.

SOFIA: Yet necessary. You've all seen over the last few days how manipulative Stephen was and the lengths he was prepared to go to in order to control people. He made it perfectly clear that if I were to do anything that would endanger his system, or his position, then my career would be over. I don't remember his actual words – I think I blocked them from memory – but he informed me that he would spread rumours about me which he said would make me unelectable and unemployable. As a woman, I'm sure you understand how difficult those sorts of accusations are to come back from.

KRISTINA: Impossible.

SOFIA: Immediately I began thinking of ways I could thwart him, and if necessary overthrow him as leader. For the good of the nation. Anyone who treats employees, the public, and indeed women, in such a way really is unfit to be a leader.

KRISTINA: I admire your strength and courage. You could have lost everything.

SOFIA: It was a gamble I had to take. It became apparent to me that the only way would be to show the people, and, with the help of DeLonzo, we managed to rig up the camera that eventually led to Renard's downfall.

KRISTINA: About that. We have a clip here of the camera being installed. I wonder if you could talk us through it.

The screen on the right fills with a grainy image. A face leans back from it, and comes into focus.

KRISTINA: What's happening here?

SOFIA: That's me in the room that housed the computers linked up to the GPS tracking everyone's phones. I'm standing on a chair, sticking the camera to the wall and checking the angle of it to make sure it's pointing towards the bank of screens and the two chairs in front of them.

KRISTINA: We can see those coming into shot now. One large central screen, several smaller ones around it.

SOFIA: That's right, and that's me typing some names into the system so that people watching can see how it works. And there I am heading out of the room.

KRISTINA: I must say, and I hope you don't mind me pointing this out, but you bear a striking resemblance to Martha Honeydew. Don't you think, audience? But slightly older of course.

The audience nod. There's a mumble of agreement.

SOFIA: Considerably older unfortunately! But you're not the first to point it out. They say everyone has a double, don't they? I wouldn't go that far, but it's probably exaggerated here as I'm wearing a hat to disguise myself, so I look much like Honeydew's shaved head.

KRISTINA: It is quite remarkable! But let's get back to Renard.

The screen changes again, the live feed from Cell 7, Renard sitting next to Martha.

KRISTINA: Does he deserve to die?

SOFIA: That's the question every member of society should be asking. Does this man, who manipulated a nation, who covered up murders, including murders of children, for his own gain, who spied on people going innocently about their business, who shot Judge Cicero, who lied to us and covertly set up an operation to blackmail people to hang on to power, does he deserve to die? Does he deserve to *live*?

KRISTINA: What will you be voting?

SOFIA: Kristina, I must stress that my opinion is simply that – one person's opinion – and I strongly believe everyone should look at the facts I've just stated and make up their own mind. If Renard is someone they believe deserves to walk freely among us, then they must vote him innocent. If they believe that someone who hides the crimes of others, who uses blackmail and a gun to protect his own power, who lies to voters for his own gain and thinks his own position more important than justice for parents whose children have been killed, should be held accountable for that, then they must vote him guilty.

KRISTINA: It's refreshing to hear a clear and impartial voice. We thank you for taking the time to join us this evening.

The audience applaud. Kristina stands and walks back to the screen.

KRISTINA: Join us again after this short –

She stops, puts a hand to her ear and frowns at the camera.

KRISTINA: It seems we have some breaking news . . . erm . . . yes, we're heading over live to the Central General Hospital. Gerome? Gerome, can you hear us?

The screen crackles with static, then slowly clears. In a thick winter coat, collar turned up and woolly hat pulled low, Gerome stands on a well-lit street with the sign 'Central General Hospital' in the background.

GEROME: Yes, Kristina, I can. It's hectic here to say the least. We've just received a message that a spokesperson from the hospital is about to issue a statement. Is that . . . ?

He turns to the main entrance of the hospital, where a man in doctor's scrubs – Pete – is walking out. Face serious and unflinching.

GEROME: Yes, here we go, let me pass you over.

The camera follows him as he pushes through the crowd, stopping with other journalists as a circle forms around Pete.

373

PETE: Good afternoon. I'm Peter Caplan, chief surgeon for emergency medicine here at Central General Hospital. It is with deepest regret that I must inform you that, a short while ago, Judge Thomas Cicero died. After his admittance yesterday, he was rushed into surgery to have the bullet removed. The operation was successful and at that stage we believed Cicero would make a full and speedy recovery.

He pauses and looks over the crowd.

PETE: Unfortunately, in the hours that followed he suffered complications, and despite my and my team's every effort he was proclaimed dead a short time ago. While Thomas Cicero leaves no family, he had a great many friends, and we ask you to show respect for them at this difficult time and offer them our sincere sympathies. Thank you.

Pete walks away. The camera refocuses on Gerome as he wipes a tear from his face.

GEROME: What a terrible shock. What is there to say? A staggering giant of a man in his time who fought tirelessly for the underdog and for truth, justice and honour. I am certain he will be remembered with respect and admiration. This tragedy may also affect the votes on death row tonight as

Renard is now guilty of the murder of a former high-court judge. Kristina, it's over to you.

Kristina shakes her head and dabs her eyes.

KRISTINA: A shock for us all there, and as Gerome says, 'a tragedy'. Join us after this short message from our sponsor, when not only will we bring you those all-important stats updates, but we'll also be looking at the life – sadly cut short – of one of our true heroes.

The screen fills with a photo of Cicero in full legal robes. RIP written across the bottom.

Max

The blue of the TV flashes across the darkness of the living room of Martha's flat in Daffodil House.

Flashes on to the bed where Isaac rested.

The chair where Cicero sat to watch Eve die.

On to Max's face as he frowns at the screen.

The fluffy white cloud of Cyber Secure appears and light spills into the room and over the makeshift curtains, still closed to keep daylight and the rest of world from him.

He flicks off the TV and blackness swallows him.

Kristina's muted voice seeps through the walls from neighbouring flats and he flinches from it, sprawling on the floor on his back.

'Cyber Secure.' The voice is just audible. 'We keep your data safe, so your mind is as clear as this sky.'

'Shut the hell up, *Cyber Secure*,' he hisses. 'I can look after my own data.'

His sigh fills the room and he stares up at the ceiling, 'What did that woman say?' he mumbles to himself, and his face creases into a frown. 'Nobody knows anything about Sofia.' He closes his eyes.

'Cyber Secure,' he whispers, and he holds his hands over his ears, filling his head with silence.

He lies there while the muffled voice from next door filters through the walls and then slowly he sits up, blinks away the darkness and drags his laptop over.

'Somebody must know something,' he mutters, and his fingers dance across the keyboard and he frowns at the screen.

Martha

Who would've thought there'd be a day when I'd be chewing the fat with the ex-Prime Minister?

Yet here we are.

'How did you stand seven days of this?' he asks.

I shrug. 'It was different. The cells were different.'

'Of course, I forgot. Warmer, more comfortable, hot running water, television –'

I laugh at him. 'You really haven't a clue, have you? It was nothing like that – that was just how they put it over to folks at home. You want to know what it was like? It was fucking shit. One was freezing cold, one had light blinding you all the time, one had dripping water, in one they me gassed me to make me hallucinate.'

'That's not . . .' His voice trails off.

'Don't play dumb with me. You know exactly what it was like; you sanctioned it.'

He looks at me.

There's something there, behind his eyes, on the tip of his tongue. I can feel it.

He looks away again.

'What?' I ask.

'Sometimes . . .' he says, but he stops. There's the whirr of the camera again. He leans in. 'They're watching, aren't they?'

I nod.

'And listening?' he whispers.

'Always,' I say.

'Sometimes,' he starts again, 'I just . . .' He leans in close to me, cups his hand over his mouth and whispers into my ear, 'I just signed things.'

Now I look at him.

'I didn't –'

'The time is 3 p.m. The current stats for Cell 7 are –'

Damn that voice interrupting. What was he about to tell me?

'– in *execution* order –'

I zone out as everyone else's names are read. Can't remember what their stats were last time and I feel bad for that.

'– Martha Honeydew: 56% in favour of execution, 44% against.'

Mine have gone up.

'Stephen Renard: 67% in favour of execution, 33% against.'

So have his.

'We will update you in: one hour.'

'What were you going to tell me?' I whisper to him.

I watch him. I can see it, something he needs to say, there, right there at the corner of his eye, the tip of his tongue and the edge of his mouth.

'What . . . ?' I start to ask again, but he shakes his head.

'I think you already know,' he replies.

Joshua's house

Standing at the top of the steps, in front of the black front double doors, a hooded figure bends down and tips the oversized plant pot to one side.

Fingers scrabble in the dirt beneath it and pull out a dirty, rusty key.

Standing back up, and hidden in the shadows, he puts the key in the lock and pushes the door open. Two minutes later, three more shadowy figures move slowly across the road, tiptoe into the house and head down into the kitchen.

'You told them I'm dead!' Cicero says, slumping down into a chair.

Joshua pulls the blinds down. 'What else would you have had us do?' he asks.

'I don't know. But how would you suggest I come back to life now?'

'Tell 'em you're Jesus!' Gus says, laughing as he leans against the door frame.

'This is a bloody mess,' Cicero says.

'Thank you,' Joshua replies. 'Thank you, Joshua, for asking your ex to go on live television and lie. Thank you, Isaac and Gus, helping me to escape the hospital and risking getting arrested. Thank you, Pete, for letting us all into your house.'

'It's your house too,' Isaac mutters.

Cicero rubs his hand over his face and exhales loudly. 'Thank you,' he says. 'All of you.' He looks around at each of them in turn. 'What do we do now?'

Nobody says anything.

'You want to stay here? Do nothing? Wait for Martha's stats all over again?'

'We go to the Old Bailey,' Isaac says. 'We get the message out. We get everyone there. And we cause a stink.'

'What good's that gonna do?' Gus asks. 'It hasn't worked before.'

'People weren't this angry before,' Isaac says. 'And now it's not just about Martha. It's about everyone.'

Martha

'Why's no one handcuffed?' I ask everyone in the cell.

They look back at me blankly. Other stuff on their minds than why the guards haven't cuffed them to the wall or whatever.

'I told you,' says the PM. 'They said they didn't have enough, or enough space, to chain us to the walls.'

'There's no need anyway,' one of the prisoners says. 'It's not like we can get out.'

'But the cell doors aren't shut either,' I say.

'Yeah, that's for the man who comes round with the camera – Gerome,' a different voice says. 'They said locking and unlocking the doors all the time was wasting too much screen time and boring the viewers. I heard him saying something about "watching how we integrate" or something.'

'More entertaining to watch us fight each other than sit quietly?' I say.

'Something like that. The doors to the outside are locked though.'

'How long have you been here?' I ask him.

'Seven days,' he says. 'I was here at the beginning. They brought me over from the death row you blew up.'

'I didn't,' I say.

He shrugs.

I follow his voice in the darkness, sit down next to him.

The camera doesn't whirr. Whoever's in charge of it must be holding it on Renard.

'How many more people are there now?' I whisper.

'It's difficult to say,' he replies. 'I don't know. Must be a lot, because when they bring meals round they come with a great big trolley.'

I stand up.

It's dark and gloomy.

Just the tiniest light through the tiniest window and flickering from the light box outside the door.

It's damp and cold.

My feet are numb on the concrete, body trembling, hands stiff.

'Where are you going?' he asks me.

I don't reply.

For a second I stand at the doorway, before I take a step out.

There's no sudden electric shock running through me, no gas in my face or anything whacking down to stop me.

The light above me flashes and hurts my eyes.

I glance left; six light boxes above six doors. Flickering on and off at random.

I glance right; one light box above the corridor leading to the execution room.

I turn to the left, walk to the next door, peer inside, waiting for my eyes to adjust to the darkness, and I can just make out the glint of light in folks' eyes as they stare at me.

'How many of you are in here?' I whisper.

'Ten,' someone says. 'We didn't do anything wrong.'

'I know,' I reply.

'Who are you?' the same voice asks, but I'm moving, at the next cell now.

I peer inside, can make out the bodies on the floor. Some of them look so small.

'There are seven of us in here,' a voice says at my feet. I glance down. A young woman, dark skin and deep eyes. 'That boy over there is only fifteen.'

I shake my head and move on before I pass out or throw up or just get so angry I thump something or scream.

I reach the next cell – nine people. The next – eight. The next – eleven. And how many are having their heads shaved and being deloused right now, ready to come in when everyone's shifted up?

I turn around, staring at the door at the far end.

The door to death.

To heaven.

Or to hell.

I walk towards it, my heart thudding, the lights flickering.

Jesus Christ.

They'll kill me this time for sure.

Keep strong, Martha, that voice in my head says, the one I imagine is Mum, or Mrs B, or Ollie.

How did this happen?

How did society come to this point?

What went wrong?

Slow build, Martha, my head says.

They played into folks' fears.

Under the promise of something good – make the streets safer.

Fear – you don't want your children to be hurt.

Manipulation – vote for keeping your family safe.

Who wouldn't want those things? I think. And still they're doing the same – voting to kill the person they believe caused danger to society.

I tilt my head back, wishing I could see the sky and the stars. I hear the whirr of the camera and I can't help but smile. As I step towards it and peer up, it tilts down to me; it's watching, *everyone's* watching. And listening.

'Kristina,' I whisper to it, 'keep the cameras rolling, and I promise you a show.'

And I wink at her.

On the streets

'There are a lot of people,' Isaac says.

'Loads,' Gus replies.

'Are they people from the Rises?' Joshua asks.

Cicero glances around and shrugs. 'How can I tell?' he asks.

They push through the crowds.

On an oversized screen above them, the view flicks from one cell to another, the latest stats running along the bottom.

They pause, glancing up as Martha appears on the screen, huddled in a corner with the other occupants of her cell. The camera zooms in but their faces are hidden and the sound fuzzes.

'What do you think she's up to?' Joshua asks.

The crowd shifts as people push through, Cicero lifts his head as he steadies himself and catches the eye of someone close by.

'Hey!' the man says. 'You look like Judge Cicero!'

'I am Judge Cicero,' he replies.

'You can't be – you're dead!'

Cicero smirks and looks over himself. 'I feel pretty alive,' he says. 'You don't want to believe all you hear in the news. They were trying to silence me. Silence us all. We need to speak out.'

The man nods. 'It is you, isn't it? I know your face. My mum was killed – this was before Votes for All – you let the guy off, said he was "mentally incapacitated" or something.'

Cicero looks away, steps to the side, but the man grabs his sleeve.

'I went to see him,' he says. 'He was a mess – didn't say anything and couldn't look me in the eye. Week later, he sent me a letter apologising. Said he'd live with that guilt for the rest of his life.'

Cicero looks at him. 'I'm sorry for your loss,' he says. 'But –'

'No, mate, you had it right. Killing them is easier, and cheaper too, but it doesn't make it the best thing to do.'

He lets go and puts his hand out; Cicero shakes it.

'Do something for that girl back in there,' he says. 'Before it's too late.'

'Cicero, look,' Isaac says, pointing to the screen.

Martha's face is close to the camera but the sound is drowned out by voices around them.

'What's she saying?' Cicero asks. 'I can't hear her.'

Next to them a woman is peering into her phone. She turns as she hears Cicero.

'Oh my God!' she says. 'She just looked right into the camera and said something about it'll be a good show.'

Cicero, Isaac and Joshua exchange a look.

'Stay here,' says Cicero. 'There's something I have to do.'

Martha

I spoke with everyone.

Quietly.

Carefully.

They were subdued but agreed. One man especially keen to do his bit.

Folks at home – Kristina and all them – will have seen me moving cell to cell. I'm certain of it.

But they won't have heard me.

Will it work?

I don't know, but it feels better than doing nothing.

We wait.

We all wait.

'The time is 6p.m. The current stats are –'

Everyone holds their breath. Even those not on their last day.

I watch the faces of the men as their fates get closer. If the stats stay around the same, we're all going to fry.

'– Martha Honeydew –'

My turn.

'– 73% in favour of execution, 27% against.'

Not much of a surprise there.

'Stephen Renard: 79% in favour of execution, 21% against.'

Lower than I thought. They're squeezing every last penny out of all those pissed-off voters.

The keys jangle in the door and everyone looks up. Here we go.

6.15 p.m. *Death is Justice*

KRISTINA: Ladies and gentlemen, welcome back after the break to our ongoing, day-long special here on *Death is Justice*!

The audience cheer and whoop.

KRISTINA: It's a special one today, not only because we have five possible executions this evening, but because we have the final episode in the ongoing Honeydew–Paige saga. Even more scandalous, we have the ex-Prime Minister himself, Stephen Renard, being judged by you, the voting public. Yes, power is well and truly in your hands today! You want to see him die? Want to see him fry in that electric chair for allowing the deaths of so many? For illegally setting up a surveillance operation allowing him to spy on your every innocent move? Then it's time to get those fingers dancing across those keys. Before we're updated on those latest stats, let's take you live to death row, with our roving reporter Gerome Sharp. Gerome, how the devil are you this evening?

She turns sideways to watch Gerome on the screen. He stands next to an old wooden door, a microphone in his hand.

GEROME: Kristina, you're joining me at a pivotal and exciting point in the proceedings. I'm here at the door to death row, and I'm just about to enter and speak to all our possible executees, especially our Martha Honeydew, and the one and only Stephen Renard. Believe me, I'm desperate to talk to him and can't wait to see what state he is in. I hope he's begging for mercy and forgiveness. Follow me inside . . .

The key jangles as the guard puts it in the lock. In the studio, Kristina touches her ear and frowns.

Gerome pushes the door open and steps inside.

Martha

'Why don't we overthrow him when he comes through the door and all run out?' someone asks me.

'They'd shoot us, you fucking numbskull,' someone else replies.

'They're not going to shoot us on live TV!'

'Why not? They execute us. What difference does it make?'

I'm not getting into it with them.

I know what I have to do.

We hear the clink of the key as it's pulled out of the lock, and the door creaks open.

Gerome steps inside, walking backwards and slowly with the cameraman following behind. 'The atmosphere along death row has been extraordinarily tense,' he says.

The guard steps in too, but we wait.

My heart's pounding fit to burst out my bloody chest, but I watch him turn the key and lock us all in.

Us prisoners.

The guard with his gun.

Gerome.

And the cameraman.

We move as one, quickly, efficiently and with utter confidence, and we overpower Gerome, and knock the cameraman to the floor.

'Fuck!' someone shouts.

I look up. It was the guard; he's fumbling with the keys. 'Don't hurt me, don't hurt me,' he's pleading, and I can see his legs are actually shaking.

'Stop,' I say to him. 'Please, just stop.' I don't know why he's bloody panicking – he's the one with a gun!

He drops the keys and remembers about the gun, his hand grabbing onto it.

'If you shoot us, you'll be in here in the morning,' I say. 'An eye for an eye, and all that.'

'S . . . self-def . . . defence . . .' he stutters.

I shake my head. 'That argument didn't work for Eve Stanton, did it?' I nod towards the camera above the door. 'And everybody's watching you.'

A muscle in his cheek twitches, his fingers tap at the barrel of the gun.

'What do you want?' he says nervously.

'To talk,' I reply, and I smile.

6.30 p.m. *Death is Justice*

Kristina stands at the screen, her mouth open at the scene unfolding. All the occupants of death row are in the corridor outside the cells, Martha at the head of them, Stephen to her right.

KRISTINA: We will be staying with this unfolding action live here on *Death is Justice*. All commercial breaks are suspended for the time being. Do not go anywhere. What *is* happening? What is the revolutionary Miss Honeydew up to now? Does she have another bomb? What plans does she have for our unfortunate cameraman, the prison guard and our heroic Gerome Sharp? Gerome, if you can hear me, then do please keep us informed with what's happening.

GEROME (whispering): Kristina, I'm not sure if you can see me right now. Charlie, our cameraman, has stayed at the front of the action. I've moved around the side and further down the corridor. It seems Honeydew has provoked a reaction from the other inmates. I'm not able to catch what she's saying at this precise moment, but –

KRISTINA: For the viewers' benefit, Gerome, can you move closer to her? We need to hear and see what's going on?

GEROME (shakily): I . . . I'm not . . .

KRISTINA: Viewers, the bravery of our reporters in such situations never fails to inspire me. Gerome, this is a once-in-a-lifetime opportunity for you to be involved in something that will go down in history. Your name –

MARTHA: Gerome, give me your microphone. I want to speak with Kristina.

The camera swings around, focusing through the crowd and down to Gerome, standing at the back, huddled in a doorway. It follows him as he scurries forward, pulls his headset off and hands it to Martha.

Martha

'Kristina? Can you hear me?'

'I sure can! It's a delight to speak to you again. Long time, no see.'

Is she fucking insane? Chit-chat when I've got an hour to live?

'What about the viewers? The folks at home. Can they hear me?'

'You are live on *Death is Justice*. The studio audience can see and hear you, and the people at home too. It's also being fed to our usual media channels, allowing everyone to follow along on their handheld devices.'

'How do I know I can trust you?'

There's a pause.

'Gerome has a screen that can link up. You can see what we're seeing.'

'Gerome,' I say. The snivelling wreck of a man's sitting on the floor in the corner, where the rats piss. I won't tell him that. 'Sort out the screen to show me what's on TV. Do it now.' He doesn't hesitate. Probably scared shitless that I'm going to blow him up or shoot him or something. He's swallowed the hype about me.

'OK, Kristina, I see it now. No tricks, right, and I promise you a show that will go down in history and be the making of your career. People will be talking about this for a long time. Do we have a deal?'

'We sure do,' she replies, and I wonder if she's got her fingers crossed behind her back.

'Come with me,' I say to the cameraman, and he follows.

I've got them all in the order I want to speak to them.

I hope I've remembered their details.

Hope I can hold it together.

And that it works.

Failing that, I reckon we shoot our way out of here and take our chances.

Because if this doesn't work, then I'm done with diplomacy.

I walk into the first cell.

'Kristina, this is Cell 1. There are ten people in here. Four women and six men. That makes ten, yeah?' I look into the camera, trying to imagine I'm actually talking to the people in the audience. 'This is Chloe; she's seventeen. You know what she did? She held a banner. It said "One Person, One Vote". Seems that was "threatening the safety and security of our nation". You know what the other folk in here did? Most of them were in a demo. A peaceful demo. They were sitting on the floor. Security guards came along, under instructions from the government, hit them, beat them up, dragged them off. Look at them.'

I stroll around, getting the camera guy to focus on each of the faces in turn. Then I walk out and into Cell 2.

'Cell 2. Eight people. Y'know how many folk in here have killed someone?'

'I don't, Martha. That's a good question,' she says in my ear.

'One,' I reply. 'You know what he did? You reckon he stabbed someone? Shot them in the head? Threw them off a cliff? No.'

I walk over to the guy – can't remember his name, there's so many of them – and I sit down next to him. He hasn't stopped crying since I met him, little hiccuping sobs. He's a mess, shaking and sniffing.

'Can you tell the viewers at home what happened to you?' I say to him.

The camera zooms in. He lifts his head. His face is blotchy, his eyes red raw.

'A girl jumped in front of my train,' he whispers. 'I couldn't do anything . . . I couldn't . . . couldn't . . .' He ugly cries now, snot and tears all over his face. Lord knows how he's going to make it through the next five bloody days if this shit carries on.

'Kristina,' I say in a low voice, 'I know your viewers are sensible folk. Gentle, kind and caring folk. Intelligent too. I know they understand that this system is wrong, and I know they want to help change it for the better.'

I'm watching the live feed on the screen as well. The camera focuses on faces in the audience, but nobody says anything. There's not the applause and cheers I wanted. Nobody's standing.

It moves to Kristina.

I stand back up, edge out of the cell and into the corridor.

'That was only a snippet of what's going on in here. This, Kristina, this insider information is such a coup for your programme. Let me tell you some more. There are fifty people in here; four of them are teenagers. This could so easily be one of your viewers, one of the voters. Kristina, this could be you.'

I stop there.

Everything falls quiet.

I go into the next cell.

'Seven people in here. Folk who did nothing more than lift a banner, question an authority figure or just be in the wrong place at the wrong time. There's a teacher, a shop assistant, a plumber, a banker, a cleaner, a vet, a full-time mum. These aren't terrorists. They're not dangerous people.'

The cameraman swoops around, zooming in on each individual's face.

'That's my wife!' the voice comes from the screen. 'Oh my God, that's my wife! She only went out for milk. She's been missing for three days. She only went –'

'People like you and me.'

'That man teaches our son!' says another voice.

'Go into the other cells,' I tell the cameraman. 'Speak to them all. Name. Occupation. Get them to talk about their families.'

You know what you're doing, Martha? That voice in my head says. *Manipulating everyone for your benefit.*

Not mine, I tell it. Everyone's.

'The time is 7 p.m. The current stats are –'

Oh Jesus. My stomach flips.

Seven o'clock. One hour till the first of us is in the execution room.

How long to stop this fucking circus?

'– Tommy Grant –'

I shut it out. Have to. Close my eyes.

'Martha Honeydew –'

I jump at the sound of my own name.

'– 78% in favour of execution, 22% against.'

Inevitable.

'Stephen Renard –'

He steps out of the cell and looks at me.

'– 80% in favour of execution, 20% against.'

Slow but sure. Still fishing for more votes, more money.

'We will update you in: 50 minutes.'

He's trembling. I'm surprised he's still upright.

The public know the truth, and they still want him dead.

7.20 p.m. *Death is Justice*

The studio is quiet. Kristina stands next to the screen, straight back, perfect hair and make-up. On the screen a man in his twenties can be seen crouched on the floor, dark skin, stubble on his face, tears in his eyes.

MAN: I went to the demo, but all I did was sit there. I wasn't threatening any safety or security. I just wanted my voice heard. I thought that was a basic human right in this country – freedom of speech. Then suddenly I'm a criminal. My wife doesn't know where I am. My kids . . . oh God, my kids are going to get the living hell taken out of them at school. Even if they don't kill me, I'll lose my job. How am I going to feed my family then? We'll end up homeless, then we'll be put in the Rises. Is that what they want for us? Is this all to segregate us? If we don't die, we'll be cast out anyway.

The camera starts to pan away, but the man grabs it.

MAN: Hey, tell my family I love them. Tricia, I miss you, darling, and I'm sorry. I'm so sorry. And Billie, Ella, work hard at school, don't give your mum any trouble. I love you.

Tears spring in his eyes. The camera moves to the side. Another face fills the screen. Another man, blond stubble, a tired swagger to his walk. He sits down in front of the cameraman and looks into the lens, his face sullen yet his eyes sincere.

Kristina staggers backwards. Her face falls.

SECOND MAN: Kristina? Can you hear me?

Kristina stands up, aghast.

CAMERAMAN (off-screen): She can hear you. If I turn this up, you can hear her too.

SECOND MAN: Kristina?

KRISTINA: Mark? What? What are you doing there?

MARK: Kristina, I love you.

KRISTINA: Mark, what's going on? This is . . . Why are you . . . what did . . . ?

MARK: I didn't do anything. This kid was . . . was running up the stairs at the train station . . . heading straight for me, and some guy was shouting after him. I thought the kid must've done something, so . . . so I . . . I went to grab him . . . but . . .

Tears fall down his cheeks and his face creases.

MARK: I bumped into him . . . and he . . . fell down. All the
way down, and he . . . he broke his neck.

KRISTINA: You killed him?

MARK (shaking his head): It was an accident. I didn't . . .
didn't . . .

His voice fades away. Kristina stands dumbfounded. The
audience are silent. Air hangs stagnant.

MARK (quietly): Kristina? If I get out, will you . . . will you
marry me?

In the audience hands go over mouths, breath is sucked in,
eyes stare from Mark, on the screen, to Kristina, right there
in front of them.

MARK: I love you. I want to spend the rest of my life with
you. You're my world, my . . . Kristina . . . you're
everything to me. Please. I love you.

A gentle 'ahh' goes over the audience.

KRISTINA: Mark . . . I . . . I can't do that.

MARK: Wha— ? Kristina? Why? You said . . . just the other

day you said about . . . about us being together . . .
What's changed?

KRISTINA: You've *killed* someone. If you're not executed,
you'll lose everything. You won't have a job, a
career, you'll lose your house.

MARK: I could live with you.

KRISTINA: But what would people think?

MARK: What does that matter? You said you love me.

KRISTINA: I did. But . . . but you're not the man I thought
you were.

Muttering spreads through the audience, slowly getting louder.

MARK: I'm still me! I feel terrible about that kid, but I told
you, it was an accident.

KRISTINA: Cameraman, move on to someone else. This is
not a discussion for –

Mark lurches towards the camera, the feed wobbles, noises
of banging, close-ups of the floor, the wall, the ceiling, the
cameraman sprawled on the floor, then back to Mark's face,
shakier than before.

MARK: This could be the last time we get to speak. Kristina, it was an accident. I told you –

KRISTINA (shouting): Didn't you stop to think how this would affect *my* career? If I marry you, who's going to employ me? I'll be 'wife of child killer'! You moron! You selfish moron!

AUDIENCE MEMBER: Bitch!

Kristina swings around to the audience. Mouth open, aghast. She makes a cutting gesture to the camera, but behind her the feed still shows Mark, looking into the camera, his eyes full of tears. Other people move into shot, trying to talk to loved ones.

AUDIENCE MEMBER: You manipulative, selfish bitch!

Kristina swishes her hair back, smiles and takes a deep breath.

KRISTINA: Ladies and gentlemen, I must apologise for the interruption.

AUDIENCE MEMBER: You heartless fucking cow!

KRISTINA: Let's get back to business and look at our accused on death row.

Audience members stand, shout and jeer. A plastic bottle explodes on to the stage, dousing Kristina's outfit in brown soda. She ducks back as a carton of popcorn hits her.

AUDIENCE MEMBER: I don't want to be part of this! It's a sham. You fucking heartless bitch. All you care about is yourself, and money, and status. You loved him when he was important, didn't you?

KRISTINA: I . . . I . . . Please keep calm!

A packet of fries scatters near her feet, a burger hits her legs, sauce splats on the white material.

KRISTINA: No! Please, listen, it's not like that!

Another soda bottle hits her in the head. She stumbles backwards, trips on her high heels, falls and bangs her head on the desk. The audience shout and jeer. People in black rush from backstage. Two of them grab Kristina and pull her away.

Someone else strides out from backstage. A microphone in his hand, he stands at the edge of the stage, then he puts his hands up and watches over the audience.

JOSHUA: Ladies and gentlemen, please, can we have some calm?

Slowly the anger dies down. One audience member starts to clap. Then another. And another, until the entire audience are on their feet applauding Joshua.

JOSHUA (shouting): I know you weren't expecting me. I had to break in!

A few people start shushing the rest.

JOSHUA: When I was a presenter I tried to do the right thing, but I failed.

Gradually the rest of them fall quiet and sit back down.

JOSHUA: I don't want Martha Honeydew to be executed. I don't want Stephen Renard to be executed. I don't want anyone to be executed. But I do want justice. I do want fairness. I do want you to listen to the person who started all this and understand, if not agree with, her point of view.

Next to him, the screen changes again. Martha's face stares out.

Martha

Jesus Christ, this is fucking scary.

How many days?

And it's all come to this.

Joshua back on *Death is Justice*.

Again.

Kristina's poor guy's a wreck!

Cameraman's back up again. Bless him.

He's doing some sort of hand gesture to me.

'Martha?' Oh, it's so good to hear Joshua's voice speaking to me. I could almost melt at the relief. 'Martha, can you hear me?'

Oh Jesus, I'm crying. I wipe my face quickly. I'm nodding at the screen.

'I can hear you. It's so good to hear you. I'm so –'

'Martha, we don't have a lot of time. You, my darling, potentially don't have a lot of time. Please, what do you have to say?'

I take a deep breath, nod my head, prep myself.

Here we go.

'I didn't . . .'

Shit, I'm shaking.

Pull yourself together.

'I didn't blow up death row. I wanted to. But I didn't. I was framed so they could get rid of me and shut me up and stop me talking to you all because they thought I, little me, little orphan girl from the Rises, was dangerous.

'All I want, all I've *ever* wanted, is justice and fairness for all. Not only for those who can afford it, and not only for those with power and influence – but for everyone.

'The Rises 7 is some ridiculous tag the media perpetuated to demonise us. That's me, sixteen years old, no mum, no dad, manipulated into a corner by grown-ups who should've known better; that's Isaac, who did shoot someone, but only because that person was threatening me; that's Cicero, who's a judge for God's sake, who knows the law and right and wrong, and has fought for justice more than anyone; that's Gus, who was manipulated for years by government, threatened constantly with being jailed; that's Joshua who's standing in front of you now, blackmailed because he's gay – I ask you, what century are we living in? That's Max, who's fifteen years old! *Fifteen!* Who's never lifted a finger to hurt anyone, who's this nerdy, geeky kid who just happens to be good with computers. And that's Eve.'

There's a lump in my throat the size of a bloody tennis ball.

'Eve,' I splutter.

'Eve.' My voice cracks, but I carry on. 'The most gentle, kindest, most sincere, most genuine person I ever met. Who did kill someone, whose husband loved her and their son so much he gave his life for them to be together. Yet they took that gift away and killed her.

'They killed her. Just like they killed Mrs B's son, knowing he was innocent. How many more?'

I pause, swallow hard, suck in a deep breath.

'The time is 7.50 p.m. The current stats are –'

Damn that fucking voice.

Shit, 7.50? That means they should be coming through for Tommy. Taking him through to the execution room.

'This is not justice!' I shout over the voice.

'This is not democracy!' As loud as I can.

'This is not right.

'And you all know it isn't.

'It's time to stand up, to take action, to fight for what you believe, for human rights, for *your* rights. For your life, and for your children's.

'And I'm not just speaking to those of you in the studio.

'I'm speaking to everyone.

'The guards holding us in here.

'The men and women tracking the votes.

'The technicians readying that machine.

'The guard about to come in here and take Tommy through to the execution room.

'Ask yourselves if what you're doing is right, all of you! If you can sleep at night, knowing not just what you've done, but what you've allowed to happen *in your name*, because while you are a member of this society, this community, while you are allowing this murder of innocent people to take place, and by innocent I mean those unable to defend themselves, then you are just as culpable as the twat who signed off on this.

'Act now, or you are guilty.

'"I was only doing my job" is not a defence.

'It's an excuse.'

I stare into the camera.

410

Has it worked?

What more can I do?

There's no guard here for Tommy.

'We're going to walk out of here now,' I say, and I'm struggling to keep the panic out of my voice. 'All of us. I'm going to bring everyone out. And you, all of you out there, are going to help us, because you are not going to stand by and allow them to shoot us or to re-arrest us.

'We are in this together.'

Folk come out of the cells.

With our heads shaved and the white prison garb on we look like prisoners of war. Maybe we are.

'Come on,' I say to them.

'Are we safe?' I ask Joshua.

'Yes,' I hear him reply. 'And someone is waiting for you.'

8 p.m. *Death is Justice*

The lights are up. Some of the audience are walking out. The air bristles with excitement.

JOSHUA: Please take your time if you're leaving, ladies and gentlemen. Be safe. For those of you staying here, we're keeping you up to date and following live updates, making sure Martha and the others find their way to safety.

He smiles and turns to the screen, where the cameraman is now standing at the doorway to death row as people flood out.

JOSHUA: It is my utmost privilege to be with you on such a momentous occasion. I can let you know, for anyone concerned, that Kristina is receiving medical attention. It's feared she may have a minor concussion.

He looks back to the screen again, the camera now focusing beyond the crowds onto a small group of people walking out of the shadows.

412

JOSHUA: And you can see there, ladies and gentlemen, as the death row occupants pour out of the building there is a small group of people walking to greet them at the exit. I can see Gus Evans, Isaac Paige, Judge Cicero . . .

The cameraman turns. Gerome comes into view, pulling his jacket around himself, shoving an earpiece in.

GEROME: Joshua? It's Gerome. What a treat to be involved with this! You certainly end up with the scoops, don't you?

JOSHUA (sighing): How good to see you there, Gerome.

GEROME: Well, it's kind of scary. All these murderers –

One of the people leaving death row lands a punch across his face and he falls to the ground.

JOSHUA: Well, that was short-lived! So, cameraman, Charlie, get that man there on your left, coming up the side now. Isaac Paige, see him?

The camera turns, focusing on Isaac as he tries to run towards the door, but it slams shut before he gets there. He pulls on the handle but it won't open.

413

ISAAC: Where's Martha?

The camera watches his face as he stares around, searching for her. Then it moves to Cicero, just as confused as Isaac.

JOSHUA: Did she already come out? Control, can we look back over the video footage?

The screen splits in two. One side with the live feed, the other with recording from moments ago.

ISAAC: Do you see her? Joshua, do you see her?

JOSHUA (quietly): No, I . . . I . . . don't.

Martha

'You fucking arse. What did you do that for?' I'm standing next to the hatch over the River Fleet. 'Why the crapping fuck would you lock us in here and throw the key in the river?'

'I can't go out there,' he says to me.

'Well, I bloody well could've, you . . . you . . . wanker!'

His arms waft around like he's trying to put a fire out or something.

'Why do you swear so much?' he says. 'You're a young lady. You shouldn't swear so much.'

'What the fucking Jesus has me being a young lady got to do with it? Maybe, just *maybe*, the swearing is something to do with you being an utter cock! How the hell are we going to get out now?'

'I've told you, I can't go out there.'

'And I've told you I bloody could've!'

He shrugs. 'Too late.'

I'm walking up and down the row. Up and down, up and down. Exasperated. What the . . .

'You could've let me go. Stayed in here by yourself.'

He shakes his head.

I slump down on the floor.

He sits opposite me.

'I need your help.'

Then he slides a gun across the floor.

'Where did you get this?' I ask.

'I stole it from the guard.'

He stares right at me, and I stare back.

'I need you to kill me.'

8.30 p.m. *Death is Justice*

The lights dip slightly.

JOSHUA: Isaac, we found her. The camera's trained on her, sound coming up now.

The audience who are left all sit back down. Joshua collapses on to the stool.

On the screen, Martha picks up the gun.

JOSHUA: Dear mother of God, don't do it.

Martha

'Go on, kill me,' he says.

It's cold in my hand. Heavy. Like Jackson's gun was.

'Why?' I ask him.

He's slumped on the floor.

'How can I walk out of here?' he says. 'I've lost everything. My career, respect, honour. My home. My friends. I have nothing left to live for.'

I don't know what to say to him. My finger touches the trigger. 'But why should *I* shoot you?'

'Because you're brave and I'm a coward. People will love you for it – saving them from someone like me. Everything in my life was tied to politics. In my job, my career. Nobody will want anything to do with me now. They'll hate me.'

'You want to die?' I say to him, and I'm waving the gun around without thinking about what I'm doing. 'I've just done all this!' I'm shouting now. 'All this to get folks out of here, that . . . that speech to the TV, fighting for all the people on this stupid, ridiculous death row, and you're tossing it back in my face?' I storm up to him. 'I've saved you from dying in the electric chair and you throw it all back at me?'

He's shaking at my feet. 'No, it's not like that. You can finish it.'

'You utter, utter tosser.'

'You'll be a hero,' he whispers.

God, I want to hit him. Swipe him round the bloody head with this gun.

'A hero?' I shout. 'Killing you wouldn't make me a hero! All it would do is make people think you were right all along – that I am a murderer! You weak, selfish man! Do you know how many lives you ruined? How many innocent people you've had put in here who were killed, leaving their families to pick up the pieces? Or innocent people who were let out but never lost the stigma of being accused? Do you, hey?'

I bend down, leering and shouting in his face.

I

am

so

fucking

angry.

'Yes, exactly. And that's why I need you to kill me. I know you want to.'

'How dare you . . . how *dare* you ask me to do that, you coward!'

'I deserve to die,' he whispers.

'Deserve? Deserve . . . what is that? Deserve to die, deserve to live, deserve to suffer. Who decides that, hey? You? What about victims? And their families? What do they deserve? You know what I think? They deserve justice! And not your sort. *Real* justice.'

'Yes!' he hisses at me, looking up, and his eyes are full of tears and fear. 'Precisely. That's why you need to kill me. You need to serve justice. I let it happen, Martha. I let them all use me. I wanted to be stronger, but I couldn't, don't you see? Not if I wanted to stay in power. I had to play the game! I knew Jackson Paige had killed your mother, I knew Lydia Barkova's son was innocent, knew about all the other innocent people too. I knew Eve Stanton's husband was innocent. I even know who killed Lydia Barkova. Do you? Or do you want me to tell you?'

Shit.

Shit.

I'm shaking.

No, come on, Martha, hold it together.

I don't want him to talk about my mum.

Or Mrs B.

Or Ollie.

Or Eve.

It's too much.

Too painful.

'Patty Paige organised it,' he says. 'She paid someone to kill Barkova. She made a hash of it though, didn't she? An utter cock-up. Why have it done where the cameras can see it happen?'

Fuck you, I think, and I swipe him across the head with the gun and he falls to the ground.

'I hate you,' I say. 'You are *evil*.'

He wipes the back of his hand across his mouth.

Blood.

And he laughs.

'I thought I was too. But I was outdone. I got my own back on Patty though. She thought she was in complete control of the bombing at death row.' He laughs and I could hit him again. 'It was a simple way of getting rid of her and framing you and your little gang.'

'The bombing of death row was you?' I hiss.

'Not exactly. I didn't *personally* do it, but I manipulated the situation. So I suppose so. Yes.'

'You nearly killed Isaac and you blamed it on me!' I can feel the blood pounding in my head.

'Yes. Nearly. It was a joint effort though. I can't take all the credit.'

'What?' I say. 'Joint effort with Patty? But you just said –'

'Not Patty!' he says, and he laughs at me. 'Not Patty!' Proper side-splitting belly laugh.

He dabs the tears at his eyes. Jesus, I hate this man.

'You know the saying? *Behind every great man . . .*'

God, I want to pull this trigger.

His laughing tails off as he watches me. 'You want to kill me now, don't you?' he hisses. 'I know you do. I had photos of your mother from when Jackson ran her down, you know – she was a mess. You should've seen her face. Oh, you did!'

'Shut up!' I shout at him, and I push the barrel of the gun on his temple.

'You know what the last words Ollie Barkova heard were?' He's grinning at me. My hand's sweating. My finger's trembling on the trigger. 'I had a guard say to him that he had a message from you.' He's laughing, shaking his head. 'It was genius! And that was me! He'd been asking people to tell you that he didn't do it. Then, just before they flicked that switch, the guard whispered in his ear.' He laughs again. I so want to pull this trigger. 'He said: "Martha says she hates you and she'll be glad when you're dead."'

He's laughing out loud, his whole body rocking with it.

How could he?

How fucking could he?

I'm shaking now, I'm so angry.

I can feel the metal of the trigger on my finger.

'It was an absolute gem! The look on his face in that split second! Oh my God, that was funny.'

I could stop this so easily.

'That's not true,' I say.

'It's absolutely true, I promise you. We all had such a laugh afterwards. Sofia was wetting herself.'

'Sofia?'

'Yes. Sofia Nachant. Genius woman. Clearly.'

'I don't believe you. Sofia's not like that.'

'He died thinking you hated him!'

My finger eases off the trigger.

But then my hand grips tighter.

I blink through the tears.

Ollie.

Ollie.

I lift the gun, I stare down the sights, and I pull the trigger.

The Old Bailey

Crowds across the pavements and road stop and stare at the screen.

But the image is gone.

And the screen hisses with static.

'She didn't . . .' Gus says. 'Did she . . . shoot him?'

'We have to get in there,' Isaac mutters.

'How?' Cicero asks.

'What's that?' Gus points through the crowd, to where a black car with flashing lights is making its way through.

'Follow it,' Isaac says.

9 p.m. *Death is Justice*

In the half-empty studio, Joshua sits on the stool, watching the screen. The remaining audience members are silent. Joshua pulls off his jacket, tosses it on the floor and rolls up his sleeves.

The screen is still split in two. But now feed from outside the Old Bailey is on the left, and on the right, where the feed from death row was, is static.

JOSHUA: Ladies and gentlemen, I'm afraid we've lost connection. I'm not sure what's happened. Please bear with us.

Martha

I bang on the door, pound and pound.

There's glass at my feet from the camera I shot out.

So angry. So fucking angry.

Never shot a gun before, wish I still hadn't, but, God, did he make me livid.

'Let me out!' I shout. I'm scared. Scared myself. Didn't think I could do that. He knew how to push me and make me do something.

The gun's still in my hand; I hate it.

I'm scared I can't control what I might do.

'There are still plenty of bullets left, Martha,' he says. 'That was a clever thing you did, because now they can't watch us in this cell. It's just me and you.'

I chuck the gun across the floor. Daren't have it in my hands.

I pound on the door again. 'Let me out!' No one's coming. I need to get out of here. Have to.

Think, Martha, think.

I could jump through the hatch and into the Fleet, but I can't swim well. I'd drown. I could run through to the execution room, try and climb over the stalls, jump across, but if I fall, I'll die.

Then what?

'I never thought it would come to this.' His voice is cold and quiet. 'I want to be brave enough, but I'm not sure I am.'

I turn around.

Now he's picking up the gun.

'I lost.'

His hand tightens on the grip.

I'm shaking, crying.

What can I do? Say? I can't move.

'Beaten by a very clever woman.'

'I didn't beat you,' I whisper. 'I beat the system.'

He laughs so loud it echoes off the walls. And he shakes his head, lifting the gun higher.

'Why is that funny?' Maybe if I can keep him talking, keep him busy, thinking.

'Because you really think that!' he says. 'You really don't see what's happened here.'

I frown at him. 'Explain it to me.'

He shakes his head. 'Ignorance is bliss, Martha Honeydew.'

He lifts the gun.

'No, no, no,' I say, 'please, no, please.'

He smiles at me.

I hear the bang.

The Old Bailey

They stop in their tracks.

The bang echoes on the other side of the door.

'Get this door open!' Cicero shouts at Sofia. 'Or get someone to knock it down! Come on. Now!'

He turns and pounds on the door. 'Martha! Martha! Can you hear me?'

He pauses; there's no reply.

Isaac stands behind him in silence.

'Martha!' Cicero shouts. 'Please, Martha!'

Still nothing.

'Stop, Cicero,' Isaac whispers. 'It's no good. She's . . . We should face it . . .'

Cicero shakes his head. 'Don't you dare give up. Maybe it's soundproofed,' he says. 'Maybe she can't hear me.'

'She's dead, Cicero,' Isaac says. 'I know she is. He's killed her. All this, and the whole thing was pointless. You heard the bang.' He pushes him away. 'I can't stay here.'

9.20 p.m. *Death is Justice*

The audience stare at the screen, now completely filled with the feed from the Old Bailey, wobbly as the camera follows Gerome, his eye swollen from the thump he received.

Suddenly it turns, someone's stumbling towards them. Gerome thrusts the microphone out.

GEROME: Isaac! Tell us what's happening.

Isaac shakes his head and carries on. The camera watches him until he disappears from view, then turns back to Gerome.

GEROME: Ahead of me you can see Cicero and Gus have now been joined by Max Stanton. This must be astonishingly painful for him; only two days ago his mother was killed in that very room at the end of the corridor.

JOSHUA (in the studio): Shut up, Gerome. We just want to know if Martha's alive. If you don't do your job properly and without exaggeration, I'm going to cut you off.

GEROME: The language of television *is* exaggeration, Joshua. And thank you for asking if I'm OK, by the way. I'm sure the viewers are relieved to know I've survived my brush with death.

JOSHUA: You were thumped – that's all.

GEROME (ignoring him): You can see our new Prime Minister – Sofia Nachant – has come to the rescue, doing as she promised and fighting for the good of those in need. She herself ordered the breaking-down of the door and –

Still trying to push through to the front, and with the camera following close behind, he flinches at the sound of the door being pummelled. Max turns to him.

MAX: Get out of here!

He shoves him in the chest and Gerome falls to the floor.

GEROME (from the ground): Tensions running high today. Don't say this reporter doesn't put his life on the line to bring you all the latest news!

In the studio Joshua stands next to the screen, oblivious to the audience, not saying a word. He watches the camera push through the doorway and swoop around the room. The sound crackles and the screen flickers with static.

CICERO (broken up): . . . dead . . . He shot . . .

MAX: Martha! Martha!

GEROME: Can see . . . over . . . blood covering . . .

GUS: No . . . Martha . . . 's . . . dead.

Joshua throws a hand over his mouth. Suddenly a face appears large through the static and stares into the camera. Cicero. Tears down his face. His moustache trembling. Shaking his head. He's grabbing the camera and trying to pull it forward but it's lurching around the room.

CICERO: . . . dead . . . not Martha . . . shot . . . he shot . . . Stephen, he . . .

The screen flickers, clears.

CICERO: You hear . . . Joshua? Joshua, can you hear me?

JOSHUA: Yes, yes! I can now! We're all listening.

CICERO: I said . . . She's not dead. It's not Martha who was shot. He shot himself. Renard, he killed himself. Martha's alive!

The audience gasp. Cicero disappears as the camera pans around the room again, a hiss of static clearing as it pauses on

Renard slumped against the wall, the gun resting in his flaccid hand. The picture spins around further, searching through the darkness, until finally it pauses on Martha.

Shivering, crying, with Cicero's arms around her as he helps her up and supports her past the camera and out of the cell.

Martha

I thought he'd shot me.

I didn't dare move.

It was like Cell 7 all over again.

Waiting to realise I'm alive.

They say the person in front of the gun doesn't hear its bang.

That he died before the sound reached his brain is a strange thought.

The smallest shaft of light ekes through the slit in the wall and falls on to him. It's sad. I never wanted him dead.

I just wanted change.

What a sad world when death is more acceptable than losing status.

I was aware of the door opening, of arms going round me and raising me.

I wish they were Isaac's, but I get why they're not.

I know where he'll be.

And I'll meet him there.

9.40 p.m. *Death is Justice*

Joshua signals a 'cut' sign to the technicians, and the massive screen to his left goes blank. No live feed. No eye logo. He lifts the microphone to his mouth and walks towards the audience.

JOSHUA: I should say something very television. I should thank you for voting, or remind you to tune in tomorrow. I should thank our sponsor or tell you that we've had record numbers of viewers or that we are cutting-edge, world leaders, that we provide once-in-a-lifetime opportunities. How many times have you heard that? But I won't. Not this time. With no help from us, Martha Honeydew is alive. With little help from us, the death row system has fallen. With a little more help from you, we can continue the fight to bring back courts, to banish injustice and to do away with corruption. Shame on us that it took a teenage girl to not only see the state of things, but to stand up and do something about it. Apathy allowed this to happen. Apathy and fear. I hope Martha Honeydew can forgive us for how we failed her. I hope we can support her while she rebuilds her life. And I hope that together we can find ourselves a fairer, safer and more just society.

A solitary spotlight focuses on him.
He stands in the pool of light, staring out over the audience.
Then he drops the microphone and walks out.
The studio goes dark.

Martha

They told me to sit and rest.

Sleep and all that.

Max appeared and hugged me, and it was so good to see him again. He told me he's been busy with something and that he'll share it with me when he's ready.

Everyone told me to wait and that Isaac would come back when he was ready.

But I didn't want to do that.

I had the quickest shower of my life, put clean clothes on, warm ones, and threw some food down my face.

And then I went out.

Now?

Now I'm walking between two fields by the light of the moon. It's been a shit couple of weeks. The very shittiest, the hardest. But you know what? In some ways, the best. My feet scuff on the dried mud, my hands brush over the long grass at my sides, and in front of me Bracken Woods looms.

The darkness swallows me as I enter it, the branches folding around me and welcoming me back.

It's been a long time, I want to tell it, and I hope it feels it in my smile.

I'm excited.

I'm happy.

Ahead of me I see the flicker of a campfire, and as I follow the path towards it, the undergrowth thins and there I am in our clearing.

There's the canopy we made, there's the shelter we lay under, there's the log we sat on.

And there you are.

Isaac.

You stand up and you walk to me.

Tears on your face and on mine.

We smile.

We laugh.

We cry.

You unclip the necklace, loop the solved puzzle ring off and place it in my hand.

Above us, the clouds pass on the wind and the sky clears.

We look up.

'Our sky, Isaac,' I say. 'And our stars. And now we can share them.'

TWENTY-FOUR DAYS LATER

Martha

We've lost a lot of people: friends, relatives, loved ones, but we still have each other.

Tomorrow is a new year.

I hope it'll be a good one.

We're all in Eve's house, which is fast becoming Cicero and Max's house. She had, after all, said in her will that if anything happened to her, she'd like Cicero to look after him. They share their loss of her. Some days the pain seems to crucify them and neither speaks, other days I see lightness in their eyes. Time won't heal – it's a lie that it will – but time will make it easier to manage.

I know this.

I still hurt from Mum, from Ollie, from Mrs B.

Joshua's here with Pete. He doesn't talk about it much, and I don't interfere with whatever's going on with them. I don't think things are perfect, but when are they for anyone?

We all went to Patty's funeral. She was a prime bitch, but . . . it felt like the right thing to do.

We waited to hear news of Hart, but he seems to have disappeared off the face of the earth. I would've liked to have seen him brought to justice, but this is the next-best thing.

DeLonzo held me to the deal we made. He interviewed me, wrote an article, and it was front page. I was surprised at how fair it was, and until I became 'yesterday's news' folks smiled and shook my hand. Now I'm fading into the background but I'm glad of that.

Sofia? I don't see her. I suppose she's busy with all her Prime-Ministering. I do wonder about her. I can fit everything else in my head, but she's like a jigsaw where someone's replaced a load of pieces with ones from a different puzzle and it doesn't fit, no matter how hard I try.

When I ask the others about her, they just shrug.

Apart from Max.

Max, I reckon, would make the world's best private investigator. When I went in his room the other day he was up to something. Loads of stuff about Cyber Secure, some Companies House information saying someone called Antonia Paige owned the whole thing. On his bed were photos of Sofia.

'You got a crush on her?' I asked him.

He laughed. 'If only it was that simple.'

I asked him to tell me, but he shrugged. 'Remember what I said the day you were released?' he asked. 'I'll share it when I know everything'.

Odd boy. But I'm glad we're friends again. I hope we always are; Max and Cicero are the only links to the woman who saved my life.

I hear the door slam.

'Food,' Isaac shouts, and he and Gus, who for once have remembered to take their shoes off, barge through and sit down in front of the open fire. Next to it still is the photo of Eve, Jim and Max.

As Gus puts the TV on for something in the background – a

new programme called *The Daily Crime* – the rest of us pull pizzas out of boxes, tear open bags of chips and pour drinks into cups.

I look around, taking it all in.

Finally I have my family, albeit a strange one, around me.

And finally I feel I'm home.

The Daily Crime

Gerome is propped on a high stool beside a tall desk. His suit is crisp, his tie straight and his hair perfectly coiffured.

GEROME: Hello, ladies and gentlemen, and welcome to our brand-new show – *The Daily Crime* – where we bring you all the latest news and developments. This evening we have a very special guest. A big welcome to none other than our youngest Prime Minister ever, and someone who clearly has her finger on the pulse of society – Sofia Nachant.

Lights flash, music blares and in a tight-fitting trouser suit Sofia steps from backstage, waves to the audience and strides across the floor to the desk, where she takes a seat on another high stool.

Gerome stands and shakes her hand.

GEROME: Thank you for coming, Prime Minister. It's a pleasure to have you here.

SOFIA: Thank you for having me, Gerome. It's a wonderful opportunity to speak to voters and keep them informed on developments. As I'm sure you're aware, after the Paige–Honeydew scandal of the last few months, there have been a number of changes. Primarily we must review the differences in society and the division between the classes, and bring in new systems to allow us to go about our lives safely and with utmost security.

GEROME: And I believe that's something you've come to inform people of today.

SOFIA: That's right, Gerome. I know voters were outraged by the grossly intrusive nature of the system Stephen Renard instigated, especially since he instigated it without anyone's knowledge. The fact that people were being watched, and were trackable, twenty-four hours a day, was shocking to the core. That is why I've come here today to explain the new system and to give the public my full reassurance.

GEROME: And what sort of system is this, Prime Minister?

SOFIA: One that will allow us to find every single person who commits a crime and bring them to justice.

GEROME: And does this justice involve the death penalty?

SOFIA: We will be moving to a referendum on the death penalty. Many people still feel very strongly that some criminals deserve it, but we will be bringing in a system that will be absolutely error-proof. I can give my complete reassurance that it is 100% accurate and that nobody, *nobody*, will be wrongly accused or convicted.

GEROME: That's quite a claim.

SOFIA: It's science, Gerome, and there is no hiding in science. We are building a DNA database which will allow us to scan through every member of society in order to find the culprit. Crime will be vastly reduced – who will commit a crime when they know they'll be discovered? We will have that safe society we dream of and that we all deserve.

The audience applaud and get to their feet. Sofia smiles at them.

GEROME: Well, I for one am so glad you've risen to power, Miss Nachant. Knowing that you have the interests of our people and our safety at heart already makes me feel safer. And when will this system be instigated?

SOFIA: Oh, it already is! Samples are being taken from anyone arrested, as well as if you visit your doctor for a blood test, or when babies are born, for example.

GEROME: Then I feel safer already! Yours has been a truly

meteoric rise to power though. How have you managed it? Many say you came from nowhere.

SOFIA (laughing): Everyone has to come from somewhere, Gerome! And I would hardly say meteoric – it's been a well-planned, hard-earned rise that I have worked consistently and conscientiously for, both in front of the cameras and behind the scenes. But I can say I am proud to lead this country, and I will do whatever it takes to ensure this leadership is a strong one, and our society a safe one. Whatever it takes.

GEROME: And we are proud to have you. We have some final news for viewers though, don't we, Sofia? Would you like the honour of explaining to our audience exactly how this new show of ours – *The Daily Crime* – works?

SOFIA: Absolutely, Gerome. This new show is all about showing you, the voting public, how we are fighting crime, and how we will eradicate it from our everyday lives using our new DNA database. Each episode will show a list of crimes that have been committed in the previous twenty-four hours and give viewers the opportunity to vote on which one the show should follow and explore. This will allow behind-the-scenes action, footage of real police investigations and live commentary as officers track down, and arrest, criminals.

GEROME: Well, there you go, ladies and gentlemen. What an exciting development! Yes, starting tomorrow, you will be able to vote, by internet, text or phone, for which crime you want us to focus on. Which one do you want special access to? Which one do you want all the gossip on? Which one do you really want to be solved, or can you solve it before our investigators and even the police? Set your alarms, folks, and tune in!

As lights flash across the studio, a jaunty theme tune begins, and the camera pans away and over the applauding audience.

The picture fades to black.

And the credits roll.

THE END

Acknowledgements

It's quite sad to come to the end of writing Cell 7. It has been wonderful to have had the space of three books to explore Martha and her gang and their individual stories, and I've become very fond of them – some more than others!

Cell 7 didn't come to my head complete, instead it slowly evolved. I wanted to write about capital punishment and explore what people facing it are going through, but after writing two very heavily research-based novels, didn't relish the thought of basing it on a factual system such as the one in the US; instead I looked for ways to set it in the UK. I spent a long time reading about the history of capital punishment in the UK and discovered it was suspended in 1965, with a second vote taken in 1969 on whether to re-instate it, or abolish it outright. In real life it was abolished, but there I found my turning point, because in my world, in the world of Cell 7, that's where I imagine it different. Instead of abolishment, I pondered on what would've happened if it had been re-instated at that point. How would it have changed in those years from 1969 to the present day and beyond? What would it have become? How would the Internet, television, media have affected it?

And with other influences, and other elements slotting in, slowly, and with many dog walks, Cell 7 came to be.

A lot of people have supported me from those initial thoughts to this final book. Emma Pass and Rebecca Mascull are my longest-standing writing buddies and I owe them a great deal. Also on the writing front are so many others who've been supportive and encouraging and generally Very Lovely Indeed – Rhian Ivory, Keris Stainton, Rae Earl, Paula Rawsthorne, Chris Callaghan, Zoe Marriott, Jo Nadin, Keren David, Sheena Wilkinson, Sarah Taylor, Liz Kessler, Liz de Jager, Susie Day, Gordon Smith, Caroline Green, Eve Ainsworth, Hayley Long – all from Camp YA/MG.

Over in 'sensible' adult corner, thanks to Sarah Jasmon, Louisa Treger, Louise Beech, Karin Salvalaggio, Vanessa Lafaye, Claire Fuller, Emma Curtis, Fionnuala Kearney, Kerry Hadley, Antonia Honeywell, Jason Hewitt and the rest of The Prime Writers.

Thank you to translator Iwona Michalowska-Gabrych – for your thoroughness. It was one of the most bizarre emails I've ever received!

Away from writing and over in the real world, big thanks to the LTC Coffee Club Biatches (my chums in triathlon) Kate Conway, Chris Giles, Jo Hunt and Tracey Wilkinson and to subsequent 'halves' Richard, Steve and Carl, who are always interested and always keep me laughing and sane. Thanks also to my iron buddies Martin Ball and Oliver Whelpton.

Simon Sharp – thank you for standing in as Jackson Paige – and Jon Bromfield, thanks to you and your twin for agreeing to be purveyors of hanging ropes.

In previous books I've thanked lots of readers, and I continue to be eternally grateful to you all. Special thanks go to Drakes Bookshop in Stockton, The Bookfayre in Woodhall Spa and Lindum Books in Lincoln. Cheers to Matthew Leach, Rebecca Veight and to school librarians up and down the country who do a sterling job often with limited resources.

Thanks to my oldest friend in the world – Matt Quinn – who does not work in Wickes and who is a worthy Scrabble opponent. Thanks for everything, Matt, and the rematch is long overdue.

I continue to be grateful for having the most supportive family I could ever wish for – Russ, Jess and Dan, Danny and Paige, Bowen, Dad and Ann, Colin, Janet and Jack, Helen and Patrick, Paul and Wendy. Thank you.

Being under the Hot Key roof for the last few years has been an honour and I'm very thankful to Emma Matthewson for taking a risk on Martha. Thanks also to the rest of the Hot Key crew – Tina Mories, Talya Baker, Ruth Logan, Jane Harris, Monique Meledje, Nicola Chapman and Charlotte Hoare.

Finally huge thanks to Jane Willis, Super-Agent, and the rest at United Agents, who are stars and are wonderful.

But before this starts to sound like a gushy acceptance speech, and I start thanking my dogs or the postman, I shall sign off. I hope you've all enjoyed following Martha and thank you all for everything.

Kerry Drewery

Kerry Drewery is the author of the CELL 7 trilogy, the first of which has been translated into more than a dozen languages, as well as two highly acclaimed, more literary YA novels: A BRIGHTER FEAR, 2012 (which was Love Reading 4 Kids' Book of the Month and shortlisted for the Leeds Book Award) and A DREAM OF LIGHTS, 2013 (which was nominated for the CILIP Carnegie Medal, awarded Highly Commended at the North East Teen Book Awards and shortlisted for the Hampshire Independent Schools Book Awards). Both were published by HarperCollins in the UK and Callenbach in The Netherlands.

HOT KEY BOOKS

Thank you for choosing a Hot Key book.

If you want to know more about our authors
and what we publish, you can find us online.

You can start at our website

www.hotkeybooks.com

And you can also find us on:

We hope to see you soon!

Want to read
NEW BOOKS
before anyone else?

Like getting
FREE BOOKS?

Enjoy sharing your
OPINIONS?

Discover

READERS FIRST

Read. Love. Share.

Get your first free book just by signing up at
readersfirst.co.uk

For Terms and Conditions see readersfirst.co.uk/pages/terms-of-service